Anonymous

Capital Stories by American Authors

Anonymous

Capital Stories by American Authors

ISBN/EAN: 9783337238407

Printed in Europe, USA, Canada, Australia, Japan

Cover: Foto ©Andreas Hilbeck / pixelio.de

More available books at **www.hansebooks.com**

BY

AMERICAN AUTHORS.

WASHINGTON IRVING

MARK TWAIN

AMELIA BARR

NATHANIEL HAWTHORN.

ELLA WHEELER WILCOX

PUBLISHED BY

THE CHRISTIAN HERALD,

LOUIS KLOPSCH, Proprietor,

BIBLE HOUSE, NEW YORK.

Press and Bindery of
HISTORICAL PUBLISHING CO.,
PHILADELPHIA.

TABLE OF CONTENTS.

CAPITAL STORIES
BY AMERICAN AUTHORS.

THE CELESTIAL RAILROAD.

BY NATHANIEL HAWTHORNE.

Not a great while ago, passing through the gate of dreams, I visited that region of the earth in which lies the famous City of Destruction. It interested me much to learn that by the public spirit of some of the inhabitants a railroad had recently been established between this populous and flourishing town and the Celestial City. Having a little time upon my hands, I resolved to gratify a liberal curiosity to make a trip thither. Accordingly, one fine morning, after paying my bill at the hotel and directing the porter to stow my luggage behind a coach, I took my seat in the vehicle and set out for the station-house. It was my good fortune to enjoy the company of a gentleman—one Mr. Smooth-it-Away—who, though he had never actually visited the Celestial City, yet seemed as well acquainted with its laws, customs, policy and statistics as with those of the City of Destruction, of which he was a native townsman. Being, moreover, a

(13)

director of the railroad corporation and one of its largest stockholders, he had it in his power to give me all desirable information respecting that praiseworthy enterprise.

Our coach rattled out of the city, and at a short distance from its outskirts passed over a bridge of elegant construction, but somewhat too slight, as I imagined, to sustain any considerable weight. On both sides lay an extensive quagmire which could not have been more disagreeable either to sight or smell had all the kennels of the earth emptied their pollution there.

"This," remarked Mr. Smooth-it-Away, "is, the famous Slough of Despond—a disgrace to all the neighborhood, and the greater that it might so easily be converted into firm ground."

"I have understood," said I, "that efforts have been made for that purpose from time immemorial. Bunyan mentions that above twenty-thousand cart-loads of wholesome instructions had been thrown in here without effect."

"Very probably! And what effect could be anticipated from such unsubstantial stuff?" cried Mr. Smooth-it-Away. "You observe this convenient bridge? We obtained a sufficient foundation for it by throwing into the slough some editions of books of morality, volumes of French philosophy and German rationalism, tracts, sermons and essays of modern clergymen, extracts from Plato, Confucius and various Hindoo sages, together with a few ingenious commentaries upon texts of Scripture—all of which, by some scientific process have been converted into a mass like granite. The whole bog might be filled up with similar matter."

It really seemed to me, however, that the bridge vibrated and heaved up and down in a very formidable manner ; and, in spite of Mr. Smooth-it-Away's testimony to the solidity of its foundation, I should be loth to cross it in a crowded omnibus, especially if each passenger were encumbered with as heavy luggage as that gentleman and myself. Nevertheless, we got over without accident, and soon found ourselves at the station-house. This very neat and spacious edifice is erected on the site of the little wicket-gate which formerly, as all old pilgrims will recollect, stood directly across the highway, and by its inconvenient narrowness was a great obstruction to the traveler of liberal mind and expansive stomach. The reader of John Bunyan will be glad to know that Christian's old friend Evangelist, who was accustomed to supply each pilgrim with a mystic roll, now presides at the ticket-office. Some malicious persons, it is true, deny the identity of this reputable character with the Evangelist of old times, and even pretend to bring competent evidence of an imposture. Without involving

myself in a dispute, I shall merely observe
that, so far as my experience goes, the square
pieces of pasteboard now delivered to passengers are much more convenient and useful along the road than the antique roll of
parchment.   Whether they will be as readily received at the gate of the Celestial City,
I decline giving an opinion.

A large number of passengers were already
at the station-house awaiting the departure
of the cars.   By the aspect and demeanor of
these persons, it was easy to judge that the
feelings of the community had undergone a
very favorable change in reference to the
celestial pilgrimage.   It would have done
Bunyan's heart good to see it.   Instead of a
lonely and ragged man with a huge burden
on his back plodding along sorrowfully on
foot, while the whole city hooted after him,
here were parties of the first gentry and
most respectable people in the neighborhood
setting forth toward the Celestial City as
if the pilgrimage were merely a summer
tour.   Among the gentlemen were charac-
ters of deserved eminence—magistrates, politicians and men of wealth, by whose
example religion could not but be greatly
recommended to their meaner brethren.   In
the ladies' department, too, I rejoiced to
distinguish some of those flowers of fashionable society, who are so well fitted to adorn
the most elevated circles of the Celestial City.
There was much pleasant conversation about

the news of the day, topics of business, politics or the lighter matters of amusement, while religion, though indubitably the main thing at heart, was thrown tastefully into the background. Even an infidel would have heard little or nothing to shock his sensibility.

One great convenience of the new method of going on pilgrimage I must not forget to mention. Our enormous burdens, instead of being carried on our shoulders, as had been the custom of old, were all snugly deposited in the baggage car, and, as I was assured, would be delivered to their respective owners at the journey's end. Another thing, likewise, the benevolent reader will be delighted to understand. It may be remembered that there was an ancient feud between Prince Beelzebub and the keeper of the wicket-gate, and that the adherents of the former distinguished personage were accustomed to shoot deadly arrows at honest pilgrims, while knocking at the door. This dispute, much to the credit as well of the illustrious potentate above mentioned, as of the worthy and enlightened directors of the railroad, has been pacifically arranged on the principle of mutual compromise. The prince's subjects are now pretty numerously employed about the station-house— some in taking care of the baggage, others in collecting fuel, feeding the engines, and such congenial occupations—and I can con-

scientiously affirm that persons more atten-
tive to their business, more willing to ac-
commodate or more generally agreeable to
the passengers are not to be found on any
railroad. Every good heart must surely
exult at so satisfactory an arrangement of
an immemorial difficulty.

"Where is Mr. Great-heart?" inquired I.
"Beyond a doubt, the directors have engaged that famous old champion to be chief
conductor on the railroad."

"Why, no," said Mr. Smooth-it-Away,
with a dry cough. "He was offered the
situation.of brakeman, but, to tell you the
truth, our friend Great-heart has grown pre-
posterously stiff and narrow in his old age.
He has so often guided pilgrims over the
road on foot that he considers it a sin to
travel in any other fashion. Beside, the old
fellow had entered so heartily into the
ancient feud with Prince Beelzebub that he
would have been perpetually at blows or ill-
language with some of the prince's subjects
and thus have embroiled us anew. So, on
the whole, we were not sorry when honest
Great-heart went off to the Celestial City in
a huff, and left us at liberty to choose a
more suitable and accommodating man.
Yonder comes the conductor of the train.
You will probably recognize him at once."

The engine at this moment took its station
in advance of the cars, looking, I must confess, much more like a sort of mechanical

demon that would hurry us to the infernal
regions than a laudable contrivance for
smoothing our way to the Celestial City.
On its top sat a personage almost enveloped
in smoke and flame, which—not to startle
the reader—appeared to gush from his own
mouth and stomach, as well as from the
engine's brazen abdomen.

"Do my eyes deceive me?" cried I.
"What on earth is this? A living creature?
If so, he is own brother to the engine he
rides upon!"

"Poh, poh! you are obtuse!" said Mr.
Smooth-it-Away, with a hearty laugh.
"Don't you know Apollyon, Christian's old
enemy, with whom he fought so fierce a
battle in the Valley of Humiliation? He
was the very fellow to manage the engine,
and so we have reconciled him to the custom
of going on pilgrimage, and engaged him
as chief conductor."

"Bravo, bravo!" exclaimed I, with irre-
pressible enthusiasm. "This shows the
liberality of the age; this proves, if anything can, that all musty prejudices are in a
fair way to be obliterated. And how will
Christian rejoice to hear of this happy transformation of his old antagonist! I promise
myself great pleasure in informing him of it
when we reach the Celestial City."

The passengers being all comfortably
seated, we now rattled away merrily, accom-
plishing a greater distance in ten minutes

than Christian probably trudged over in a
day. It was laughable, while we glanced
along, as it were, at the tail of a thunderbolt,
to observe two dusty foot travelers, in the
old pilgrim guise, with cockle-shell and
staff, their mystic rolls of parchment in their
hands, and their intolerable burdens on their
backs. The preposterous obstinacy of these
honest people in persisting to groan and
stumble along the difficult pathway rather
than take advantage of modern improvements excited great mirth among our wiser
brotherhood. We greeted the two pilgrims
with many pleasant gibes and a roar of
laughter ; whereupon they gazed at us with
such woful and absurdly compassionate
visages that our merriment grew tenfold
more obstreperous. Apollyon, also, entered
heartily into the fun, and contrived to flirt
the smoke and flame of the engine or of his
own breath into their faces, and envelop
them in an atmosphere of scalding steam.
These little practical jokes amused us mightily, and doubtless afforded the pilgrims the
gratification of considering themselves mar-
tyrs.

At some distance from the railroad Mr.
Smooth-it-Away pointed to a large, antique
edifice which he observed, was a tavern of
long standing, and had formerly been a
noted stopping place for pilgrims. In Bunyan's road-book it is mentioned as the Inter-
preter's House.

" I have long had a curiosity to visit that old mansion," remarked I.

" It is not one of our stations, as you perceive," said my companion. "The keeper was violently opposed to the railroad, and well he might be, as the track left his house of entertainment on one side, and thus was pretty certain to deprive him of all his reputable customers. But the footpath still passes his door, and the old gentleman now and then receives a call from some simple traveler and entertains him with fare as old-fashioned as himself."

Before our talk on this subject came to a conclusion we were rushing by the place where Christian's burden fell from his shoulders at the sight of the cross. This served as a theme for Mr. Smooth-it-Away, Mr. Live-for-the-World, Mr. Hide-Sin-in-the-Heart, Mr. Scaly-Conscience and a knot of gentlemen from the town of Shun-Repentance, to descant upon the inestimable advantages resulting from the safety of our baggage. Myself—and all the passengers, indeed—joined with great unanimity in this view of the matter, for our burdens were rich in many things esteemed precious throughout the world, and especially we each of us possessed a great variety of favorite habits which we trusted would not be out of fashion even in the polite circles of the Celestial City. It would have been a sad spectacle to see such an assortment of

valuable articles tumbling into the sepul-
chre.

Thus pleasantly conversing on the favorable circumstances of our position as compared with those of past pilgrims and of
narrow-minded ones at the present day, we
soon found ourselves at the foot of the Hill
Difficulty. Through the very heart of this
rocky mountain a tunnel has been constructed, of most admirable architecture,
with a lofty arch and a spacious double track;
so that, unless the earth and rocks should
chance to crumble down, it will remain an
eternal monument of the builders' skill and
enterprise. It is a great though incidental
advantage that the materials from the heart
of the Hill Difficulty have been employed in
filling up the Valley of Humiliation, thus
obviating the necessity of descending into
that disagreeable and unwholesome hollow.

"This is a wonderful improvement indeed," said I, "yet I should have been glad
of an opportunity to visit the palace Beautiful and be introduced to the charming
young ladies—Miss Prudence, Miss Piety.
Miss Charity, and the rest—who have the
kindness to entertain pilgrims there."

"Young ladies!" cried Mr. Smooth-it-
Away as soon as he could speak for laughing. "And charming young ladies! Why,
my dear fellow, they are old maids, every
soul of them—prim, starched, dry and
angular—and not one of them, I will venture

to say, has altered so much as the fashion
of her gown since the days of Christian's
pilgrimage."

"Ah, well!" said I, much comforted;
"then I can very readily dispense with their
acquaintance."

The respectable Apollyon was now putting
on the steam at a prodigious rate—anxious,
perhaps, to get rid of the unpleasant remin-
iscences connected with the spot where he
had so disastrously encountered Christian.

Consulting Mr. Bunyan's road-book, I
perceived that we must now be within a few
miles of the Valley of the Shadow of Death,
into which doleful region, at our present
speed, we should plunge much sooner than
seemed at all desirable. In truth, I expected nothing better than to find myself in
the ditch on one side of the quag or the
other. But on communicating my appre-
hensions to Mr. Smooth-it-Away he assured
me that the difficulties of this passage, even
in its worst condition, had been vastly exaggerated, and that in its present state of
improvement I might consider myself as safe
as on any railroad in Christendom.

Even while we were speaking the train
shot into the entrance of this dreaded valley. Though I plead guilty to some foolish
palpitations of the heart during our head-
long rush over the causeway here constructed, yet it were unjust to withhold the
highest encomiums on the boldness of its

original conception and the ingenuity of those who executed it. It was gratifying, likewise, to observe how much care had been taken to dispel the everlasting gloom and supply the defect of cheerful sunshine, not a ray of which has ever penetrated among these awful shadows. For this purpose the inflammable gas which exudes plentifully from the soil is collected by means of pipes, and thence communicated to a quadruple row of lamps along the whole extent of the passage. Thus a radiance has been created even out of the fiery and sulphurous curse that rests forever upon the Valley—a radiance hurtful, however, to the eyes, and somewhat bewildering, as I discovered by the changes which it wrought in the visages of my companions. In this respect, as compared with natural daylight, there is the same difference as between truth and falsehood ; but if the reader has ever traveled through the dark valley, he will have learned to be thankful for any light that he could get—if not from the sky above, then from the blasted soil beneath. Such was the red brilliancy of these lamps that they appeared to build walls of fire on both sides of the track, between which we held our course at lightning speed, while a reverberating thunder filled the valley with its echoes. Had the engine run off the track—a catastrophe, it is whispered, by no means unprecedented—the bottomless pit,

if there be any such place, would undoubt-
edly have received us. Just as some dismal
fooleries of this nature had made my heart
quake there came a tremendous shriek
careering along the Valley as if a thousand
devils had burst their lungs to utter it, but
which proved to be merely the whistle of
the engine on arriving at a stopping place.
The spot where he had now paused is the
same that our friend Bunyan—truthful man,
but infected with many fantastic notions—
has designated in terms plainer than I like
to repeat, as the mouth of the infernal
region. This, however, must be a mistake,
inasmuch as Mr. Smooth-it-Away, while we
remained in the smoky and lurid cavern,
took occasion to prove that Tophet has not
even a metaphorical existence. The place,
he assured us, is no other than the crater
of a half extinct volcano, in which the directors had caused forges to be set up for
the manufacture of railroad-iron. Hence,
also, is obtained a plentiful supply of fuel
for the use of the engines. Whoever had
gazed into the dismal obscurity of the broad
cavern-mouth, whence ever and anon darted
huge tongues of dusky flame, and had seen
the strange, half-shaped monsters and vi-
sions of faces horribly grotesque into which
the smoke seemed to wreath itself, and had
heard the awful murmurs and shrieks and
deep shuddering whispers of the blast,
sometimes forming themselves into words

almost articulate, would have seized upon Mr. Smooth-it-Away's comfortable explanation as greedily as we did. The inhabitants of the cavern, moreover, were unlovely personages—dark, smoke begrimed, generally deformed, with misshapen feet and a glow of dusky redness in their eyes, as if their hearts had caught fire and were blazing out of the upper windows. It struck me as a peculiarity that the laborers at the forge and those who brought fuel to the engine, when they began to draw short breath, positively emitted smoke from their mouth and nostrils.

Among the idlers about the train, most of whom were puffing cigars, which they had lighted at the flame of the crater, I was perplexed to notice several who, to my certain knowledge, had heretofore set forth by railroad for the Celestial City. They looked dark, wild and smoky, with a singular resemblance, indeed, to the native inhabitants, like whom, also, they had a disagreeable propensity to ill-natured gibes and sneers, the habit of which had wrought a settled contortion of their visages. Having been on speaking terms with one of these persons—an indolent, good-for-nothing fellow who went by the name of Take-it-Easy—I called him and inquired what was his business there.

"Did you not start," said I, "for the Celestial City?"

"That's a fact," said Mr. Take-it-Easy, carelessly puffing some smoke into my eyes; "but I heard such bad accounts that I never took pains to climb the hill on which the city stands—no business doing, no fun going on, nothing to drink, and no smoking allowed, and a thrumming of church music from morning till night. I would not stay in such a place if they offered me house-room and living free."

"But, my good Mr. Take-it-Easy," cried I, "why take up your residence here of all places in the world?"

"Oh," said the loafer, with a grin, "it is very warm hereabouts, and I meet with plenty of old acquaintances, and altogether the place suits me. I hope to see you back again some day soon. A pleasant journey to you!"

While he was speaking the bell of the engine rang, and we dashed away after dropping a few passengers, but receiving no new ones.

Rattling onward through the valley, we were dazzled with the fiercely gleaming gas-lamps, as before, but sometimes, in the dark of intense brightness, grim faces that bore the aspect and expression of individual sins or evil passions seemed to thrust themselves through the veil of light, glaring upon us and stretching forth a great dusky hand as if to impede our progress. I almost thought that they were my own sins that appalled

me there. These were freaks of imagination—nothing more, certainly; mere delu-
sions which I ought to be heartily ashamed
of—but all through the dark valley I was
tormented and pestered and dolefully bewildered with the same kind of waking
dreams. The mephitic gases of that region
intoxicate the brain. As the light of natural
day, however, began to struggle with the
glow of the lanterns, these vain imagina-
tions lost their vividness, and finally vanished with the first ray of sunshine that
greeted our escape from the Valley of the
Shadow of Death. Ere we had gone a mile
beyond it I could well-nigh have taken my
oath that this whole gloomy passage was a
dream.

At the end of the valley, as John Bunyan
mentions, is a cavern where in his days
dwelt two cruel giants, Pope and Pagan,
who had strewn the ground about their
residences with the bones of slaughtered
pilgrims. These vile old troglodytes are no
longer there, but in their deserted cave
another terrible giant has thrust himself,
and makes it his business to seize upon
honest travelers and fat them for his table
with plentiful meals of smoke, mist, moon-
shine, raw potatoes and sawdust. He is a
German by birth, and is called Giant Trans-
cendentalist, but as to his form, his features,
his substance, and his nature generally,
it is the chief peculiarity of this huge

miscreant that neither he for himself nor anybody for him has ever been able to describe
them. As we rushed by the cavern's mouth
we caught a hasty glimpse of him, looking
somewhat like an ill-proportioned figure,
but considerably more like a heap of fog
and duskiness. He shouted after us, but in
so strange a phraseology that we knew not
what he meant, nor whether to be encouraged or affrighted.

It was late in the day when the train
thundered into the ancient City of Vanity,
where Vanity Fair is still at the height of
prosperity and exhibits an epitome of whatever is brilliant, gay and fascinating beneath
the sun. As I purposed to make a considerable stay here, it gratified me to learn
that there is no longer the want of harmony
between the townspeople and pilgrims which
impelled the former to such lamentably
mistaken measures as the persecution of
Christian and the fiery martyrdom of Faithful. On the contrary, as the new railroad
brings with it great trade and a constant in-
flux of strangers, the lord of Vanity Fair is
its chief patron and the capitalists of the
city are among the largest stockholders.
Many passengers stop to take their pleasure
or make their profit in the fair, instead of
going onward to the Celestial City. Indeed,
such are the charms of the place that people
often affirm it to be the true and only
heaven, stoutly contending that there is no

other, that those who seek farther are mere
dreamers, and that if the fabled brightness
of the Celestial City lay but a bare mile
beyond the gates of Vanity they wou.d not
be fools enough to go thither. Without
subscribing to these perhaps exaggerated
encomiums, I can truly say that my abode
in the city was mainly agreeable and my
intercourse with the inhabitants productive
of much amusement and instruction.

Being naturally of a serious turn, my
attention was directed to the solid advantages derivable from a residence here, rather
than to the effervescent pleasures which are
the grand object with too many visitants.
The Christian reader, if he have had no accounts of the city later than Bunyan's time,
will be surprised to hear that almost every
street has its church, and that the reverend
clergy are nowhere held in higher respect
than at Vanity Fair. And well do they
deserve such honorable estimation, for the
maxims of wisdom and virtue which fall
from their lips come from as deep a spiritual
source and tend to as lofty a religious aim
as those of the sagest philosophers of old.
In justification of this high praise I need
only mention the names of the Rev. Mr Shal-
low-Deep, the Rev. Mr. Stumble-at-Truth,
that fine old clerical character the Rev. Mr.
This-to Day, who expects shortly to resign
his pulpit to the Rev. Mr. That-to-Morrow,
together with the Rev. Mr. Bewilderment,

the Rev. Mr. Clog-the-Spirit, and, last and
greatest, the Rev. Dr. Wind-of-Doctrine.
The labors of these eminent divines are
aided by those of innumerable lecturers,
who diffuse such a various profundity in all
subjects of human or celestial science that
any man may acquire an omnigenous erudi-
tion without the trouble of even learning to
read. Thus literature is etherealized by assuming for its medium the human voice,
and knowledge, depositing all its heavier
particles—except, doubtless, its gold—becomes exhaled into a sound which forthwith
steals into the ever-open ear of the community. These ingenious methods consti-
tute a sort of machinery by which thought
and study are done to every person's hand
without his putting himself to the slightest
inconvenience in the matter. There is
another species of machine for the whole-
sale manufacture of individual morality.
This excellent result is effected by societies
for all manner of virtuous purposes, and
with which a man has merely to connect
himself, throwing, as it were, his quota of
virtue into the common stock, and the presi-
dent and directors will take care that the
aggregate amount be well applied. All
these, and other wonderful improvements in
ethics, religion and literature, being made
plain to my comprehension by the ingenious
Mr. Smooth-it-Away, inspired me with a
vast admiration of Vanity Fair.

It would fill a volume in an age of pam-
phlets were I to record all my observations in
this great capital of human business and
pleasure. There was an unlimited range of
society—the powerful, the wise, the witty
and the famous in every walk of life, princes,
presidents, poets, generals, artists, actors
and philanthropists—all making their own
market at the fair, and deeming no price
too exorbitant for such commodities as
hit their fancy. It was well worth one's
while, even if he had no idea of buying or
selling, to loiter through the bazaars and
observe the various sorts of traffic that were
going forward.

Some of the purchasers, I thought, made
very foolish bargains. For instance, a
young man having inherited a splendid
fortune laid out a considerable portion of it
in the purchase of diseases, and finally
spent all the rest for a heavy lot of repentance and a suit of rags. A very pretty girl
bartered a heart as clear as crystal, and
which seemed her most valuable possession,
for another jewel of the same kind, but so
worn and defaced as to be utterly worthless.
In one shop there were a great many crowns
of laurel and myrtle, which soldiers,
authors, statesmen, and various other people
pressed eagerly to buy. Some purchased
these paltry wreaths with their lives, others
by a toilsome servitude of years, and many
sacrificed whatever was most valuable, yet

finally slunk away without the crown.
There was a sort of stock or scrip called
Conscience which seemed to be in great demand and would purchase almost anything.
Indeed, few rich commodities were to be
obtained without paying a heavy sum in
this particular stock, and a man's business
was seldom very lucrative unless he knew
precisely when and how to throw his hoard
of Conscience into the market. Yet, as this
stock was the only thing of permanent
value, whoever parted with it was sure to
find himself a loser in the long run. Several
of the speculations were of a questionable
character. Occasionally a member of Congress recruited his pocket by the sale of his
constituents, and I was assured that public
officers have often sold their country at very
moderate prices. Thousands sold their
happiness for a whim. Gilded chains were
in great demand, and purchased with almost
any sacrifice. In truth, those who desired,
according to the old adage, to sell anything
valuable for a song, might find customers
all over the fair, and there were innumerable messes of pottage, piping hot, for such
as chose to buy them with their birthrights.
A few articles, however, could not be found
genuine at Vanity Fair. If a customer
wished to renew his stock of youth, the
dealers offered him a set of false teeth and an
auburn wig ; if he demanded peace of mind,
they recommended opium or a brandy-bottle.

Tracts of land and golden mansions situate in the Celestial City were often exchanged at very disadvantageous rates for a few years' lease of small, inconvenient tenements in Vanity Fair. Prince Beelzebub himself took great interest in this sort of traffic, and sometimes condescended to meddle with smaller matters. I once had the pleasure to see him bargaining with a miser for his soul, which after much ingenious skirmishing on both sides His Highness succeeded in obtaining at about the value of sixpence. The prince remarked with a smile that he was a loser by the transaction.

Day after day, as I walked the streets of Vanity, my manners and deportment became more and more like those of the inhabitants. The place began to seem like home : the idea of pursuing my travels to the Celestial City was almost obliterated from my mind. I was reminded of it, however, by the sight of the same pair of simple pilgrims at whom we had laughed so heartily when Apollyon puffed smoke and steam into their faces at the commencement of our journey. There they stood amid the densest bustle of Vanity, the dealers offering them their purple and fine linen and jewels, and men of wit and humor gibing at them, a pair of buxom ladies ogling them askance, while the benevolent Mr. Smooth-it-Away whispered some of his wisdom at their elbows and pointed to a newly-erected

temple ; but there were these worthy sim-
pletons making the scene look wild and
monstrous merely by their sturdy repudia-
tion of all part in its business or pleasures.

One of them—his name was Stick-to-the-
Right—perceived in my face, I suppose, a
species of sympathy, and almost admiration, which, to my own great surprise, I
could not help feeling for this pragmatic
couple. It prompted him to address me.

"Sir," inquired he, with a sad yet mild
and kindly voice, "do you call yourself a
pilgrim?"

"Yes," I replied; "my right to that
appellation is indubitable. I am merely a
sojourner here in Vanity Fair, being bound
to the Celestial City by the new railroad."

"Alas, friend!" rejoined Mr. Stick-to-
the-Right; "I do assure you, and beseech
you to receive the truth of my words, that
that whole concern is a bubble. You may
travel on it all your lifetime, were you to
live thousands of years, and yet never get
beyond the limits of Vanity Fair. Yea,
though you should deem yourself entering
the gates of the blessed city, it will be nothing but a miserable delusion."

"The Lord of the Celestial City," began
the other pilgrim, whose name was Mr.
Foot-it-to-Heaven, "has refused, and will
ever refuse, to grant an act of incorporation
for this railroad, and unless that be obtained

no passenger can ever hope to enter his do-
minions; wherefore every man who buys a
ticket must lay his account with losing the
purchase-money, which is the value of his
own soul."

"Poh! nonsense!" said Mr. Smooth-it-
Away, taking my arm and leading me off;
"these fellows ought to be indicted for a
libel. If the law stood as it once did in
Vanity Fair, we should see them grinning
through the iron bars of the prison window."

This incident made a considerable impression on my mind, and contributed with
other circumstances to indispose me to a
permanent residence in the City of Vanity,
although, of course, I was not simple
enough to give up my original plan of gliding along easily and commodiously by railroad. Still, I grew anxious to be gone.
There was one strange thing that troubled
me: amid the occupations or amusements
of the fair, nothing was more common than
for a person—whether at a feast, theatre or
church, or trafficking for wealth and honors,
or whatever he might be doing and however
unseasonable the interruption—suddenly to
vanish like a soap-bubble and be nevermore
seen of his fellows; and so accustomed were
the latter to such little accidents that they
went on with their business as quietly as if
nothing had happened. But it was otherwise with me.

Finally, after a pretty long residence at

the fair, I resumed my journey toward the
Celestial City, still with Mr. Smooth-it-
Away at my side. At a short distance beyond the suburbs of Vanity we passed the
ancient silver-mine of which Demas was the
first discoverer, and which is now wrought
to great advantage, supplying nearly all the
coined currency of the world. A little
farther onward was the spot where Lot's
wife had stood for ages under the semblance
of a pillar of salt. Curious travelers have
long since carried it away piecemeal. Had
all regrets been punished as rigorously as
this poor dame's were, my yearning for the
relinquished delights of Vanity Fair might
have produced a similar change in my own
corporeal substance, and left me a warning
to future pilgrims.

The next remarkable object was a large
edifice constructed of moss-grown stone, but
in a modern and airy style of architecture.
The engine came to a pause in its vicinity
with the usual tremendous shriek.

"This was formerly the castle of the re-
doubted Giant Despair," observed Mr.
Smooth-it-Away, "but since his death Mr.
Flimsy-Faith has repaired it, and now keeps
an excellent house of entertainment here.
It is one of our stopping-places."

"It seems but slightly put together,"
remarked I, looking at the frail yet ponderous walls. "I do not envy Mr. Flimsy-
Faith his habitation. Some day it will

thunder down upon the heads of the occupants.''

"We shall escape, at all events," said
Mr. Smooth-it-Away, "for Apollyon is
putting on the steam again."

The road now plunged into a gorge of
the Delectable Mountains, and traversed the
field where in former ages the blind men
wandered and stumbled along the tombs.
One of these ancient tombstones had been
thrust across the track by some malicious
person, and gave the train of cars a terrible
jolt. Far up the rugged side of a mountain I perceived a rusty iron door half over-
grown with bushes and creeping plants, but
with smoke issuing from its crevices.

"Is that," inquired I, "the very door in
the hillside which the shepherds assured
Christian was a by-way to hell?"

"That was a joke on the part of the
shepherds," said Mr. Smooth-it-Away, with
a smile. "It is neither more nor less than
the door of a cavern which they use as a
smoke-house for the preparation of mutton-
hams."

My recollections of the journey are now
for a little space dim and confused, inasmuch as a singular drowsiness here overcame me, owing to the fact that we were
passing over the Enchanted Ground, the
air of which encourages a disposition to
sleep. I awoke, however, as soon as we
crossed the borders of the pleasant Land of

Beulah. All the passengers were rubbing
their eyes, comparing watches and congrat-
ulating one another on the prospect of arriving so seasonably at the journey's end.
The sweet breezes of this happy clime came
refreshingly to our nostrils ; we beheld the
glimmering gush of silver fountains overhung by trees of beautiful foliage and de-
licious fruit, which were propagated by
grafts from the celestial gardens. Once, as
we dashed onward like a hurricane, there
was a flutter of wings, and the bright appearance of an angel in the air speeding
forth on some heavenly mission.

The engine now announced the close
vicinity of the final station-house by one
last and horrible scream in which there
seemed to be distinguishable every kind of
wailing and woe and bitter fierceness of
wrath, all mixed up with the wild laughter
of a devil or a madman. Throughout our
journey, at every stopping-place, Apollyon
had exercised his ingenuity in screwing the
most abominable sounds out of the whistle
of the steam-engine, but in this closing
effort he outdid himself, and created an infernal uproar which, besides disturbing the
peaceful inhabitants of Beulah, must have
sent its discord even through the celestial
gates.

While the horrid clamor was still ringing
in our ears we heard an exulting strain, as
if a thousand instruments of music with

height and depth and sweetness in their tones, at once tender and triumphant, were struck in unison to greet the approach of some illustrious hero who had fought the good fight and won a glorious victory, and was come to lay aside his battered arms forever. Looking to ascertain what might be the occasion of this glad harmony, I perceived, on alighting from the cars, that a multitude of shining ones had assembled on the other side of the river to welcome two poor pilgrims who were just emerging from its depths. They were the same whom Apollyon and ourselves had persecuted with taunts and gibes and scalding steam at the commencement of our journey—the same whose unworldly aspect and impressive words had stirred my conscience amid the wild revelers of Vanity Fair.

"How amazingly well those men have got on!" cried I to Mr. Smooth-it-Away. "I wish we were secure of as good a reception."

"Never fear! never fear!" answered my friend. "Come! make haste. The ferry-boat will be off directly, and in three minutes you will be on the other side of the river. No doubt you will find coaches to carry you up to the city gates."

A steam ferry-boat—the last improvement on this important route—lay at the river-side puffing, snorting and emitting all those other disagreeable utterances which betoken the departure to be immediate. I hurried on board with the rest of the passengers, most of whom were in great perturbation, some bawling out for their baggage, some tearing their hair and exclaiming that the boat would explode or sink, some already pale with the heaving of the stream, some gazing affrighted at the ugly aspect of the steersman, and some still dizzy with the slumberous influences of the Enchanted Ground.

Looking back to the shore, I was amazed to discern Mr. Smooth-it-Away waving his hand in token of farewell.

" Don't you go over to the Celestial City ? " exclaimed I.

" Oh, no ! " answered he, with a queer smile and that same disagreeable contortion of visage which I had remarked in the inhabitants of the dark valley—" oh, no ! I have come thus far only for the sake of your pleasant company. Good-bye ! We shall meet again."

And then did my excellent friend, Mr. Smooth-it-Away, laugh outright ; in the midst of which cachinnation a smoke-wreath issued from his mouth and nostrils, while a twinkle of lurid flame darted out of either eye, proving indubitably that his heart was all of a red blaze. The impudent fiend ! To deny the existence of Tophet when he felt its fiery tortures raging within his breast ! I rushed to the side of the boat, intending to fling myself on shore, but the wheels, as they began their revolutions, threw a dash of spray over me, so cold—so deadly cold with the chill that will never leave those waters until Death be drowned in his own river—that with a shiver and a heartquake I awoke.

Thank Heaven it was a dream !

A CHASE FOR A WIFE.

BY T. C. HALIBURTON.

In the morning all the guests assisted Mr. Neal and his men in endeavoring to cut a passage through the enormous drift that had obstructed our progress on the night of our arrival. Although apparently a work of vast labor, the opening was, in fact, effected with great ease, and in an incredibly short space of time. The drift shovel is made of dry wood, weighs very little, and lifts a large quantity of snow at once. There were no arrivals during the day, nor did any of the party at Mount Hope venture to leave it and become pioneers. In the afternoon we adjourned again, for the last time, to the Keeping Room, for Barclay expressed his determination to force his way to Illinoo on the

following day, and Mr. Stephen Richardson
said, as the road to Halifax would, from its
position, be so much more obstructed than
that which lay through the woods, he had
resolved to leave his horse, and perform the
remaining part of the journey on snow-
shoes.

" I can't say my business is so very ur-
gent, neither," he observed ; "but I can't
bear to be idle, and when a man's away
from home things don't, in a general way,
go ahead so fast, or get so well done, as
when he is to the fore. Them that work
never think ; and if the thinking man is
away, the laboring men may as well be
away also, for the chances are they will
work wrong, and, at any rate, they are sure
to work badly. That's my idea, at any
rate. But there is one comfort, anyhow ;
there is no fishery law where I live ; and if
there was, I don't think Mrs. Richardson,
my wife, would be altogether just so sharp
upon me as Luke Loon's was. I must tell
you that story, Miss Lucy. For instance,
folks like you have no idea of what is going
on sometimes seaboard ways. Plowing the
land and plowing the sea is about as
different things as may be, and yet they
ain't more different than them who turn the
furrows or hold the tiller. It ain't no easy
matter to give you an idea of a fishing-
station ; but I'll try, miss.

" We have two sorts of emigrants to this

province of Nova Scotia, do you observe ; droves of paupers from Europe, and shoals of fish from the sea ; old Nick sends one, and the Lord sends the other ; one we have to feed, and the other feeds us ; one brings destitution, distress, and disease, and the other health, wealth, and happiness. Well, when our friends the mackerel strike in toward the shore, and travel round the province to the northward, the whole coasting population is on the stir, too. Perhaps there never was seen, under the blessed light of the sun, anything like the everlasting number of mackerel in one shoal on our sea-coast. Millions is too little a word for it ; acres of them is too small a term to give a right notion ; miles of them, perhaps, is more like the thing ; and when they rise to the surface, it's a solid body of fish you sail through. It's a beautiful sight to see them tumbling into a harbor, head over tail, and tail over head, jumping and thumping, sputtering and fluttering, lashing and thrashing, with a gurgling kind of sound, as much as to say, ' Here we are, my hearties ! How are you off for salt ? Is your barrels all ready ?—because we are. So bear a hand, and out with your nets, as we are off to the next harbor to-morrow, and don't wait for such lazy fellows as you be.' Well, when they come in shoals that way, the fishermen come in swarms, too. Oh, it beats all natur—that's a fact ! Did you

ever stand on a beach, miss, or on a pasture,
that's on a river, or on a bay, and see a great
flock of plover, containing hundreds, and
hundreds, and hundreds of birds, come and
light all at once in one spot, where a minute
afore there warn't one? Well, that's the
way with humans on the fishery-stations.
Take Crow Harbor now, or Fox Island, or
Just-au-Corps Point, or Louisburg, or any
of them places, whenever the fish strike in,
they are all crowded right up in a minute,
chock full of people from all parts of these
colonies and Eastern States of America, in
flats and boats, and decked vessels, and
shallops, and schooners, and pinks, and
sloops, and smacks, and every kind and
sort of small craft ; and, in course, where
there are such a number of men, the few
women that live near at hand just lay down
the law their own way, and carry things
with a high hand. Like all other legis-
lators, too, they make 'nactments to suit
themselves. Petticoat government is a petty
tyrannical government, I tell you."

" Why, Mr. Stephen ! " said Miss Lucy.

" Beg your pardon, miss, I actilly forgat
that time," he continued. " I did make a
hole in my manners that pitch, I grant, and
I am sorry for it. It don't do to tell the
truth at all times, that's a fact. The fishery
regulation that I am a-going to speak of is
repealed now, I guess, everywhere a'most,
except at the Magdalen Islands, and there,

I believe, it is in full force yet, and carried
out very strict; but I recollect when it prevailed here at Shad Harbor, and poor Luke
Loon suffered under it.   Time flies so, a
body can hardly believe, when they look
back, that things that seem as if they happened yesterday, actilly took place twenty
years ago : but so it is, and it appears to me
sometimes, as if the older events are, the
clearer they be in the mind ; but I suppose
it is because they are like the lines of our
farms in the woods, so often blazed anew,
by going over agin and agin, they are kept
fresh and plain.   Howsumever that may be,
it's about the matter of nineteen years ago
come next February, when that misfortunate crittur, Luke Loon, came to me in a
most desperate pucker of a hurry—

   " ' Steve,' says he, ' for Heaven's sake !
let me have a horse, that's a good fellow—
will you? to go to Shad Harbor ; and I'll
pay you anything in the world you'll ask
for it.'

   " ' Are you in a great hurry ? ' said I.

   " ' I must clap on all sail and scud before
the wind like the mischief.   I haven't a
minit to lose,' said he.

   " ' Then you can't have him,' said I, ' for
you will ride the beast too fast.'

   " You never saw a feller so taken a-back,
and so chap-fallen, in all your life.   He
walked about the room, and wrung his
hands, and groaned as if his heart was

breaking, and at last he fairly boo-hooed right out——

" ' O my soul ! ' said he, ' I shall lose Miss Loon, my wife, for a sartenty ! I shall be adrift again in the world, as sure as fate ! I have only to-morrow to reach home in ; for, by the law of the fishery, if a man is absent over three months, his wife can marry again ; and the time will be up in twenty-four hours. What onder the sun shall I do ? '

" ' If that's the sort of gal she is, Luke,' said I, 'she won't keep; let her run into another man's net if she likes, for she won't stand the inspection brand, and ain't a No. 1 article ! Do you just bait your hook and try your luck again, for there is as good fish in the sea as was ever hauled out of it ! '

" But he carried on so after the gal, and took it so much to heart, I actilly pitied the crittur ; and at last consented to let him have the horse. Poor fellow ! he was too late, after all. His wife, the cunning minx, to make up time, counted the day of sailing as one day, which was onfair, oncustomary, and contrary to the fishery laws ; and was married again the night before he arrived to big Tom Bullock, of Owl's Head. When Luke heard it he nearly went crazy ; he raved and carried on so, and threatened to shoot Tom, seeing that he wasn't able to thrash him ; but the more he raved the more the neighbors' boys and gals made

game of him, following him about and singing out—

" 'Get out of the way, old Dan Tucker.
You are too late to come to supper ! '

And fairly tormented him out of the fishery-
station."

"Ah !" said Miss Lucy, "I know you
made up that story—didn't you, now? It
ain't true, is it ?"

"Fact ! I assure you," said Stephen.
" There is others besides me that's a knowing to it."

" Well, I never ! " said the young lady.
" That beats all I ever heard. Oh, my! what
folks fishing people must be ! "

" Well, there are some droll things done,
and droll people to do them in this world,"
replied Stephen.

An exclamation from one of the little boys
called Miss Lucy's attention to him, and
she sent the little culprit off to bed, not-
withstanding Mr. Stephen's earnest en-
treaties to the contrary. The young lady
was inexorable. She said—

" That in an establishment like that of
Mount Hope, nothing could be accomplished
without order and regularity ; and that there
were certain rules in the household which
were never deviated from on any account
whatever."

" You don't mean to say," inquired Stephen, " that you have rules you never alter

or bend a little on one side, if you don't break them, do you? "

" Yes, I do," said Miss Lucy; " I couldn't keep house if I didn't."

" Well, you must break one of them for me to-night, my little rosebud ! "

" Indeed, I shall not ! "

" Oh, but you must ! "

" Oh, but I must not ! "

" Oh, but you will, tho' ! "

" Oh, but I won't, tho' ! "

" Well, we shall see," said Stephen ; "but you are too hard on those poor little fellows. They are nice, manly little boys, and I love them ; and, after all, what is it they did, now?"

" What became of poor Luke ?" said the inflexible hostess, in order to turn the conversation. " I should like to hear the rest of that story."

" Poor little dears !" said Stephen, regardless of the question.

" Oh, never mind the boys, Mr. Stephen," she replied. " It's time they went to bed, at any rate ; but Luke !—did you ever hear of him afterward ?"

" I didn't think you would be so hard-hearted, now, Miss Lucy," he said, pursuing the subject.

" Now, Mr. Stephen, there is just one favor I have to ask of you."

" Granted before told," he replied. " Anything under the sun I can do for you,

miss, either by day or by night, I am ready
to do. I only wish we had plenty more of
such well broughten up, excellent house-
keepers as you be, and such rail right down
hand ——''

'' Now, don't talk nonsense,'' she said,
'' or I am done. But just tell me, that's a
good soul, is that story of yours about Luke
Loon true, or were you only romancing?
Is it a bam or a fact?''

'' Fact, miss, and no mistake. Do you
think, now, I would go for to deceive you
that way? No, not for the world. It's as
true as I am here.''

'' Well, it's a very odd story, then,'' said
Miss Lucy—'' the oddest story I ever heard
in all my life. What a wretch that woman
must have been. And poor Luke, what
became of him?''

'' Oh, don't ask me,'' replied Stephen,
with a serious air—'' don't ask me that;
anything else but that.''

'' Ah, do!''

'' I'd rather not, excuse me, miss.''

'' Did he die of a broken heart?''

'' Worse than that.''

'' Did he make 'way with himself?''

'' Worse than that.''

'' Get desperate, do something awful, and
get hanged for it?''

'' Worse than that.''

'' Oh, my! didn't you say just now you'd
do anything for me—Oh! you false man!

And now you have raised my curiosity so,
I actilly can't go to sleep till I hear it. Do
you know the story, Mr. Barclay?"

"No ; if I did, I would tell it to you with
pleasure."

"Do you, sir?" applying to the commis-
sary.

"No, I never heard it."

"Is there no one knows it? Oh, how
stupid of you, Mr. Stephen, to tease a body
so ! You might, now—— Come, that's a
dear man, do tell me !' "

"My dear friend," said Stephen, with a
sad and melancholy air, "it's a dismal,
shocking story ; and I can't bear to think
of it, much less to talk of it. You won't
sleep to-night, if I tell it to you, neither
shall I : and I know you will wish I had let
it alone. It was an untimely thing."

"What?"

"The end of poor Luke !"

"Then he is dead—is he ? "

"I didn't say he was dead."

"Ah, Mr. Stephen," she said, "don't
tease, now, that's a good man !" and she
rose up, and stood behind his chair, and
patted his cheek with her hand coaxingly.
"I'll do anything in the world for you, if
you will tell me that story."

"Well," said Stephen, "I give in ; if I
must, I suppose I must ; but mind, I warned
you beforehand !"

And then, looking round, and taking up

an empty decanter, as if to help himself to
some more lemonade before he began, he
affected surprise at there being nothing in it,
and, handing it to the young hostess said—

"I must have the matter of half-a-pint
of lemonade to get through with this dismal
affair."

"Certainly, certainly; anything you
please!" said Miss Lucy, who immediately
proceeded to a room, situated in the other
part of the house, to procure it.

As soon as she left the room, Stephen
looked up and laughed, saying—

"Didn't I manage that well? They are
very strict people here about hours, and
nothing in the world will tempt them to
open the door after twelve at night. That is
one of the rules she never breaks, she says;
but I told her I'd make her do it, and I have
succeeded unbeknown to her. I never saw
it fail yet: pique a woman's curiosity, and
she'll unlock her door, her purse, her heart,
or anything, for you. They can't stand it.
In fact, it aint a bad story, but it's too long
to get through without moistening one's
lips. Ah, miss, there is no resisting you!"
he continued, as the young lady returned.

"No resisting the lemonade, you mean!"
retorted Miss Lucy. "I believe in my soul,
you did it a purpose to make me break
rules; but, come, begin now."

"Well, here's my service to you, miss,
and your very good health! Now, poor

Luke Loon, arter his wife gin him the dodge
(like all other water fowl when they are
scared out of one harbor light in another),
made for Snug Cove in Micmac Bay, where
there is a'most a grand mackerel fishery.
At the head of the cove there lived one old
Marm Bowers, a widow woman, with whom
Luke went to board. Poor crittur! he was
very dull and downhearted, for he was raily
wery fond of the gal : and, besides, when a
man is desarted that way, it's a kind of sight
put on him that nobody likes——"

" I guess not," said Miss Lucy ; "but he
was well rid of that horrid wretch."

" People kind of look at him and whisper,
and say, ' That's Luke Loon—him that big
Tom Bullock cut out!' And then sarcy
people are apt to throw such misfortunes
into a man's face. It ain't pleasant, I don't
suppose. Well, Luke said nothing to anybody, minded his own business, and was
getting on well, and laying by money hand
over hand, for he was a great fisherman,
and understood the Yankee mode of feeding
and enticing mackerel. Everybody liked
him, and Mother Bowers pitied him, and
was very kind to him. The old woman had
three daughters ; two of them were nothing
to brag on, but the other—that is, the
youngest—was a doll. Oh, she was a little
beauty, you may depend ! She was generally allowed to be the handsomest gal out
of sight on the whole coast, far and near, by

high and low, black or white, rich or poor.
But that warn't all ; perhaps there never
was one that was so active on her pins as
she was. She could put her hands on the
highest fence (that is, anything she could
reach), and go sideways over it like anything ; or step back a few paces, hold up her
little petticoats to her knees, and clear it like
a bird. Stumps, gates, brooks, hillocks,
nor hollows, never stopped her. She scarcely
seemed to touch the ground, she was so
light of foot. When she was a half-grown·
gal, she used to run young men across the
field as the crows flies for a dollar or a
pound of tea agin a kiss, and she kept up
the practice after she had grown up a young
woman ; but she raised her price to two
dollars, so as not to be challenged too often.
Many a young man, in follering her over a
fence, has fell, and sprained his ankle, or
put his shoulder out, or nearly broke his
neck ; while she was never known to trip,
or to be caught and kissed by no one."

" Well, well," said Miss Lucy, " what
carryings on ! What broughtens up ! What
next, I wonder ! "

" Well, Luke, though he warn't so large,
or so tall, bony, and strong as Tom Bullock,
was a withy, wiry active man—few like him
anywhere ; wrestling, running, rowing,
jumping, or shinning up rigging ; and he
thought he'd have a trial with Sally Bowers,
for a kiss or a forfeit."

" He seems to have got over his troubles very easy, I think," said Miss Lucy, "to begin racing so soon with that forward, sarcy gal. Don't you think so?"

" Tell you what, miss," he replied, " man was never made to live alone, as is shown by his being able to talk, which no other animal is, and that is a proof he must have a woman to talk to. A man's heart is a cage for love ; and, if one love gives him the dodge, there's the cage, and the perch, and the bars, and the water-glass, all so lonely and desolate, he must get another love and put into it. And therefore it was natural for Luke to feel all-over-like when he looked upon such a little fairy as Sally."

" Pooh !" said Miss Lucy. " Go on."

" ' So,' says he, ' mother,' says he, ' here's the money ; I should like to run Sally ; I kind of consait I can go it as fast as she can, although she *is* a clinker-built craft.'

" ' Nonsense, Luke,' she said ; ' you are no touch to a fore-and-after like Sally. Don't be foolish ; I don't want your money. Here, take it ! You have lost enough, already, poor fellow, without losing your money !'

" That kind of grigged Luke, for no one likes to have mishaps cast up that way, even in pity.

" ' What will you bet I don't catch her ?' says he.

" 'I'll bet you a pound,' said she. 'No, I won't either, 'cause it's only a robbing of you ; but Sally shall give you a chance, at any rate, if it's only to take the consait out of you.'

" So she called in her darter.

" 'Sally,' says she, 'Luke is teasing me to let him run a race to kiss or forfeit with you.'

" 'Who—you ? ' said she.

" 'Yes, me ! ' said Luke.

" 'Why, you don't mean to say you have the vanity to run me, do you ? '

" 'I do, though.'

" She made a spring right up an eend, till her head touched the ceiling a'most, came down with one foot out a good piece afore the other, and one arm akimbo ; then, stooping forward, and pointing with the other close into his face—

" 'You ! ' she said—'you ! Well, if that don't pass ! I wonder who will challenge me next ! Why, man alive, I could jump over your head so high you couldn't touch my foot ! But here's at you, at any rate. I'll go and shoe, and will soon make you look foolish, I know.'

" Well, she took the twenty yards' start which she always had, and off they sot, and she beat him all holler, and would haul up now and then, turn round, and step backward, with short, quick, light steps, a-tiptoe, and beckon him with her hand, and

say, 'Don't you hope you may ketch me?
Do I swim too fast for you, my young blowing porpoise?' And then point her finger
at him, and laugh like anything, and round
agin, and off like the wind, and over a fence
like a greyhound. Luke never said a word,
but kept steadily on, so as to save his wind
(for it warn't the first time he had run foot-
races); and at last he began to gain on her
by main strength. Away she flew, when she
found that, over stump land, wild pasture,
windfalls, and everything, turned at the
goal-tree, and pulled foot for home for dear
life. Luke reached the tree soon after, and
then came the tug of the race; but he had
the endurance and the wind, and overhauled
her as she ascended the hill behind the
house, and caught her just as she was falling. She was regularly beat out, and panted
like a hare, and lay in his arms, with her
head on his shoulder and her eyes shut, almost insensible.

"'Sally, dear!' said he; and he kissed
her, but she didn't speak.

"'Dear Sally! Oh, what shall I do?'
and he kissed her again and again.

"'Speak, for Heaven's sake, dear, or you
will break my heart! Oh, what an unfortunate man I be!'

"At last she kind of woke up.

"'Luke,' said she, 'don't tell mother
that you caught me, that's a good soul!
There, now!'—and she put her arms round

his neck and kissed him—'there, now, is your forfeit! I've come to, now; let me go: and do you follow, but don't push me too hard, for I'm fairly blown,' and she took over the hill, and he after her at a considerable distance.

"When they got back, said old Mother Bowers—

"'Didn't I tell you so, Luke! I knowed you couldn't do it: no man ever did it yet! I hope you feel easier, now your comb is cut. Here's your forfeit, I don't want it! But this I will say, you have made a great run for it, at any rate—the best I ever see any one make yet!'

"'Who?' said Sally. 'Do you mean him?' and she sprung up as before, and, coming down the same way on her feet, and pointing at him with her fingers, jeering like, said, 'Who?—him!—him!—why the clumsy lumokin feller don't know how even to begin to run! I hope you feel better, sir?'

"'Well, I do,' said Luke, 'that's a fact; and I should like to run you again, for I have an idea next time I could catch you in rail airnest!'

"'You do, do you?' said she; 'then your "like" is all you are likely to get, for I never run any one twice.'"

"O my!" said Miss Lucy, "what an artful, false girl! Well, I never! But is that all? is that what you call such a dismal story?"

"Oh, I wish it was," said Stephen. " The other is the end, but this is the beginning. I'll tell you the next to-morrow ; it's getting late now. Don't press me, my little rosebud ; it's really too sad."

" Ah, now, you promised me," she replied, "and it's so different from anything I ever heard before ! Ah, do, that's a good man ! "

" It's too long a story, it will take all night."

" I don't care if it does take all night, I want to hear the end of it ! "

" Well, then, I am afraid I must trouble you again, miss," handing her the empty decanter, " for I've drank it all before I've got to the part that touches the heart ! "

" Ah, Mr. Stephen," she replied, " I'll get it for you, though I know you are making game of me all the time ; but if you are, I'll be upsides with you some of these days, see if I don't !—What an awful man to drink you are !" she said, as she returned with the liquor. " Here it is : now go on."

" Well, arter the race, Luke felt a kind of affection for the young gal, and she for him. And he proposed to the old woman to marry her, but she wouldn't hear to it at no rate. Women don't much care to have a jilted man that way for their darters ; cast-off things ain't like new, and second-hand articles ain't prized in a general way ; and beside, the old lady was kind of proud

of her girl, and thought she might make a
better match than taking up with the likes
of him. At last winter came, and things
were going on in this dissatisfactory kind
of way, when a thought struck Luke.
Sally was a'most a beautiful skater. She
could go the outside edge, cut circles one
inside the other, write her name, and
figures of the year, and execute all sorts of
things on the ice with her skates; and
Luke proposed to run her that way for marriage, or twenty pounds forfeit if he didn't
catch her. It was a long time before the
old woman would consent; but at last, seeing that Sally had beat him so easy afoot,
she knowed, in course, she could outskate
him on the ice like nothing; and, therefore,
she gave in, on condition that Luke, if he
was beat, should clear out and leave the
Cove, and, as he couldn't get no better
terms, he agreed to it, and the day was
fixed and arrangements made for the race,
and the folks came from far and near to see
it. Some backed Sally and bet on her, and
some backed Luke and betted on him, but
most people wished him to win; and there
never was, perhaps, a horse-race, or foot-
race, or boat-race, or anything excited and
interested folks like this ' Race for a Wife.'
     '' The Cove was all froze over with beau-
tiful glassy ice, and the day was fine and
the company assembled, and out came the
two racers. Sally was dressed in long cloth

dress, only covered by her skirt as far as the knees, so as to admit of a free use of her limbs, and a close-fitting body with narrow sleeves, and wore a black fur cap on her head. Luke had on a pair of sea-men's trousers, belted tight round the waist, and a loose, striped Guernsey shirt, open at the neck, and a knowing little seal-skin cap, worn jauntingly a one side. It ain't often you see such a handsome couple, I can tell you. Before Sally left the house, her mother called her a one side, and said—

" ' Sally, dear, do your best, now, that's a good gal ; if you get beat, people will say you let him do it a purpose, and that ain't womanly. If such a thing was to be that you had to marry him, marry him conquer-ing and not beaten. It's a good thing to teach a man that the gray mare is the better horse. Take the conceit out of him, dear !'

" ' Never fear, mother,' said she ; ' I'll lead him a dance that goes so fast he won't know the tune he is keeping step to, I know.'

" Well, they walked hand in hand down to the Cove, and the folks cheered them again and again when they arrived on the ice. After fitting on their skates, they slowly skimmed about the Cove, showing off, cutting all sorts of feats, shines, evolu-tions, and didoes, and what not ; when they come together again, tightened their straps, shook hands, and took their places, twenty

yards apart, and, at the sound of a conch-
shell, off they started, like two streaks of
lightning. Perhaps it was the most splendid thing ever seen in this country. Sally
played him off beautifully, and would let
him all but catch her, then stop short,
double on him, and leave him ever so far
behind. Once she ran right round him, so
near as to be able to lay her little balance-
stick across his shoulders, whack with all
her might. Oh, what a laugh it raised, and
what shouts of applause, every cutting off
or heading of his received, or sudden pull
up, sharp turn, or knowing dodge of hern,
was welcomed with ! It was great sport.''

''Sport, indeed !'' said Miss Lucy. ''I
never heard anything so degrading; I
couldn't have believed it possible that a
woman would make a show of herself that
way before men, and in such an unusual
way, too !''

'' The Cove fairly rung with merriment.
At last the hour for the race was drawing
near its close (for it was agreed it should
only last an hour), and she began to lead
him off as far as possible, so as to double
on him, and make a dash for the shore, and
was saving her breath and strength for the
last rush, when, unfortunately, she got un-
awares into what they call blistered ice
(that is, a kind of rough and uneven freez-
ing of the surface), tripped, and fell at full
length on her face ; and, as Luke was in full

pursuit, he couldn't stop himself in time, and fell also right over her.

"'She is mine!' said he; 'I have her! Hurrah, I have won!'"

"Oh, yes!" said Lucy, "it's very easy to win when it's all arranged beforehand. Do you pretend to tell me, after the race in the field, that that wasn't done on purpose? I don't think I ever heard tell of a more false, bold, artful woman!"

"Oh," continued Mr. Stephen, "what a cheer of praise and triumph that caused! It rang over the ice, and was echoed back by the woods, and was so loud and clear you might have heard it clean away out to sea, as far as the light-house a'most!"

"And this is your dismal story, is it?" said the young hostess, with an air of disappointment.

"Such a waving of hats and throwing up of fur caps, was never seen; and when people had done cheering, and got their heads straight again, and looked for the racers, they was gone——"

"Gone!" said Lucy. "Where?"

"To heaven, I hope!" said Stephen.

"Why, you dont mean to say they were lost, do you?"

"Yes, I do!"

"Drowned?"

"Yes, drowned."

"What, both of them?"

"Yes, both of them."

"What, did they go through the ice?"

"Yes, through the ice. It was an airhole where they fell?"

"Oh, my, how awful!"

"I told you so, miss," said Stephen, "but you wouldn't believe me. It was awful, that's a fact!"

"Dear me!" ejaculated Lucy. "Only think of poor Luke; he was a misfortunate man, sartainly! Were they ever found?"

"Yes, when the ice broke up, the next eastwardly gale, they floated ashore, tightly clasped in each other's arms, and were buried in one grave and in one coffin. It was the largest funeral ever seen in them parts; all the fishermen from far and near attended, with their wives and darters, marching two and two; the men all dressed in their blue trousers and check shirts, and the women in their gray homespun and white aprons. There was hardly a dry eye among the whole of them. It was a most affecting scene.

"When the service was over, the people subscribed a handsome sum on the spot, and had a monument put up there. It stands on the right hand of the gate as you go into the churchyard at Snug Harbor. The school-master cut their names and ages on the stone, and also this beautiful inscription, or epitaph, or whatever it is called—

"' *This* loving pair went out to skate,
 Broke through the ice and met their fate,
 And now lie buried near this gate ;
 Year, eighteen hundred twenty-eight.'"

"Dear me, how very awful!" said Miss Lucy. "I don't think I shall sleep to-night for thinking of them ; and, if I do, I know I shall dream of them. Still, it's a pretty story, after all. It's out of the common way, like. What a strange history Luke's is! First, losing his wife by the fishery-law, then a race on foot for the tea or a forfeit, and at last, skating for a wedding or a grave! It's quite a romance in real life, isn't it? But, dear me, it's one o'clock in the morning, as I'm alive! Mr. Barclay, if you will see to the fire, please, before you go to bed, that it's all made safe (for we are great cowards about fire here), I believe I will bid you all good-night."

"It ain't quite finished yet," said Stephen. "There was another young lady."

"Who?" said Miss Lucy.

"A far handsomer and far more sensible gal than Sally, one of the best broughten up in the whole country, and one that would be a fortin to a man that was lucky enough to get her for a wife."

"Who was she, and where did she live?" inquired Lucy, who put down her candle, and awaited the reply.

"To home with her own folks," said Stephen ; "and an excellent, and comfortable, and happy home she made it, too. It's a pity Luke's wife hadn't seen her to take pattern by her ; though Luke's wife warn't fit to hold a candle to her. They hadn't ought to be mentioned in the same day. Nobody that ever see her that didn't love her—old or young, gentle or simple, married or single."

"She was no great shakes, then," said the young hostess. "She must have been a great flirt, if that was the case."

"Well, she warn't then; she was as modest, and honest, and well-conducted a gal as you ever laid your eyes on. I only wish my son, who is to man's estate now, had her, for I should be proud of her as a darter-in-law; and would give them a farm, and stock it with a complete fit-out of everything."

"If he's like his father," said Lucy, "may be he'd be a hard bargain for all that. Who is your sampler that set off with such colors, and wants the word 'Richardson' worked on it?"

"But then she has one fault," continued Stephen.

"What's that? Perhaps she's ill-tempered, for many beauties are so."

"No, as sweet-tempered a gal as ever you see. Guess agin."

"Won't take your son, may be?"

"No; she never seed him, I don't think; for, if she did, it's my notion her heart would beat like a town-clock; so loud you could hear it ever so far. Guess agin."

"Oh! I can't guess if I was to try till

to-morrow, for I never was a good hand at
finding out riddles. What is it?"

"She is a leetle, jist a leetle, too con-
saited, and is as inquisi*tive* as old Marm
Eve herself. She says she has rules that
can't never be bended nor broken, on no
account; but yet her curiosity is so great,
she will break the best regulation she has;
and that is, not to sit up after twelve o'clock
at night more than once the same evening
to hear a good story."

"Ah, now, Mr. Stephen," said the young
lady, "that's a great shame! Only to
think I should be such a goose as to be
took in so, and to stand here and listen to
all that nonsense! And then being made
such a goose of to my face, is all the thanks
I get for my pains of trying to please the
like of you! Well, I never! I'll be even with
you yet for that, see if I don't! Good night."

"One word more, please, miss. Keep
to your rules, they are all capital ones, and
I was only joking; but I must add this
little short one to them. *Circumstances
alters cases.* Good-night, dear," and he
got up and opened the door for her, and
whispered in her ear, "I am in earnest
about my son: I am, upon my soul! I'll
send him to see you. Don't be scorney,
now, that's a darling!"

"Do get away," she replied, "and don't
tease me! Gentlemen, I wish you all good-
night!"

CLARENCE'S COURTSHIP.

BY IK MARVEL.

You are at home again ;—not your own
home, that is gone ; but at the home of
Nelly and of Frank. The city heats of
summer drive you to the country. You
ramble, with a little kindling of old desires
and memories, over the hillsides that once
bounded your boyish vision.   Here, you
netted the wild rabbits, as they came out at
dusk, to feed ; there, upon that tall chestnut
you cruelly maimed your first captive
squirrel.   The old maples are even now
scarred with the rude cuts you gave them,
in sappy March.

You sit down upon some height, over-
looking the valley where you were born ;
you trace the faint, silvery line of river ; you
detect by the leaning elm, your old bathing
place upon the Saturdays of Summer. Your
eye dwells upon some patches of pasture
wood, which were famous for their nuts.
Your rambling and saddened vision roams
over the houses ; it traces the familiar chimney stacks ; it searches out the low-lying
cottages ; it dwells upon the gray roof, sleeping yonder under the sycamores.

Tears swell in your eye as you gaze ; you
cannot tell whence or why they come. Yet
they are tears eloquent of feeling.   They
speak of brother children—of boyish glee,—

of the flush of young health,—of a mother's devotion,—of the home affections,—of the vanities of life,—of the wasting years, of the Death that must shroud what friends remain, as it has shrouded what friends have gone,—and of that GREAT HOPE, beaming on your seared manhood dimly, from the upper world.

Your wealth suffices for all the luxuries of life: there is no fear of coming want; health beats strong in your veins ; you have learned to hold a place in the world, with a man's strength and a man's confidence. And yet in the view of those sweet scenes which belonged to early days, when neither strength, confidence, nor wealth was yours, days never to come again,—a shade of melancholy broods upon your spirit, and covers with its veil all that fierce pride which your worldly wisdom has wrought.

You visit again, with Frank, the country homestead of his grandfather ; he is dead ; but the old lady still lives ; and blind Fanny, now drawing toward womanhood, wears yet through her darkened life the same air of placid content and of sweet trustfulness in Heaven. The boys whom you astounded with your stories of books are gone, building up now with steady industry the queen cities of our new Western land. The old clergyman is gone from the desk and from under his sounding-board ; he sleeps beneath a brown stone slab in the churchyard. The

stout deacon is dead ; his wig and his wick-
edness rest together. The tall chorister
sings yet : but they have now a bass-viol—
handled by a new schoolmaster, in place of
his tuning-fork ; and the years have sown
feeble quavers in his voice.

Once more you meet at the home of Nelly,
—the blue-eyed Madge. The sixpence is
all forgotten ; you cannot tell where your
half of it is gone. Yet she is beautiful—
just budding into the full ripeness of womanhood. Her eyes have a quiet, still joy, and
hope beaming in them, like angel's looks.
Her motions have a native grace and freedom that no culture can bestow. Her words
have a gentle earnestness and honesty that
could never nurture guile.

You had thought, after your gay experi-
ences of the world, to meet her with a kind
condescension, as an old friend of Nelly's.
But there is that in her eye which forbids
all thought of condescension. There is that
in her air which tells of a high womanly
dignity, which can only be met on equal
ground. Your pride is piqued. She has
known—she must know your history ; but
it does not tame her. There is no marked
and submissive appreciation of your gifts,
as a man of the world.

She meets your happiest compliments
with a very easy indifference ; she receives
your elegant civilities with a very assured
brow. She neither courts your society nor

avoids it. She does not seek to provoke any special attention. And only when your old self glows in some casual kindness to Nelly, does her look beam with a flush of sympathy.

This look touches you. It makes you ponder on the noble heart that lives in Madge. It makes you wish it were yours. But that is gone. The fervor and the honesty of a glowing youth is swallowed up in the flash and splendor of the world. A half-regret chases over you at nightfall, when solitude pierces you with the swift dart of gone-by memories. But at morning, the regret dies in the glitter of ambitious purposes.

The summer months linger ; and still you linger with them. Madge is often with Nelly ; and Madge is never less than Madge. You venture to point your attentions with a little more fervor ; but she meets the fervor with no glow. She knows too well the habit of your life.

Strange feelings come over you ; feelings like half-forgotten memories—musical—dreamy—doubtful. You have seen a hundred faces more brilliant than that of Madge; you have pressed a hundred jeweled hands that have returned a half-pressure to yours. You do not exactly admire ;—to love, you have forgotten ;—you only—linger !

*   *   *   *   *   *   *

It is a soft autumn evening, and the harvest moon is red and round over the eastern skirt of woods. You are attending Madge to that little cottage home, where lives that gentle and doting mother, who in the midst of comparative poverty, cherishes that re-fined delicacy which never comes to a child but by inheritance.

Madge has been passing the day with Nelly. Something—it may be the soft autumn air wafting toward you the fresh-ness of young days—moves you to speak, as you have not ventured to speak,—as your vanity has not allowed you to speak before.

" You remember, Madge (you have guarded this sole token of boyish intimacy), our split sixpence ? "

" Perfectly ! " It is a short word to speak, and there is no tremor in her tone—not the slightest.

" You have it yet ? "

" I dare say, I have it somewhere : " no tremor now : she is very composed.

" That was a happy time : " very great emphasis on the word happy.

" Very happy : "—no emphasis anywhere.

" I sometimes wish I might live it over again."

" Yes ? "—inquiringly.

" There are after all no pleasures in the world like those."

" No ? "—inquiringly again.

You thought you had learned to have language at command : you never thought, after so many years schooling of the world, that your pliant tongue would play you truant. Yet now,—you are silent.

The moon steals silvery into the light. flakes of cloud, and the air is soft as May. The cottage is in sight. Again you risk: utterance :

" You must live very happily here."

" I have very kind friends : "—the "very " is emphasized.

" I am sure Nelly loves you very much."

" Oh, I believe it ! "—with great earnest· ness.

You are at the cottage door :—

" Good-night, Maggie,"—very feelingly.

" Good-night, Clarence,"—very kindly ; and she draws her hand coyly, and half tremulously, from your somewhat fevered grasp.

You stroll away dreamily,—watching the moon,—running over your fragmentary life ;—half moody, — half pleased,—half hopeful.

You come back stealthily and with a heart throbbing with a certain wild sense of shame to watch the light gleaming in the cottage. You linger in the shadows of the trees, until you catch a glimpse of her figure gliding past the window. You bear the image home with you. You are silent on your return. You retire early ;—but you do not sleep early.

—If you were only as you were :—if it

were not too late ! If Madge could only love
you, as you know she will and must love
one manly heart, there would be a world of
joy opening before you.

You draw out Nelly to speak of Madge :
Nelly is very prudent.   " Madge is a dear
girl,"—she says.   Does Nelly even distrust
you ? It is a sad thing to be too much a man
of the world.

You go back again to noisy, ambitious
life : you try to drown old memories in its
blaze and its vanities.   Your lot seems cast
beyond all change ; and you task yourself
with its noisy fulfillment.   But amid the
silence, and the toil of your office hours, a
strange desire broods over your spirit ;—a
desire for more of manliness—that manliness
which feels itself a protector of loving and
trustful innocence.

You look around upon the faces in which
you have smiled unmeaning smiles ;—there
is nothing there to feed your dawning desires.   You meet with those ready to court
you by flattering your vanity—by retailing
the praises of what you may do well,—by
odious familiarity,—by brazen proffer of
friendship ; but you see in it only the emptiness, and the vanity, which you have studied
to enjoy.

Sickness comes over you, and binds you
for weary days and nights ;—in which life
hovers doubtfully, and the lips babble secrets that you cherish.   It is astonishing

how disease clips a man from the artificiali-
ties of the world. Lying lonely upon his bed,
moaning, writhing, suffering, his soul joins
on to the universe of souls by only natural
bonds. The factitious ties of wealth, of
place, of reputation, vanish from his bleared
eyes ; and the earnest heart, deep under all,
craves only—heartiness.

The old yearning of the office silence comes
back ;—not with the proud wish only—of
being a protector, but—of being protected.
And whatever may be the trust in that
beneficent Power, who "chasteneth whom
He loveth,"—there is yet an earnest, human
leaning toward some one, whose love—most,
and whose duty—least, would call her to
your side ;—whose soft hands would cool
the fever of yours—whose step would wake
a throb of joy,—whose voice would tie you
to life, and whose presence would make the
worst of Death—an Adieu !

As you gain strength once more, you go
back to Nelly's home. Her kindness does
not falter ; every care and attention belong
to you there. Again your eye rests upon
that figure of Madge, and upon her face,
wearing an even gentler expression, as she
sees you sitting pale and feeble by the old
hearth-stone. She brings flowers—for Nelly :
you beg Nelly to place them upon the little
table at your side. It is as yet the only taste
of the country that you can enjoy. You
love those flowers.

After a time you grow strong, and walk in the fields. You linger until nightfall. You pass by the cottage where Madge lives. It is your pleasantest walk. The trees are greenest in that direction ; the shadows are softest ; the flowers are thickest.

It is strange—this feeling in you. It is not the feeling you had for Laura Dalton. It does not even remind of that. That was an impulse ; but this is growth. That was strong ; but this is—strength. You catch sight of her little notes to Nelly ; you read them over and over ; you treasure them ; you learn them by heart. There is something in the very writing that touches you.

You bid her adieu with tones of kindness that tremble ;—and that meet a half-trembling tone in reply. She is very good.

——If it were not too late !

* * * * * * *

And shall pride yield at length ?

——Pride !——and what has love to do with pride ? Let us see how it is.

Madge is poor ; she is humble. You are rich ; you are a man of the world ; you are met respectfully by the veterans of fashion ; you have gained perhaps a kind of brilliancy of position.

Would it then be a condescension to love Madge ? Dare you ask yourself such a question ? Do you not know—in spite of your worldliness—that the man or the

woman who *condescends* to love, never loves
in earnest?

But again, Madge is possessed of a purity,
a delicacy, and a dignity that lift her far
above you, that make you feel your weakness
and your unworthiness ; and it is the deep
and the mortifying sense of this unworthiness that makes you bolster yourself upon
your pride. You *know* that you do yourself
honor in loving such grace and goodness ;—
you know that you would be honored tenfold more than you deserve, in being loved—
by so much grace and goodness.

It scarce seems to you possible ; it is a joy
too great to be hoped for ; and in the doubt
of its attainment, your old worldly vanity
comes in, and tells you—to beware ; and to
live on, in the splendor of your dissipation,
and in the lusts of your selfish habit. Yet
still, underneath all, there is a deep, low
heart-voice,—quickened from above,—which
assures you that you are capable of better
things ;—that you are not wholly lost ; that
a mine of unstarted tenderness still lies
smoldering in your soul.

And with this sense quickening your
better nature, you venture the wealth of your
whole heart-life upon the hope that now
blazes on your path.

——You are seated at your desk, working
with such zeal of labor as your ambitious
projects never could command. It is a letter
to Margaret Boyne that so tasks your love,

and makes the veins upon your forehead
swell with the earnestness of the employ.

——" DEAR MADGE—May I not call you
thus, if only in memory of our childish affections ;—and might I dare to hope that a
riper affection which your character has
awakened may permit me to call you thus
always?

" If I have not ventured to speak, dear
Madge, will you not believe that the consciousness of my own ill-desert has tied my
tongue ;—will you not, at least, give me
credit for a little remaining modesty of
heart? You know my life, and you know
my character—what a sad jumble of errors
and of misfortunes have belonged to each.
You know the careless and the vain purposes
which have made me recreant to the better
nature which belonged to that sunny childhood, when we lived and grew up—together.
And will you not believe me when I say
that your grace of character, and kindness
of heart, have drawn me back from the
follies in which I lived, and quickened new
desires, which I thought to be wholly dead?
Can I indeed hope that you will overlook all
that has gained your secret reproaches, and
confide in a heart which is made conscious
of better things by the love—you have inspired?

" Ah, Madge, it is not with a vain show
of words, or with any counterfeit of feeling,

that I write now ;—you know it is not ;—
you know that my heart is leaning toward
you with the freshness of its noblest in-
stincts ;—you know that—I love you !

"Can I, dare I hope that it is not spoken
in vain ? I had thought in my pride never
to make such avowal,—never again to sue
for affection ; but your gentleness, your
modesty, your virtues of life and heart, have
conquered me. I am sure you will treat me
with the generosity of a victor.

"You know my weaknesses ;—I would
not conceal from you a single one,—even to
win you. I can offer nothing to you which
will bear comparison in value with what is
yours to bestow. I can only offer this feeble
hand of mine—to guard you ; and this poor
heart—to love you !

"Am I rash ? Am I extravagant in
word, or in hope ? Forgive it, then, dear
Madge, for the sake of our old childish
affection ; and believe me when I say that
what is here written,—is written honestly
and tearfully.

"Adieu."

It is with no fervor of boyish passion that
you fold this letter ; it is with the trembling
hand of eager and earnest manhood. They
tell you that man is not capable of love ;—so
the September sun is not capable of warmth.
It may not indeed be so fierce as that of
July ; but it is steadier. It does not force

great flaunting leaves into breadth and suc-
culence ; but it matures whole harvests of
plenty.

There is a deep and earnest soul pervading
the reply of Madge that makes it sacred ; it
is full of delicacy and full of hope. Yet it is
not final. Her heart lies intrenched within
the ramparts of Duty and of Devotion. It
is a citadel of strength, in the middle of the
city of her affections. To win the way to
it, there must be not only earnestness of
love, but earnestness of life.

Weeks roll by ; and other letters pass and
are answered,—a glow of warmth beaming
on either side.

You are again at the home of Nelly ; she
is very joyous ; she is the confidant of
Madge. Nelly feels that, with all your
errors, you have enough inner goodness of
heart to make Madge happy ; and she feels
doubly—that Madge has such excess of
goodness as will cover your heart with joy.
Yet she tells you very little. She will give
you no full assurance of the love of Madge ;
she leaves that for yourself to win.

She will even tease you in her pleasant
way until hope almost changes to despair ;
and your brow grows pale with the dread—
that even now your unworthiness may con-
demn you.

It is summer weather ; and you have been
walking over the hills of home with Madge
and Nelly. Nelly has found some excuse to

leave you,—glancing at you most teasingly as she hurries away.

You are left sitting with Madge, upon a bank tufted with blue violets. You have been talking of the days of childhood, and some word has called up to the old chain of boyish feeling, and joined it to your new hope.

What you would say crowds too fast for utterance ; and you abandon it. But you take from your pocket that little broken bit of sixpence,—which you have found after long search,—and without a word, but with a look that tells your inmost thought, you lay it in the half opened hand of Madge.

She looks at you with a slight suffusion of color,—seems to hesitate a moment,— raises her other hand and draws from her bosom, by a bit of blue ribbon, a little locket. She touches a spring, and there falls beside your relique,—another, that had once belonged to it.

Hope glows now like the sun.

——" And have you worn this, Maggie?"

——" Always ! "

" Dear Madge ! "

" Dear Clarence ! "

——And you pass your arm now, un-checked, around that yielding, graceful figure ; and fold her to your bosom, with the swift and blessed assurance that your fullest and noblest dream of love is won.

MISFORTUNE'S FAVORITE.

BY CARLOTTA PERRY.

I.

Everybody said that Dick Andrews was born to ill luck ; and what everybody says comes in time to be believed. He almost believed it himself; he knew that, as he put it, "the wind always blew in his face." In his boyhood, if any one of the children of the family was late at school, it was sure to be Dick ; if any skates got broken or any sled lost a runner, there was no need to ask to which of the boys the property belonged. If either of the boys went without mittens or an overcoat, it was Dick, of course. If any one stayed at home from church or merry-making to tend to the fires or keep the mother company, Dick was the one.

No one could tell exactly why. To be sure, his brothers and sisters appropriated his property without scruple, which was one reason of its often being out of repair ; besides, if any one wanted to borrow sled or skates, it was supposed that it was less of a denial for him than for Tom, his brother, to go without them ; and it grew to be an accepted belief that he didn't care very much for merry-making anyway, and then, too, one couldn't go without suitable clothes, and after getting Tom all he needed, and

providing suitable garments for Sue and
Mary, there wasn't so very much left. Not
that he was an abused or neglected child.
His mother loved him tenderly, and to his
sisters and one brother there was nobody
like dear old Dick ; but it was discovered
that he had one talent—the talent for self-
denial, and it was allowed full opportunity
for development, as it generally is.

Tom wanted to go out into the world, and
he went. Dick wanted to go, but there
were the widowed mother and the two sisters
and the farm, and Dick stayed. So he
worked faithfully and prospered in worldly
things. The girls .went to school ; they
came home and filled the old house with
their wonderful paintings, their fancy-
work, their marvelous music and still more
marvelous French. And Dick, plain, simple, unlearned Dick, stood in much awe of
the girls, who in turn patronized him. To
be sure, there were books in Dick's room of
whose very names they were ignorant, and
curious mechanical devices that would have
bewildered them, but that was only Dick's
oddity. He was never like other people
anyway, and it was just like him to be
spending the time, when he ought to be
sleeping, in poring over some dull scientific
nonsense or constructing some foolish una-
vailable machine, that ought to work but
wouldn't. So they talked, and life moved
on for all. The early morning found him

at his duty, the evening found his duty done. He had grown used to his life, he had ceased to think much about it, further than to do everything he could for everybody around him.

He thought his sisters the most beautiful and accomplished women in the world, and all women were in his eyes to be admired and reverenced. About the fittest use he deemed that his life could be put to was to make their lives fair and full of ease.

When Agatha Dale came to visit his sisters his world widened. He had seen no woman like her; he had seen very few women anyway, and that the world held any such as she he had not imagined. She talked to him more than anyone else had ever done, and one day, when a rain had driven him in from the field, she followed him out on the porch where he stood watching the storm, and said:

"Mr. Andrews, Sue tells me that you have a den filled not with wild beasts, but with wonderful machines and inventions of your own ; and though she speaks of them rather lightly, I am inclined to suspect that you are a genius—and I have a perfect craze for making discoveries, and if I could only discover a *genius* hidden away on this great farm of yours I should die content."

"Oh, don't talk of dying, Miss Dale," he replied, while a great flush of color swept into his face ; "don't talk of dying."

'' No, I don't intend to ; that I hope is to be deferred till I have made the discovery I spoke of.''

'' There's nothing to discover that I know of, nothing at least that you would care to know.''

'' I want to see that room where you burn the midnight oil. I want you to show me what you are trying to do, though I cannot help you, only as interest and sympathy help one,'' and she looked up into his honest eyes with a look that set his honest heart beating wildly. And she gained what she asked. He told her of dreams and hopes that had stirred the brain that every one else thought dull and sluggish. He explained how nearly he had achieved the perfect working of an invention that should be of priceless value in a certain department of labor. Only it was not *quite* perfect. If this wheel were a little larger or smaller, and that band or pulley could be made to work a little different, or if this spring were a little stronger or more flexible, it would be all right. And it would be after a little ; he was sure he had the right idea. And then here was something else that if he had time he could develop, but he had not been able to get the time, and so there it was !

'' But I guess I'll make it out yet, Miss Dale.''

'' Yes, I think you will, Mr. Andrews. I think you will.''

"Everybody in these parts calls me Dick,"
he said ; "maybe you would."

"No," she replied, "I shall not call you
Dick ; that is no name to call such a man
as you by.   I will call you Richard, if you
are willing.   You are my host, besides.   I
see what these around you do not see, and
what I think you are too modest to believe,
that something akin to the wonderful thing
we call genius is yours."

"I don't know," he said.   "I don't
know as all this means anything, but I've
kind o' thought sometimes that if I'd had a
chance—but you see, Miss Dale, Tom he
had to go, and the girls they had to go and
be educated, and there was the farm and
mother, and so I had to stay ; there was no
other way, you see."

"Yes ; I see, Richard, I see."

It was food and drink to him, this appar-
ent sympathy of hers.   To have her choose
to call him Richard was a sweet thing to
him.   It gave him a kind of dignity in his
own eyes that he had never thought of
claiming.

He regretted more than he had ever done
in his life that he had lived so ignorant of
the ways of the world in which *she* lived,
that he was not master of any of the arts
and graces which women love.

She saw all this.   She was a clear, quick-
brained woman, with intellect enough to see
the sweetness, the unselfishness of such a

character as his, but without heart enough to reverence it. She saw, too, how nearly he came to having the divine gift of genius; but she saw also that while these machines worked without flaw, and the thought-engine rolled with perfect motion through his brain, that not for him would their grand possibilities be realized. Some more practical hand would execute what his brain conceived, the flower would blossom but not for him, from the seed of his sowing great harvest should come, but not for his hands to gather.

How he grew to worship her! with all the earnest unselfishness of his nature he worshiped her. She permitted it; she liked it. It interested her to see what love would do for such a man. He was no common lover; had he been she would have grown weary of him, as she had of many others. But it was delightful to waken this soul to a new life. It was charming to read to him, to sing to him, and see him draw in her voice as though it were the breath of life. It was interesting to see the fire in the eyes, and know that it burned outward from the soul.

It was pleasant to see how happy he could be made by a little warmer smile than usual, by a little kindlier glance. She reasoned with herself that it would do no harm; that his life had been so empty, that this experience, while it could end in but one way, would still be good for him. She was one of those, who, having known little of sorrow, had a high opinion of its disciplinary advantages.

*   *   *   *   *

Then one day there came a letter from Tom ; he was coming home. The old mother was trembling for happiness. The girls were delighted that Tom was coming while Agatha was there. She would like Tom, everybody did. Agatha thought to herself that it might be a good thing. She was about satisfied with the result of her experiment. Dick said little ; he would be glad, too, it could not make much difference, he thought. Tom Andrews was one of those men who seem to fill a house. Gay, handsome, selfish, acquainted with the world and fond of it, with a gift for getting money, but a greater gift for spending it ; he was one of those men whom men like without having any great respect for, and whom women love half-knowing his unworthiness.

Then such pain came to Dick as he had not supposed the world could hold. He could understand why a woman might prefer Tom to himself, but his simple, honest soul could not see why an interest and sympathy so true as Agatha's had been could wane so suddenly. With an abject admiration for Tom and his attractions, he had still such absolute constancy himself that he could not understand how any one could

be swayed in love or friendship, and of in-
sincerity he had no knowledge. But he saw
without understanding that his little lease
of happiness was gone. It was the old
way, the way he thought he was used to.
The best of everything for Tom, always
Tom.

He said over and over to himself that it
was all right. That she had done nothing
wrong. Then he remembered how she
looked in his eyes the day she gave him the
rose out of her hair, and how she had once
put her soft hand on his forehead, and how
pleased she looked when he brought her the
lilies from the pond, and called him a dear,
good fellow ; but it must be that it was the
way women did, and must be right. She
meant to be kind to him. In his simple
heart he never once thought that she was to
blame for his heart-ache, that she had
amused herself with him never once crossed
his mind. She was so good, so high, so
beautiful, besides she was a woman, and he
had not learned that women could be anything but true and noble.

And he ought not to begrudge Tom any
happiness. But one night he saw Tom and
Agatha standing together under the tree in
front of his window. The moonlight shone
on her fair hair, and he thought he could
see the very smile on her red lips. He saw
the red geranium on the bosom of her white
gown, he noticed how white her arms were,

and how lithe and graceful her form as she stood looking up into Tom's eyes as she had looked into his. And then, yes, he saw Tom put his arms around her and draw her close, close to his breast ; he saw the red lips lifted to his ; he saw the fair head droop to the strong shoulder.

He did not groan nor rave, he did not curse nor swear, he did not rail against man's treachery nor woman's perfidy, but he went slowly down the back stairs and out to the stable. He pretended to himself that he wanted to see if everything was all right. He heard his sisters' voices in the sitting-room. They had each a lover, and there was singing and merry sounds coming from happy hearts. His pet horse whinnied as he came into the barn. A great creature, magnificent in strength and limb, which no one but Dick could ever manage. He put his arms round the horse's neck and bowed his head on the glossy mane.

"It's all right, Charley ; but it's hard, isn't it, old fellow ? "

That was all ; then he went back. Passing his mother's bedroom door, she called out, " Good-night, Tom."

" It's Dick, mother," he replied.

"Oh, I thought it was Tom."

"No, it's me."

Then he remembered that Agatha had told him that he should not say, " It's me," and he softly corrected himself. Then he

saw the girls bidding a gay good-night to
their lovers, and heard Agatha at the piano.
He sat at his window long, looking at the
stars that shone brighter as the moon paled ;
he remembered what she had called their
names. Then he called himself a foolish
fellow. It was all right, only the great ache
in his bosom he could not help ; he did not
understand why he should be so hurt in his
heart by anything that was all right, as that
surely was.

II.

The next morning Mrs. Andrews was
found dead in her bed. Heart-disease, the
doctor called it. There was sincere grief,
for she was beloved of her children and respected of all. But the suddenness of the
blow unnerved them all, all but Dick. He
told with a mighty struggle against his
tears how she had called out "good-night,
Tom," the night before; he would have
given half his life if that last good-night
had been for him. Tom made him say it
over and over, and told it over to others
how her last word heard by mortal ears was
tor him. And they all wept and sobbed,
and wondered that Dick could do the things
he did, for it was he who attended to all the
details of the funeral, he who sat in the
still night in the same room with the still
body, and he who insisted upon helping to

lay it in the coffin. It was a comfort to do
these things ; it was an escape for the terrible pain in his heart. The others had words
and tears and moans ; his sorrow was dumb,
only by these sad ministries could it find
relief. Hungry and thirsting for pity, he
heard them say, "It was strange how little
Dick felt it, they did not see how he could
do the things he did ; they knew they could
not, but Dick was always queer." He
supposed it was because he was queer that
he could not cry, but he thought that maybe
Agatha understood that he cared, for he
had heard her say once that the deepest
sorrow was silent. It would be some comfort to know that she understood. She was
so busy that he had not seen her much, for
she was attending to the funeral garments
for his sisters. She was arranging the
house, and conferring with the singers. But
a little box came from the city for her that
last morning, and as she took it in the room
where the dead lay, he followed her.

He untied the box, and helped take out
the mass of white carnations and lay them
on the foot of the casket. "Just sixty-five,"
she said ; "just as many as she had lived
years."

As they laid the flowers down their hands
met an instant ; he felt the ring on her
finger, and he saw that it was one Tom had
worn for years, and she was wearing it now.
The touch of the ring brought it all back,

all the agony of that night when all his hope died, and a vague thought came that he too was dead, dead with the breath yet in him, and the world fair around him, only not dead to pain. as they thought he was.

*   *   *   *   *

It was said a few days after the funeral that Agatha was going home. The girls pleaded for a longer stay, but she had been with them more than two months, and she must go. Tom said nothing ; but Dick said to her as they met on the stairs an hour later :

"I want to say a word to you, Agatha."

"Yes, Richard ;" and she said, "let's take a little walk."

She would have gone out in the shade of the big tree in front of the window, but he said no, not there. She sat down in a chair on the porch, and he stood beside her.

"Going away, Agatha ?"

"Yes, I have been here a long time. It has been such a pleasant time ; except for this dreadful sorrow for you all, which I, too, feel keenly, I should say it was the happiest summer I had known for a long, long time. It has been almost perfect, has it not, Richard ?"

He had not dreamed of saying the words that came to his lips, he had only meant to speak of Tom, and of the engagement which he supposed existed, and to ask her to stay right along ; but the calm way in which she spoke of her happy summer was too much ; he surprised her and himself not less by saying :

"It has been heaven and hell both, and you've made both for me."

"What do you mean, Richard?"

"If you don't know what I mean, nothing that I can say would make you, and maybe you don't know, maybe you don't. Of course you don't if you say so. Perhaps I never should have told you how much I loved you, for I knew all the time it was no use ; but, though I'd got used to giving up before Tom, it was mighty hard to see you go with the rest. But it's all right, and I won't blame you for loving Tom. You do love him, I suppose?" There was a look in his eyes that was touchingly pathetic. A look in which he seemed to be trying to hide the little hope that seemed determined to live.

"Yes, I love Tom ; but I like you, Richard, and I hope we shall be friends. I'm sorry that you feel so bad ; but you are strong, and you will conquer it."

"I reckon trouble is something like sickness ; it goes hardest with the strongest sometimes," he said.

"I've helped you some this summer, Richard. I've given you some pleasure," she said. She *was* sorry for him as he stood there. So strong in frame and muscle. So strong in his faith and patience, with such a capacity for endurance in suffering.

Though she had been cruel to him, she understood him better than the others did, perhaps because her wrongs toward him were greater than theirs. Something like this she thought as she said, "I've helped you some, Richard."

"I don't know ; you've meant to, perhaps, and if you meant to and hurt me instead, why, you're not to blame, I suppose."

The old platitudes rose to her lips. "Sometimes troubles are good for us. Sometimes they make us stronger and nobler, and in the end happier. The greatest deeds have been done by men who had hard lives, and the greatest poems have been written by men who had sad hearts."

"But I'm not that kind, and I know it," he said, simply. "I guess they didn't do all these great things because of the trouble, but in spite of it ; besides, if they did, seems 'twouldn't hardly pay 'em. I've read somewhere that when men want the turtle shell that is made into pretty combs and such for women to wear, they catch the turtle and tie a string to him so he can't get away, then put hot coals on his back, more and more of 'em, and hotter and hotter, till the shell cracks ; the poor turtle is just crazy with the pain, but it can't get away ; and they get the shell, and the pretty women wear the combs ; but seems to me the turtle has a hard time of it.''

"That's horrible, Richard, and I don't think it's true, either.''

"No, I don't know as it's true, but I've read it somewhere.''

"Then you don't think that sorrow ever helps anybody ? ''

"Seems to me, it depends a good deal on what sort of sorrow it is, and how it comes to a body. I've read again somewhere that there is in some far-off country a little fly or insect, or something of that sort, that the people take a great deal of pains to have live because the sting of it ripens a little quicker a certain sort of fruit that the people are fond of. It sort o' *stings* it into ripeness. It isn't quite perfect fruit, but it has ripened quicker for the sting. But that isn't what I was going to talk about. Sue will be married this winter, and Mary, too, perhaps ; and as I'm going away, seems to me it would be the right thing for you and Tom to be married, and—and to keep the old place up ; that is, if you and he could be contented on the farm. I'd like to think that you were here.''

"I don't know—when are you going ?'' She tried to ask the question sympathetically. She was ashamed not to care when in his heart-break he was making such plans for her, but he only answered, "I'll talk to Tom, and see what he says, and if he'll consent to stay it'll be all right.''

III.

Tom would stay, nothing could suit him better ; he had indulged his fancy for roving, he had spent all the money he had, and he had very small fondness, and still smaller talent, for making money. The farm was in good order, there was no incumbrance upon it, he would be able to keep all the necessary help for himself and his wife, thanks to Dick's economy and management ; and altogether he imagined that though his experience was limited, it would not be a difficult thing to make life a pleasant thing on the farm, and it was his firm belief that life should be a pleasant thing—his life, anyway. And so it was arranged.

Agatha went home, and in a few weeks Tom went for her and they were married. The house was in order for their return. The day they were to come, Dick was in the little room all day. He packed up the models of the inventions over which he had had such dreams, and his trunks and boxes were taken from the house. Then, when night came, he went out to his mother's grave, for she was buried in her own ground in sight of her own door. He heard the whistle of the engine at the station two miles away ; he stayed there at the grave till the old-fashioned rockaway drove up to

the door of the house ; he strained his eyes
to see the bride as she crossed the threshold
of the home, her home henceforth.   Then
he walked away toward the village and the
train which he knew would be due there in
an hour.   It was the only cowardice and
deception of his life, but he said over and
over to himself as he walked along, " I
couldn't bear any more—I couldn't bear
any more."   In a little note in his room
they found his simple good-by.

They were sorry, so they said, that he
had gone ; and so they were—sorry as people are whose own lives are full of their own
hopes and plans and pleasures.

In midwinter the sisters both married,
and their portion was given to them. There
was a verbal understanding that a certain
part of the profits from the farm were to
be placed in the bank subject to Dick's
order.

He went West. The wonderful stories
of the Pacific coast lured him on, and it
made little difference.   He had no great
plans or aims ; he had no great dream or
hopes.   His heart-ache, heavy, dull, and
constant, left him no room for sweet imag-
inings, had he ever been given to such.

His wants were simple, but, simple as
they were, they were not always met.   Always the wind blew in his face.

A little mining, a little stock-raising, a
little working as a common farm-hand, and

the months went by. Then, after a little, he went into the sunny Southern California. Nature was warm of heart toward him. Fruits and flowers seem to know his hand. And here three serene years went by. The curious people, made up of many peoples, learned to know and love him. Cunning Spaniards, wily French, and the sharp, shrewd men from his own land. The pretty Señoritas and the practical, ambitious women from Yankee-land all learned to know the simple stranger, whose inability to learn the world's wisdom made them place him now in the category of saints, and now in that of fools. At long intervals he wrote home, and at longer intervals they wrote to him. Three children had been born to Tom and Agatha. Once they wrote of alterations and improvements they had been making in the old house ; then of failures in this or that crop ; then of ill-health. Then again of good times and new expenditures.

And he wrote very simply of himself, making no murmurs, telling not a word of the loneliness and emptiness of life, saying nothing of the pain of his constant nature.

But after a time he turned again to his models. The old love came upon him, and again his nights saw him repeating the old attempts to realize his dreams. Then he thought success stood at his side. Ah ! he had what he sought ! Then he remembered that a certain share of the profits of the old farm was lying in the bank at home, and he had learned the lesson that all men, wise or foolish, learn, that though his invention was one that would move the world it would take money to prove the fact.

He wrote to Tom to send the money. Tom wrote, or Agatha wrote, that they were sorry, but Tom had used it. It wasn't a great sum any way, and their expenses had been large the last two years, and they had improved the old place, and of course that had cost a large sum, and altogether there wasn't much due him, but by-and-by, when he came home, they would make it all right.

He read the letter twice slowly. He had seen dishonesty; he had seen men shot down in broad day without a moment's warning; he had seen vileness flaunting the streets, and vice in high places, and virtue cold and hungry; still his honest heart made no accusation against his brother. It was all right; at any rate the woman he had loved had been made happier by it, and what more could he ask that his money should do; it was right. Then once more he locked the docr upon his hopes, and turned away to fight this last disappointment. If he had made any moans, none heard them. If he whispered his griefs sometimes to his beloved grape-vines to whose service he gave his heart, that was

all. They gave generous return for his service, but they never betrayed his secrets.

The poetic people about him, the smooth-
voiced Señors and Señoritas spoke of him as
the gentle Señor who had no gray hairs nor
wrinkles in his heart.

Then one day there came a letter from
Agatha. Tom was dead! He had died
three months before the letter reached Dick.
There were many expressions of sorrow ;
there were laments over the sad condition in
which affairs were left. Tom had been
careless, and there were four children, and
she did not know what she should do under
her burdens. She asked for nothing, but
there was no need. The next mail took all
the money which Dick could control, and it
took also many kind words, awkwardly expressed, but beating with the sincerity of
his soul, and also the promise of more help
speedily.

He would have gone home, but something, a feeling he could not give a name to,
held him back. He wanted to know more
of them all than the infrequent letters told ;
he wanted, God only knew how fervently,
to see the old home, his mother's grave, and
that new one beside it ; he wanted to see his
sisters' faces, and Agatha, and Agatha's
children. More deeply than he could tell
almost more wildly than he acknowledged to
himself, did his starved heart cry out against
its hunger that had fed upon famine only.

By and by he would go home, but not yet. He grew wildly ambitious to make money—money so that he could take care of Tom's children, and make the way smooth for Agatha—only for that.

He told his wants one day to a friend ; told simply that he wanted more money than he had or saw any way of getting. And then in a burst of confidence, he said, "I've got something that I'm going to show you. I've had a notion that it was worth something, but I don't know sure, leastways it can do no harm to show it." So half the night they sat examining and talking about the invention which Dick had thought he had forever given up.

Josiah Green was a quick, clear-headed man, and, after the fashion of the worldly business man, he was honest. At a glance, almost, he saw the value of Dick's invention, and after examining it closely he thought he saw the remedy for certain flaws which seemed to exist in it. But he met the imploring, doubting look in Dick's eyes with a cool and an almost discouraging look. "What did he think of it?" Well, he couldn't just tell ; it might be good for something, and then again it mightn't. He'd think about it and tell him next day.

The next day he said : "I think, Dick, that if that machine of yours was just right, it would be a mighty big thing, but 'taint just right, or that's the way it looks to me, and if it comes within an inch of perfection, it might as well be a mile, you know."

"Perhaps I can make it right."

"Perhaps you can ; but you've been ten years about it, haven't you ? "

"Yes ; ten years."

"And then, you've to get it patented, and I've had some experience in patents. A man said to me once : 'Whatever else you do in the world, Green, don't invent anything.' You hear me! And I've kept clear of it. And then when you apply for a patent you've got to be mighty sure that there's no fellow ahead of you, or you're in trouble, and after the thing *is* patented, and is all right, why you've got to have money and lots of experience and good hard sense of a practical sort to get it on the market, and you won't mind my telling you, Dick, that you're not that sort. You'd be the round peg in the square hole, eh?"

"What would you do?"

"I'll tell you what *I'll* do. I'll buy that thing of you, outright. I'll take my chances on perfecting it. I'll get it patented, and if it is a success I'll make money out of it, and if it isn't, why, it'll take its place with the rest of the trash the world is full of. I'll give you five thousand dollars for it just as it is. What do you say?"

Dick showed the simplicity of his nature by asking, "What would you do if you were me?"

The man from Maine, as Josiah Green was always called, looked with half-pity on Dick as he answered in entire honesty, "If I were *you* I'd take it quicker than lightning!"

"Do you think that's as much as it's worth?"

"You are the strangest man I ever set eyes on. You act as though a man making a bargain was bound to work for the other party's interest as well as his own. Now, your confounded faith in me leads me to say, that I think I've offered you all that the thing is worth to *you;* all and more than you'll be likely to get for it from anybody else, or through any effort of your own ; but if it were mine, I wouldn't sell it for what I advise you to take,—all because I'm a different sort of man from what you are. I couldn't have done what you have so far— head isn't shaped right ; but now, I can take it, and make something out of it, I think. You can't. Your head isn't shaped right for that. See? Now you can think about it, and let me know, and if you say yes, we'll go up to 'Frisco, and have it all arranged whenever you say so."

And Dick accepted the offer. They went to 'Frisco, and it was legally arranged. When he saw the model, the child of his heart, carried out of his room, he bent his head and wept. But there was the money, and what would not that do toward the comfort of those he loved? And added to this were the proceeds of the well-beloved vines and fig-trees. All that he cared most for that was really his own, was represented by the yellow gold and crisp bank-notes.

It was more than a year since Tom died, and he would go home. It was his home, save such portion of it as would come to Agatha, as Tom's widow, and surely he had a right to seek his own. He found all so changed; the "slight improvements" meant bay-windows, and porches, and wonderful painting, and tiling, and all the æsthetic decorations of the day. There were fine furnishings inside, and a fountain on the lawn. There were shabby out-buildings, and empty granaries, and ill-cared-for stock, and worse-cared-for fields. There were debts, debts, debts. And there was Agatha, older, but scarcely less beautiful, wearing her widow's weeds, and the children, who at once loved the "Uncle Dick," who had lots of money and would spend it with them.

It was easy to understand why all had gone so ill. Extravagance rather than misfortune had wrought all the trouble, and Dick's work was plain to his eyes.

Steadily he looked into matters, and patiently he set about in his slow fashion to mend them. The neighbors said that the coming home of Dick Andrews, queer as he was, was a blessing to the widow and the children. In a year's time there was less display at the front of the house and more comfort inside. He assumed the burdens, and no one objected to his bearing burdens. He enjoyed it. Agatha was very kind ; with returning prosperity her spirits returned. There was no comfort or pleasure that could be laid at her feet that was not provided. A little remonstrance she would offer, but the reply always came : " I've no other use for money, and I shan't buy anything I can't afford." Dick was almost happy ; it seemed to him that if he were as strong as he used to be, he would be quite happy ; but the years, and the roving life, and the exposures, had told upon him ; he was not quite strong.

But home was so pleasant ! Agatha was so sweet and kind ! They had in the summer evenings pleasant rides over the old familiar roads. Always at night he rode to the village for the mail, and two or three times each week she would go with him, for she had a correspondence—business letters, she said, and it did not occur to Dick to wonder what the business could be that he did not know.

He was almost happy, and the old dream of being entirely happy came back. Who knew ? Perhaps it might be, after all ; perhaps, after all these years, it would come to him—the hope of his soul, the desire of his life. Perhaps the winds of fate would blow fairly for him yet.

That night they sat together by the fire after the children had gone to bed, and talked of the past. With her Dick was at his best. Almost he had spoken his thought, when she said: " Dick, there's something I want to tell you. I was not quite heart-whole when I married Tom. I loved "— Great God ! what was she going to say ?— " I loved another, or I had loved another man before I saw him or you." Ah, what a ridiculous thought that was that flashed upon Dick for an instant ! " And six months ago, one day when you happened to be away, he came, this old lover, and, Dick, you un-derstand—he wants me to marry him—and —and——"

" You want to marry him ? "

" I have said that I would—in the spring, perhaps. We shall go away from here, and then, Dick, dear, you must marry and stay in the old home. The old place is yours, anyway, Dick, or ought to be."

" The place will be yours and your chil-dren's after you."

" You are glad that I am going to find love and care and the protection of a strong heart again ? Oh, you've been good and kind, Dick, but you know—or no, you don't know —how lonesome a heart can be, after all."

How could he make her understand his life ·long hunger ; what was the use of saying anything? So he said only, "I suppose not."

"And are you glad?"

What was the use of saying anything, except what she seemed to want him to say? what did it matter if he lied? So he looked her straight in the eyes and said he was glad, glad for anything that made her happy.

*   *   *   *   *

Then death, which, it is said, to every mortal thing comes too early or too late, remembered him. Death, pityingly, took him out of the warm, cruel hands of life. It was a general decline, the doctor said, brought about by exposure, together with an inherited "tendency to pulmonary troubles." His father and Tom had gone in something the same way. They did not know that he was dying of a broken heart —men do not die of broken hearts, the doctors say. He made his will, and the lawyer, a little keener of sight, said to himself, "He is not the first man who has wasted heart and soul and substance on a woman too blind to see and too selfish to care for it."

The day before he died came a lot of papers, giving an account of the trial and perfect success of a certain invention which was to work wonders in the world of mechanical labor. It was spoken of as the product of great inventive genius wedded to patience and skill.

There came also a line from Josiah Green.

"It's all right, old honest heart, a great success! I found the 'missing link,' just enough to make it honest for me to call it mine. Already I see a big fortune in it; and the world, quick to see a good thing, sees it also, and there are plenty with money ready to take hold of it if I want, which I don't. If there's anything I can do for you let me know."

"There's nothing that can be done for me," said Dick. "I wish that this child of mine could have borne my name. I wish I could have left something, that the world would have known I had given it something. But it's like all the rest of my life, and it's all right. I hope that somewhere there is a world where all the failures and the blunders of this will be understood. I have wished and longed so much, and could not tell. I could never make you know, Agatha, but some time and some where you will see, I hope, not what I did, or failed to do, but what I would have done; not what I was, but what I would have been if I could. If I only could! But it was all wrong from the beginning; the wind always blew in my face, and—it—was—too—strong—for me. But I think the wind is changing, dear. It is blowing soft and cool and sweet, and I am going with it now at last, at last." So Death remembered him.

Then the kisses his living lips never knew were given to him dead, the flowers that had never blossomed for him living were piled upon his coffin. And they wept and lamented and wished that they had loved him more. They saw the sweetness and the sadness of his unselfish, denied life when it was too late to love the one or help the other. 'Tis the world's way.

A TRUE STORY.

BY MARK TWAIN.

It was summer time and twilight. We were sitting on the porch of the farm-house, on the summit of the hill, and "Aunt Rachel" was sitting respectfully below our level, on the steps, for she was our servant and colored. She was of mighty frame and stature ; she was sixty years old, but her eye was undimmed and her strength unabated. She was a cheerful, hearty soul, and it was no more trouble for her to laugh than it is for a bird to sing. She was under fire now, as usual when the day was done. That is to say, she was being chaffed without mercy, and was enjoying it. She would let off peal after peal of laughter, and then sit with her face in her hands and shake with throes of enjoyment which she could no longer get breath enough to express. At

such a moment as this a thought occurred
to me, and I said :

"Aunt Rachel, how is it that you've
lived sixty years and never had any
trouble?"

She stopped quaking. She paused, and
there was a moment of silence. She turned
her face over her shoulder toward me, and
said without even a smile in her voice :

"Misto C——, is you in 'arnest?"

It surprised me a good deal; and it
sobered my manner and my speech, too.
I said :

"Why, I thought—that is, I meant—
why, you *can't* have had any trouble. I've
never heard you sigh, and never seen your
eye when there wasn't a laugh in it."

She faced fairly around now, and was full
of earnestness.

"Has I had any trouble! Misto C——,
I's gwyne to tell you, den I leave it to you.
I was bawn down 'mongst de slaves; I
knows all 'bout slavery, 'case I been one of
'em my own se'f. Well, sah, my ole man,
—dat's my husban'—he was lovin' an' kind
to me, jist as kind as you is to yo' own
wife. An' we had chil'en—seven chil'en—
an' we loved dem chil'en jist de same as
you loves yo' chil'en. Dey was black, but
de Lord can't make no chil'en so black but
what dey mother loves 'em an' wouldn't
give 'em up, no, not for anything dat's in
this whole world.

"Well, sah, I was raised in old Fo'ginny, but my mother she was raised in Maryland; an' my *souls!* she was turrible when she'd git started. My *lan!* but she'd make de fur fly! When she'd git into dem tantrums, she always had one word dat she said. She'd straighten herse'f up an' put her fists in her hips an' say, 'I want you to understan' dat I wa'nt bawn in de mash to be fool' by trash! I's one o' de old Blue Hen's Chickens, *I* is!' 'ca'se, you see, dat's what folks dat's bawn in Maryland calls deyselves, an' dey's proud of it. Well, dat was her word. I don't ever forgit it, beca'se she said it so much, an' beca'se she said it one day when my little Henry tore his wris' awful, and most busted his head, right up at the top of his forehead, an' de niggers didn't fly aroun' fas' enough to 'tend to him. An' when dey talk' back at her, she up an' she says, 'Look-a-heah!' she says, 'I want you niggers to understan' that I wa'nt bawn in de mash to be fool' by trash! I's one o' de ole Blue Hen's Chickens, *I* is!' an' den she clar' dat kitchen an' bandage' up de chile herse'f. So I says dat word, too, when I's riled.

"Well, bymeby my ole mistis says she's broke, an' she' got to sell all de niggers on de place. An' when I hear dat dey gwyne to sell us all off at oction in Richmon', oh de good gracious! I know what dat mean!"

Aunt Rachel had gradually risen, while she warmed to her subject, and now she towered above us, black against the stars.

" Dey put chains on us an' put us on a stan' as high as dis po'ch,—twenty foot high,—an' all de people stood aroun', crowds an' crowds. An' dey'd come up dah an' look at us all roun', an' squeeze our arm, an' make us git up an' walk, an' den say, ' Dis one too ole,' or ' Dis one lame,' or ' Dis one don't 'mount to much.' An' dey sole my ole man, an' took him away, an' dey begin to sell my chil'en an' take *dem* away, an' I begin to cry; an' de man say, ' Shet up yo fool blubberin',' an' hit me on de mouf wid his han'. An' when de las' one was gone but my little Henry, I grab' *him* clost up to my breas' so, an' I ris up an' says, ' You shan't take him away,' I says ; ' I'll kill de man that tetches him !' I says. But my little Henry whisper an' say, ' I gwyne to run away, an' den I work an' buy yo' freedom.' Oh, bless de chile, he always so good ! But dey got him —dey got him, de men did ; but I took an' tear de clo's mos' off of 'em an' beat 'em over de head wid my chain ; and *dey* give it to *me*, too, but I didn't mind dat.

" Well, dah was my ole man gone, an' all my chil'en, all my seven chil'en—an' six of 'em I hain't set eyes on ag'in to dis day, an' dat's twenty-two years ago las' Easter. De man dat bought me b'long in

Newbern, an' he took me dah. Well, by-meby de years roll on an' de wah come. My marster he was a Confedrit colonel, an' I was his family's cook. So when de Unions took dat town, dey all run away an' lef' me all by myse'f wid de other niggers in dat mons'us big house. So de big Union offi-cers move in dah, an' dey ask me would I cook for *dem.* 'Lord bless you,' says I, 'dat's what I's *for.*'

"Dey wa'nt no small-fry officers, mine you, dey was de biggest dey *is;* an' de way dey made dem sojers mosey roun'! De Gen'l he tole me to boss dat kitchen; an' he say, 'If anybody come meddlin' wid you, you jist make 'em walk chalk; don't you be afeard,' he says; 'you's 'mong frens, now.'

"Well, I thinks to myse'f, if my little Henry ever got a chance to run away, he'd make to de Norf, o' course. So one day I comes in dah whar de big officers was, in de parlor, an' I drops a kurtchy, so, an' I up an' tole 'em 'bout my Henry, dey a-listenin' to my troubles jist de same as if I was white folks; an' I says, 'What I come for is beca'se if he got away and got up Norf whar you gemmen comes from, you might 'a' seen him, mabe, an' could tell me so as I could fine him ag'in; he was very little, an' he had a sk-yar on his lef' wris', an' at de top of his forehad.' Den dey look mournful, an de Gen'l say, 'How

long since you los' him?' an' I say,
'Thirteen year.' Den de Gen'l say, 'He
wouldn't be little no mo', now—he's a
man!'

"I never thought o' dat befo'! He was
only dat little feller to *me*, yit. I never
thought 'bout him growin' up and bein' big.
But I see it den. None o' de gemmen had
run acrost him, so dey couldn't do nothin'
for me. But all dat time, do' *I* didn't know
it, my Henry *was* run off to de Norf, years
an' years, an' he was a barber, too, an'
worked for hisse'f. An' bymeby, when de
wah come, he ups an' he says: 'I's done
barberin',' he says, 'I's gwyne to fine my
ole mammy, less'n she's dead.' So he sole
out an' went to whar dey was recruitin', an'
hired hisse'f out to de colonel for his servant; an' den he went all froo de battles
everywhah, huntin' for his ole mammy; yes
indeedy, he'd hire to fust one officer an' den
another, tell he'd ransacked de whole Souf;
but you see *I* didn't know nuffin 'bout *dis*.
How was *I* gwyne to know it?

"Well, one night we had a big sojer ball;
de sojers dah at Newbern was always havin'
balls an' carryin' on. Dey had 'em in my
kitchen, heaps o' times, 'case it was so big.
Mine you, I was *down* on sich doins; beca'se
my place was wid de officers, an' it rasp me
to have dem common sojers cavortin' roun'
my kitchen like dat. But I alway' stood
aroun' an' kep' things straight, I did; an'

sometimes dey'd git my dander up, an' den
I'd make 'em clar dat kitchen, mine I *tell*
you!

"Well, one night—it was a Friday night
—dey comes a whole platoon f'm a *nigger*
ridgment dat was on guard at de house,—
de house was head-quarters, you know,—an'
den I was jist a-*bilin*' ! Mad? I was jist
a-*boomin*' ! I swelled aroun', an swelled
aroun' ; I jist was a-itchin' for 'em to do
somefin for to start me. *An*' dey was
a-waltzin' an' a-dancin' ! *my* ! but dey was
havin' a time! an' I jist a-swellin' an'
a-swellin' up! Pooty soon, 'long comes
sich a spruce young nigger a-sailin' down de
room with a yaller wench roun' de wais' ;
an' roun' an' roun' an' roun' dey went,
enough to make a body drunk to look at
'em; an' when dey get abreas' o' me, dey
went to kin' o' balancin' aroun' fust on one
leg an' den on t'other, an smilin' at my big
red turban, an' makin' fun, an' I ups an'
says ' *Git* along wid you!—rubbage !' De
young man's face kin' o' changed, all of a
sudden for 'bout a second, but den he went
to smilin' ag'in, same as he was befo'.
Well, 'bout dis time, in comes some niggers
dat played music and b'long' to de ban', an'
dey *never* could git along without puttin' on
airs. An' de very fust air dey put on dat
night, I lit into 'em! Dey laughed, an' dat
made me wuss. De res' o' de niggers got
to laughin', an' den my soul *alive* but I was

hot! My eye was jist a-blazin'! I jist
straightened myself up, so,—jist as I is now,
plum to de ceilin', mos',—an' I digs my fists
into my hips, an' I says, 'Look-a-heah!' I
says, 'I want you niggers to understan' dat
I wa'nt bawn in the mash to be fool' by
trash! I's one o' de ole Blue Hen's Chickens, *I* is!' an' den I see dat young man
stan' a-starin' an' stiff, lookin' kin' o' up at
de ceilin' like he fo'got somefin, an' couldn't
'member it no mo'. Well. I jist march on
dem niggers,—so, lookin' like a gen'l,—an'
dey jist cave' away befo' me an' out at de
do'. An' as dis young man was a-goin' out,
I heah him say to another nigger, 'Jim,' he
says, 'you go 'long an' tell de cap'n I be on
han' 'bout eight o'clock in de mawnin';
dey's somefin on my mine,' he says; 'I don't
sleep no mo' dis night. You go 'long,' he
says, 'an' leave me by my own se'f.'

"Dis was 'bout one o'clock in de mawnin'.
Well, 'bout seven, I was up an' on han',
gittin' de officers' breakfast. I was a-stoop-
in' down by de stove,—jist so, same as if
yo' foot was de stove,—an' I'd opened de
stove do' wid my right han',—so, pushin' it
back, jist as I pushes yo' foot,—an' I'd jist
got de pan o' hot biscuits in my han' an'
was 'bout to raise up, when I see a black
face come aroun' under mine, an' de eyes
a-lookin' up into mine, jist as I's a-lookin'
up clost under yo' face now; an' I jist
stopped *right dah*, an' never budged! jist

gazed, an' gazed, so; an' de pan begin to tremble, an' all of a sudden I *knowed!* De pan drop' on de flo' an' I grab his lef' han' an' shove back his sleeve,—jist so, as I's doin' to you,—an' den I goes for his fore-head an' push de hair back, so, an' ' Boy ! ' I says, ' if you an't my Henry, what is you doin' wid dis welt on yo' wris' an' dat sk-yar on yo' forehead ? De Lord God ob heaven be praise', I got my own ag'in ! '

" Oh, no, Misto C——, I hain't had no trouble.   An' no *joy !* "

MINISTERS' SUNSHINE.

BY T. DE WITT TALMAGE.

So much has been written of the hardships of clergymen, small salaries, unreasonable churches, mean committees, and impudent parishioners, that parents seeking for their children's happiness are not wont to desire them to enter the sacred calling.   Indeed, the story of empty bread-trays and cheerless parsonages has not half been told. But there is another side to the picture.   Ministers' wives are not all vixens, nor their children scapegraces.   Pastors do not always step on thorns and preach to empty benches.   The parish sewing-society does not always roast their pastor over the slow fires of tittle-tattle. There is no inevitable connection between the gospel and bronchitis. As far as we have observed the brightest sunshine is ministers' sunshine. They have access to refined circles, means to give a good education to their children, friends to stand by them in every perplexity, and through the branches that drop occasional shadows on their way sifts the golden light of great enjoyment.

It was about six o'clock of a June afternoon, the sun striking aslant upon the river, when the young minister and his bride were riding toward their new home. The air was bewitched with fragrance of field and garden, and a hum with bees out honey-making. The lengthening shadows did not fall on the road the twain passed ; at least, they saw none. The leaves shook out a welcome, and as the carriage rumbled across the bridge in front of the house at which they were for a few days to tarry, it seemed as if hoof and wheel understood the transport of the hour. The weeks of bridal congratulation had ended, and here they were at the door of the good deacon who would entertain them. The village was all astir that evening. As far as politeness would allow, there was peering from the doors, and looking through the blinds, for everybody would see the new minister's wife ; and children, swinging on the gate, rushed in the back way to cry out, '' They are coming ! ''

The minister and his bride alighted amid
hearty welcomes, for the flock had been for
a long while without a shepherd, and all
imagined something of the embarrassment
of a young man with the ink hardly dry on
his parchment of licensure, and a girl just
entering into the responsibility of a clergyman's wife.

After tea, some of the parishioners came
in ; old Mr. Bromlette stepped up to offer a
greeting. He owned a large estate, had been
born in high life, was a genuine aristocrat,
and had in his possession silver plate which
his father used in entertaining General
Washington. He had no pretension or
pomp of manner, but showed by his walk
and his conversation that he had always
moved in polite circles. He was a fat man,
and wiped the perspiration from his brow—
sweat started not more by his walk than the
excitement of the occasion—and said, " Hot
night, dominie ! " He began the conversation by asking the minister who his father
was, and who his grandfather ; and when
he found that there was in the ancestral line
of the minister a dignitary, seemed delighted, and said, " I knew him well.
Danced forty years ago with his daughter at
Saratoga." He added, " I think we will be
able to make you comfortable here. We
have in our village some families of highly
respectable descent. Here is our friend over
the way ; his grandfather was wounded at

Monmouth. He would have called in to-night, but he is in the city at a banquet given in honor of one of the English lords. Let me see ; what's his name?'' At this point the door opened, and the servant looked in and said, ''Mr. Bromlette, your carriage is waiting.'' ''Good-night, dominie !'' said the old gentleman ; ''I hope to see you at my house to-morrow. The Governor will dine with us, and about two o'clock my carriage will call for you. You look tired. Better retire early. Good-night, ladies and gentlemen !''

MacMillan, the Scotchman, now entered into conversation. He was brawny and blunt. Looked dead in earnest. Seldom saw anything to laugh it. He was of the cast-iron make, and if he had cared much about family blood, could no doubt have traced it back to Drumclog or Bothwell Bridge. He said, ''I came in to-night to welcome you as a minister of the New Covenant. Do not know much about you. What catechism did you stoody?'' ''Westminster !'' replied the clergyman. ''Praise God for that !'' said the Scotchman. '' I think you must belong to the good old orthodox, out-and-out Calvinistic school. I must be going home, for it is nine o'clock, and I never allow the children to go to bed until I have sung with them a Psalm of David. Do not like to suggest, but if parfactly convainiant, give us next

Sabbath a solid sermon about the eternal decrees. Suppose you have read ' McCosh on the Divine Government.' Do not think anything surpasses that, unless it be ' Edwards on the Will.' Good-night ! '' he said as he picked up his hat, which he had persisted in setting on the floor beside him. '' Hope we will meet often in this world, and in the next ; we most certainly will if we have been elected. Good-night ! I will stand by you as long as I find you contending earnestly for the faith once delivered to the saints.'' And without bowing to the rest he started through the hall, and began to rattle the front door, and shouted, '' Here, somebody ! open this door ! Hope we shall not have as much trouble in getting open the door of heaven ! ''

Mrs. Durbin was present that evening. She was always present when pleasant words were to be uttered, or kind deeds done. She was any minister's blessing. If the pastor had a cough, she would come right into his house, only half knocking, and in the kitchen, over the hot stove, she would stand mixing all sorts of pleasant things to take. From her table often came in a plate of biscuit, or a bowl of berries already sugared. If the pulpit must be upholstered, she was head of the committee. If money was to be raised for a musical instrument, she begged it, no man saying nay, even if he could ill afford to contribute. _ Everybody liked her.

Everybody blessed her. She stepped quick ; had a laugh that was catching; knew all the sick ; had her pocket full of nuts and picture-books. When she went through the poorer parts of the village, the little ragamuffins, white and black, would come out and say, " Here comes Mrs. Durbin ! "

But do not fall in love with Mrs. Durbin, for she was married. Her husband was a man of the world, took things easy, let his wife go to church as much as she desired, if she would not bother him with her religion, gave her as much money as she wanted, but teased her unmercifully about the poor urchins who followed her in the street, and used to say, "My dear ! have you found out any new Lazarus? I am afraid you will get the small-pox if you don't stop carrying victuals into those nigger shanties !"

Mrs. Durbin talked rapidly that night, but mostly to the pastor's wife. Was overheard to be laying plans for a ride to the Falls. Hoped that the minister would not work too hard at the start. Told him that after he got rested he might go and visit a family near by who were greatly distressed, and wanted a minister to pray with them. As she rose to go, she said, "If you need anything at all, be at perfect liberty to send." Her husband arose at the same time. He had not said a word, and felt a little

awkward in the presence of so many church-
people. But he came up and took the
minister's hand, and said, " Call and see us !
I am not a church-man, as you will soon
find out. I hardly ever go to church, except on Thanksgiving Days, or now and
then when the notion takes me. Still, I
have a good horse. Anybody can drive him,
and he is any time at your disposal. All
you have to do is just to get in and take up
the ribbons. My wife takes care of the religion, and I mind the horses. She has
what our college-bred Joe calls the ' *Suaviter
in modo*,' and I have the ' *Fortiter in re*.'
Good-bye ! Take care of yourself ! "

Elder Lucas was there ; a man of fifty.
His great characteristic was, that he never
said anything, but always acted. Never ex-
horted or prayed in public : only listened.
One time at the church-meeting, called for
the purpose of increasing the minister's
salary, where Robert Cruikshank spoke
four times in favor of the project, and afterward subscribed one dollar ; Lucas was
still, but subscribed fifty dollars. On the
evening of which we chiefly write, he sat
silently looking at his new pastor. Those
who thought he felt nothing were greatly
mistaken. He was all kindness and love.
Much of the time there were emotional tears
in his eyes, but few saw them, for he had a
sly habit of looking the other way till they
dried up, or if they continued to run he

would rub his handkerchief across his nose,
allowing it accidentally to slip up to the
corner of his eyes, and so nothing of emotion was suspected. He never offered to do
anything, but always did it. He never
promised to send a carriage to take his
minister a riding, but often sent it. Never
gave notice two weeks before of an intended
barrel of flour. But it was, without any
warning, rolled into the back entry. He did
not some day in front of the church, in the
presence of half the congregation, tell the
minister that he meant to give him a suit of
clothes, but slyly found out who was the
clergyman's tailor, and then by a former
measurement had the garments made and
sent up on Saturday night with his compliments, for two weeks keeping out of the
way for fear the minister would thank him.

When Elder Lucas left that evening, he
came up, and without saying a word, gave
the minister a quick shake of the hand, and
over forehead, cheek and hands of the bash-
ful man passed a succession of blushes.

But the life of the little company that
night was Harry Bronson. Probably in no
other man was there ever compressed more
vivacity of nature. He was a wonderful
compound of mirthfulness and piety. Old
men always took his hand with affection,
and children ran wild when they saw him.
On Sunday he prayed like a minister, but
on Monday, among the boys, he could jump

the highest, run the swiftest, shout the loudest, bat the truest, and turn somersault the easiest. Indeed, there were in the church two or three awful-visaged people who thought that Harry Bronson ought to be disciplined, and that santification was never accompanied by kicking up of the heels. They remonstrated with him, but before he got out of sight, and while they were yet praying for the good effect of their admonition, he put his hand on the top of the fence, and, without touching, leaped over, not because there was any need of crossing the fence, for, showing that he was actuated by nothing but worldliness and frivolity, he put his hand on the top of the rail and leaped back again. If there was anything funny, he was sure to see it, and had a way of striking attitudes, and imitating peculiar intonations, and walked sometimes on his toes, and sometimes on his heels, till one evening at church, one of the brethren with a religion made up of equal portions of sour-krout, mustard and red pepper, prayed right at him, saying, " If there is any brother present who does not walk as he should, we pray Thee that Thou wouldst do with him as Thou didst with Sennacherib of old, and put a hook in his nose and turn him back ! " To which prayer Harry Bronson responded, "Amen ! " never supposing that the hook was meant for his own nose. The reprimanding

brother finding his prayer ineffectual, and
that the Lord was unwilling to take Harry
in His hands, resolved to attend to the case
himself, and the second time proposed to
undertake the work of admonition, not in
beseeching terms as before, but with a fiery
indignation that would either be, as he expressed it, a savor of life unto life, or of
death unto death. But entering Harry
Bronson's house that evening, he found him
on his hands and knees playing " Bear "
with his children, and cutting such a ludicrous figure, that the lachrymose Elder for
once lost his gravity, and joined in the
merriment with such a full gush of laughter
that he did not feel it would be consistent to
undertake his mission, since the facetious
Harry might turn on him and say, " Physician ! heal thyself ! "

That night at the minister's welcome
Harry was in full glee. The first grasp he
gave on entering the room, and the words of
greeting that he offered, and the whole-
souled, intense manner with which he con-
fronted the young clergyman, showed him
to be one of those earnest, active, intelligent.
loving and lovable Christian men, who is a
treasure to any pastor.

He had a story for every turn of the evening's entertainment, and took all the spare
room in the parlor to tell it. The gravest
men in the party would take a joke from
him. When MacMillan asked the minister

about his choice of catechism, Harry ventured the opinion that he thought "Brown's Shorter" good enough for anybody. "Ah!" said MacMillan, "Harry, you rogue, stop that joking!" When Mr. Bromlette offered his carraige, Bronson offered to loan a wheel-barrow. He asked Mrs. Durbin if she wanted any more combs or castile soap for her mission on Dirt Alley. He almost drew into conversation the silent Mr. Lucas asking a strange question, and because Lucas, through embarrassment, made no response, saying, "Silence gives consent!" Was full of narratives about weddings, and general trainings, and parish meetings. Stayed till all the rest were gone, for he never was talked out.

"Well, well!" said two of the party that night as they shut the front door; "we will have to tell Harry Bronson to serve God in his own way." I guess there may sometimes be as much religion in laughing as in crying. We cannot make such a man as that keep step to a "Dead March." I think the dew of grace may fall just as certainly on a grotesque cactus as a precise primrose. Indeed, the jubilant palm-tree bears fruit, while the weeping-willow throws its worthless catkins into the brook.

The first Sunday came. The congregation gathered early. The brownstone church was a beautiful structure, within and

without. An adjacent quarry had furnished
the material and the architect and builder,
who were men of taste, had not been interfered with. A few creeping vines had been
planted at the front and side, and a white
rose-bush stood at the door, flinging its fragrance across the yard. Many had gone in
and taken their seats, but others had stayed
at the door to watch the coming of the new
minister and his bride. She is gone now,
and it is no flattery to write that she was fair
to look upon, delicate in structure of body,
eye large and blue, hair in which was
folded the shadows of midnight, erect carraige, but quite small. She was such a one
as you could pick up and carry over a stream
with one arm. She had a sweet voice, and
had stood several years in the choir of the
city churches, and had withal a magic of
presence that had turned all whom she ever
met into warm personal admirers. Her
hand trembled on her husband's arm as
that day they went up the steps of the
meeting house, gazed at intently by young
and old. The pastor looked paler even than
was his wont. His voice quavered in read-
ing the hymn, and he looked confused in
making the publications. That day, a
mother had brought her child for baptism,
and for the first time he officiated in that
ceremony. Had hard work to remember
the words, and knew not what to do next.
When he came to preach, in his excitement

he could not find his sermon. It had fallen back of the sofa. Looked up and down, and forward and backward. Fished it out at last, just in time to come up, flushed and hot to read the text. Made a very feeble attempt at preaching. But all were ready to hear his words. The young sympathized with him, for he was young. And the old looked on him with a sort of paternal indulgence. At the few words in which he commended himself and his to their sympathy and care, they broke forth into weeping. And at the foot of the pulpit, at the close of service, the people gathered, poor and rich, to offer their right hand.

MacMillan the Scotchman said, "Young man! that's the right doctrine; the same that Dr. Duncan taught me forty years ago at the kirk in the glen!" Mr. Bromlette came up, and introduced to the young minister a young man who was a baronet, and a lady who was somehow related to the Astors. Harry Bronson took his pastor by the hand, and said, "That sermon went right to the spot. Glad you found it. Was afraid you would never fish it out from behind that sofa. When I saw you on all-fours, looking it up, thought I should burst." Lucas, with his eyes red as a half-hour of crying could make them, took the minister's hand, but said nothing, only looked more thanks and kindness than words could have expressed. Mr. Durbin said, " How are

you? Broke in on my rule to-day and came
to church. Little curious, you see. Did
not believe it quite all, but that will do.
Glad you gave it to those Christians. Saw
them wince under it!'' Mrs. Durbin was
meanwhile employed in introducing the
bride to the people at the door who were a
little backward. Begged them to come up.
Drew up an array of four or five children
that she had clothed and brought out of the
shanties to attend church. Said, '' This is
Bridget Maloy, and that Ellen Haggerty.
Good girls they are, too, and like to come
to church!''

For a long while the hand-shakings continued, and some who could not get confidence to even wait at the door, stretched
their hands out from the covered wagon,
and gave a pleasant '' How do you do?'' or
'' God bless you,'' till the minister and his
wife agreed that their happiness was full,
and went home, saying, '' This, indeed, is
MINISTER'S SUNSHINE!''

The parsonage was only a little distance
off, but the pastor had nothing with which
to furnish it. The grass was long, and
needed to be cut, and the weeds were covering the garden. On Monday morning the
pastor and his wife were saying what a
pity it was that they were not able to take
immediate possession. They could be so
happy in such a cozy place. Never mind.
They would out of the first year's salary

save enough to warrant going to housekeeping.

That afternoon the sewing society met.
That society never disgraced itself with
gossip. They were good women, and met
together, sometimes to sew for the destitute
of the village, and sometimes to send garments to the suffering home missionaries.
For two hours their needles would fly, and
then off for home, better for their phil-
anthropic labors. But that afternoon the
ladies stood round the room in knots, a-whis-
pering. Could it be that the society was
losing its good name, and was becoming a
school of scandal? That could not be, for
Mrs. Durbin seemed the most active in the
company, and Mrs. Durbin was always
right.

Next morning, while the minister and his
wife were talking over the secrecy of conversation at the sewing-circle, Harry Bronson came in and asked the young pastor if
he was not weary with last Sunday's work.
He answered, " No ! " " Well," suggested
Harry, " I think you had better take a few
days' rest anyhow. Go off and see your
friends. My carriage will, in about an hour,
go to the cars, and I will meet you on Saturday night. Think it will do you both
good."

" Well, well," said the minister, while
aside consulting with his wife, " what does
this mean ? Are they tired of us so soon ?

Is this any result of yesterday's whispering? But they make the suggestion, and I shall take it.'' So that Tuesday evening found them walking the streets of the neighboring city, wondering what all this meant. Saturday came, and on the arrival of the afternoon train Harry Bronson was ready to meet the young parson and his wife. They rode up to the place of their previous entertainment. After tea, Bronson said : '' We have been making a little alteration at the parsonage since you were gone.'' '' Have you?'' exclaimed the minister. ''Come, my dear! let us go up and see!'' As they passed up the steps of the old parsonage, the roses and the lilacs on either side swung in the evening air. The river in front glowed under the long row of willows, and parties of villagers in white passed by in the rocking boat, singing '' Life on the Ocean Wave.'' It was just before sunset, and what with the perfume, and the roseate clouds, and the rustling of the maples, and the romance of a thousand dawning expectations—it was an evening never to be forgotten. Its flowers will never close. Its clouds will never melt. Its waters will never lose their sheen. Its aroma will never float away.

The key was thrust into the door and it swung open. ''What does this mean?'' they both cried out at the same time. '' Who put down this carpet, and set here these chairs, and hung this hall lamp?''

They stood as if transfixed. It was no shabby carpet, but one that showed that many dollars had been expended, and much taste employed, and much effort exerted. They opened the parlor door, and there they all stood—sofa, and whatnot, and chair, and stand, and mantel ornament, and picture. They went upstairs, and every room was furnished ; beds with beautiful white coun-terpanes, and vases filled with flowers, and walls hung with engravings. Everything complete.

These surprised people came downstairs to the pantry. Found boxes of sugar, bags of salt, cans of preserves, packages of spices, bins of flour, loaves of bread. Went to the basement, and found pails, baskets, dippers, cups, saucers, plates, forks, knives, spoons, strainers, bowls, pitchers, tubs, and a huge stove filled with fuel, and a lucifer match lying on the lid ; so that all the young married pair would have to do in going to housekeeping, would be to strike the match and apply it to the shavings. In the study, adorned with lounge and flowers, and on the table, covered with bright green baize, lay an envelope enclosing a card, on which was written : '' Please accept from a few friends.''

Had Aladdin been around with his lamp? Was this a vision such as comes to one about half awake on a sunshiny morning? They sat down, weak and tearful from

surprise, thanked God, blessed Mrs. Durbin,
knew that Mr. Bromlette's purse had been
busy, felt that silent Mr. Lucas had at last
spoken, realized that Harry Bronson had
been perpetrating a practical joke, were certain that MacMillan had at last been brought
to believe a little in "works," and exclaimed,
"Verily, this is Ministers' Sunshine!" and
as the slanting rays of the setting day struck
the porcelain pitcher, and printed another
figure on the carpet, and threw its gold on
the cushion of the easy-chair, it seemed as
if everything within, and everything
around, and everything above, responded,
"Ministers' Sunshine!"

The fact was, that during the absence of
the new pastor that week, the whole village
had been topsy-turvy with excitement.
People standing together in knots, others
running in and out of doors; the hunting
up of measuring-rods; the running around
of committees with everything to do, and so
little time in which to do it. Somebody had
proposed a very cheap furnishing of the
house, but Mr. Bromlette said : "This will
never do. How can we prosper, if, living
in fine houses ourselves, we let our minister
go half cared for? The sheep shall not be
better off than the shepherd!" and down
went his name on the subscription with a
liberal sum.

MacMillan said, "I am in favor of taking
care of the Lord's anointed. And this young

minister of the everlasting gospel hinted that he believed in the perseverance of the saints, and other cardinal doctrines, and you may put me down for so much, and that is twice what I can afford to give, but we must have faith, and make sacrifices for the kingdom of God's sake."

While others had this suggestion about the window shades, and that one a preference about the figure of the carpets, and another one said he would have nothing to do with it unless it were thus and so, quiet Mr. Lucas said nothing, and some of the people feared he would not help in the enterprise. But when the subscription paper was handed to him, he looked it over, thought for a minute or two, and then set down a sum that was about twice as much as any of the other contributions. Worldly Mr. Durbin said at the start : "I will give nothing. There is no use of making such a fuss over a minister. You will spoil him at the start. Let him fight his own way up, as the rest of us have had to do. Delia (that was his wife's name), nobody furnished our house when we started." But Mrs. Durbin, as was expected, stood in front of the enterprise. If there was a stingy fellow to be approached, she was sent to get the money out of him, and always succeeded. She had been so used to begging for the poor of the back street, that when any of the farmers found her coming up the lane, they would

shout : '' Well, Mrs. Durbin, how much will
satisfy you to-day ? '' She was on the committee that selected the carpets. While
others were waiting for the men to come and
hang up the window shades, she mounted a
table and hung four of them. Some of the
hardest workers in the undertaking were
ready to do anything but tack down carpets.
'' Well,'' she said, '' that is just what I am
willing to do ; '' and so down she went,
pulling until red in the face to make the
breadths match, and pounding her finger
till the blood started under the nail, in trying
to make a crooked tack do its duty. One
evening her husband drove up in front of
the parsonage with a handsome bookcase.
Said he had come across it, and had bought
it to please his wife, not because he approved
of all this fuss over a minister, who might
turn out well, and might not. The next
morning there came three tons of coal that
he had ordered to be put in the cellar of the
parsonage. And though Durbin never ac--
knowledged to his wife any satisfaction in
the movement, he every night asked all
about how affairs were getting on, and it
was found at last that he had been among
the most liberal.

Harry Bronson had been all around during
the week. He had a cheerful word for every
perplexity. Put his hand deep down in his
own pocket. Cracked jokes over the cracked
crockery. Sent up some pictures, such as

"The Sleigh-riding Party," "Ball Playing," and "Boys Coasting." Knocked off Lucas' hat, and pretended to know nothing about it. Slipped on purpose, and tumbled into the lap of the committee. Went up stairs three steps at a time, and came down astride the banisters. At his antics some smiled, some smirked, some tittered, some chuckled, some laughed through the nose, some shouted outright, and all that week Harry Bronson kept the parsonage roaring with laughter. Yet once in a while you would find him seated in the corner, talking with some old mother in Israel, who was telling him all her griefs, and *he* offering the consolations of religion. "Just look at Bronson!" said some one. "What a strange conglomeration! There he is crying with that old lady in a corner. You would not think he had ever smiled. This truly is weeping with those who weep, and laughing with those who laugh. Bronson seems to carry in his heart all the joys and griefs of this village."

It was five o'clock of Saturday afternoon, one hour before the minister was expected, that the work was completed, entry swept out, the pieces of string picked up, shades drawn down, and the door of the parsonage locked. As these church-workers went down the street, their backs ached, and their fingers were sore, but their hearts were light, and their countenances happy, and every

step of the way from the parsonage door to
their own gate they saw scattered on the
graveled sidewalk, and yard-grass, and
door-step, broad flecks of Ministers' Sunshine !

But two or three days had passed, and
the young married couple took possession of
their new house. It was afternoon, and the
tea-table was to be spread for the first time.
It seemed as if every garden in the village
had sent its greeting to that tea-table.
Bouquets from one, and strawberries from
another, and radishes, and bread, and cake,
and grass-butter with figure of wheat-sheaf
printed on it. The silver all new, that which
the committee had left added to the bridal
presents. Only two sat at the table, yet the
room seemed crowded with emotions, such
as attend only upon the first meal of a newly
married couple, when beginning to keep
house. The past sent up to that table a
thousand tender memories, and the future
hovered with wings of amber and gold.
That bread-breaking partook somewhat of
the solemnity of a sacrament. There was
little talk and much silence. They lingered
long at the table, spoke of the crowning of
so many anticipations, and laid out plans for
the great future. The sun had not yet set.
The castor glistened in it. The glasses
glowed in the red light. It gave a roseate
tinge to the knives, and trembled across the
cake-basket, as the leaves at the window

fluttered in the evening air ; and the twain continued to sit there, until the sun had dropped to the very verge of the horizon, and with nothing to intercept its blaze, it poured in the open windows, till from ceiling to floor and from wall to wall the room was flooded with Ministers' Sunshine.

A year passed on, and the first cloud hovered over the parsonage. It was a very dark cloud. It filled the air, and with its long black folds seemed to sweep the eaves of the parsonage. Yet it parted, and through it fell as bright a light as ever gilded a hearthstone. The next day all sorts of packages arrived ; little socks, with a verse of poetry stuck in each one of them —socks about large enough for a small kitten ; and a comb with which you might imagine Tom Thumb's wife would comb his hair for him. Mrs. Durbin was there— indeed had been there for the last twenty- four hours. Mr. Bromlette sent up his coachman to make inquiries. MacMillan called to express his hope that it was a child of the " Covenant." Lucas came up the door-step to offer his congratulation, but had not courage to rattle the knocker, and so went away, but stopped at the store to order up a box of farina. Harry Bronson smiled all the way to the parsonage, and smiled all the way back. Meanwhile the light within the house every moment grew brighter. The parson hardly dared to touch the little delicate thing for fear he would break it; and walked around with it upon a pillow, wondering what it would do next, starting at every sneeze or cry, for fear he had done some irreparable damage; wondering if its foot was set on right, and if with that peculiar formation of the head it would ever know anything, and if infantile eyes always looked like those. The wonder grew, till one day Durbin, out of regard for his wife, was invited to see the little stranger, when he declared he had during his life seen fifty just like it, and said, "Do you think that worth raising, eh?"

All came to see it, and just wanted to feel the weight of it. The little girls of the neighborhood must take off its socks to examine the dimples on its fat feet. And, although not old enough to appreciate it, there came directed to the baby, rings and rattles, and pins, and bracelets, and gold pieces with a string through, to hang about the neck, and spoons for pap, and things the use of which the parson could not imagine. The ladies said it looked like its father, and the gentlemen exclaimed, "How much it resembles its mother!" All sorts of names were proposed, some from novels and some from Scripture. MacMillan thought it ought to be called Deborah or Patience. Mr. Bromlette wished it called Eugenia Van Courtlandt. Mrs. Durbin thought it would be nice to name it Grace. Harry

Bronson thought it might be styled Humpsy Dumpsy. A young gentleman suggested Felicia, and a young lady thought it might be Angelina. When Lucas was asked what he had to propose, he blushed, and after a somewhat protracted silence, answered, "Call it what you like. Please yourselves and you please me." All of the names were tried in turn, but none of them was good enough. So a temporary name must be selected, one that might do till the day of the christening. The first day the pet was carried out was a very bright day, the sun was high up, and as the neighbors rushed out to the nurse, and lifted the veil that kept off the glare of the light, they all thought it well to call it the Ministers' Sunshine.

And so the days and the months and the years flew by. If a cloud came up, as on the day mentioned, there was a Hand behind it to lift the heavy folds. If there was a storm, it only made the shrubs sweeter, and the fields greener. If a winter night was filled with rain and tempest, the next morning all the trees stood up in burnished mail of ice, casting their crowns at the feet of the sun, and surrendering their gleaming swords to the conqueror. If the trees lost their blossoms, it was to put on the mellowness of fruit; and when the fruit was scattered, autumnal glories set up in the tops their flaming torches. And when the leaves fell it was only through death to come

singing in the next spring-time, when the
mellow horn of the south wind sounded the
resurrection. If in the chill April a snow-
bank lingered in the yard, they were apt to
find a crocus at the foot of it. If an early
frost touched the corn, that same frost un-
locked the burr of the chestnut, and poured
richer blood into the veins of the Catawba.
When the moon set, the stars came out to
worship and counted their golden beads in
the Cathedral of the Infinite.

On the petunias that all over the knoll
shed their blood for the glory of the garden ;
on the honeysuckle where birds rested, and
from which fountains of odor tossed their
spray ; on the river, where by day the barge
floated, and by night the moon-tipped oars
came up tangled with the tinkling jewels
of the deep ; at eventide in the garden,
where God walked in the cool of the day ;
by the minister's hearth, where the child
watched the fall of the embers, and congenial spirits talked, and ministering angels
hovered, and in the sounds of the night-fall
there floated the voices of bright immortals,
bidding the two, "Come up higher !"—
there was calm, clear MINISTERS' SUN-
SHINE !

MRS. BULLFROG.

BY NATHANIEL HAWTHORNE.

It makes me melancholy to see how like fools some very sensible people act in the matter of choosing wives. They perplex their judgments by a most undue attention to little niceties of personal appearance, habits, disposition, and other trifles which concern nobody but the lady herself. An unhappy gentleman, resolving to wed nothing short of perfection, keeps his heart and hand till both get so old and withered that no tolerable woman will accept them. Now, this is the very height of absurdity. A kind Providence has so skillfully adapted sex to sex and the mass of individuals to each other that, with certain obvious exceptions, any male and female may be moderately happy in the married state. The true rule is to ascertain that the match is fundamentally a good one, and then to take it for granted that all minor objections, should there be such, will vanish if you let them alone. Only put yourself beyond hazard as to the real basis of matrimonial bliss, and it is scarcely to be imagined what miracles in the way of reconciling smaller incongruities connubial love will effect.

For my own part, I freely confess that in my bachelorship I was precisely such an over-curious simpleton as I now advise the reader not to be. My early habits had gifted me with a feminine sensibility and too exquisite refinement. I was the accomplished graduate of a dry-goods store, where by dint of ministering to the whims of fine ladies, and suiting silken hose to delicate limbs, and handling satins, ribbons, chintzes, calicoes, tapes, gauze and cambric needles, I grew up a very ladylike sort of a gentleman. It is not assuming too much to affirm that the ladies themselves were hardly so ladylike as Thomas Bullfrog. So painfully acute was my sense of female imperfection, and such varied excellence did I require in the woman whom I could love, that there was an awful risk of my getting no wife at all, or of being driven to perpetuate matrimony with my own image in the looking-glass. Besides the fundamental principle already hinted at, I demanded the fresh bloom of youth, pearly teeth, glossy ringlets, and the whole list of lovely items, with the utmost delicacy of habits and sentiments, a silken texture of mind, and, above all, a virgin heart. In a word, if a young angel just from Paradise, yet dressed in earthly fashion, had come and offered me her hand, it is by no means certain that I should have taken it. There was every chance of my becoming a most miserable old bachelor, when by the best luck in the world I made a journey into another State and was smitten by and smote again, and wooed, won and married the present Mrs. Bullfrog, all in the space of a fortnight. Owing to these extempore measures, I not only gave my bride credit for certain perfections which have not as yet come to light, but also overlooked a few trifling defects, which, however, glimmered on my perception long before the close of the honeymoon. Yet, as there was no mistake about the fundamental principle aforesaid, I soon learned, as will be seen, to estimate Mrs. Bullfrog's deficiencies and superfluities at exactly their proper value.

The same morning that Mrs. Bullfrog and I came together as a unit we took two seats in the stage-coach and began our journey toward my place of business. There being no other passengers, we were as much alone and as free to give vent to our raptures as if I had hired a hack for the matrimonial jaunt. My bride looked charmingly in a green silk calash and riding-habit of pelisse cloth ; and whenever her red lips parted with a smile, each tooth appeared like an inestimable pearl. Such was my passionate warmth that—we had rattled out of the village, gentle reader, and were as lonely as Adam and Eve in Paradise—I plead guilty to no less freedom than a kiss. The gentle eye of Mrs. Bullfrog scarcely rebuked me for the profanation. Emboldened by her indulgence, I threw back the calash from her polished brow, and suffered my fingers, white and delicate as her own, to stray among those dark and glossy curls which realized my day-dreams of rich hair.

" My love," said Mrs. Bullfrog tenderly, " you will disarrange my curls."

" Oh, no, my sweet Laura," replied I, still playing with the glossy ringlet. " Even your fair hand could not manage a curl more delicately than mine. I propose myself the pleasure of doing up your hair in papers every evening at the same time with my own."

" Mr. Bullfrog," repeated she, " you must not disarrange my curls."

This was spoken in a more decided tone than I had happened to hear until then from my gentlest of all gentle brides. At the same time she put up her hand and took mine prisoner, but merely drew it away from the forbidden ringlet, and then immediately released it. Now, I am a fidgety little man and always love to have something in my fingers ; so that, being debarred from my wife's curls, I looked about me for any other plaything. On the front seat of the coach there was one of those small baskets in which traveling ladies who are too delicate to appear at a public table generally carry a supply of gingerbread, biscuits and cheese, cold ham, and other light refreshments, merely to sustain nature to the journey's end. Such airy diet will sometimes keep

them in pretty good flesh for a week together. Laying hold of this same little
basket, I thrust my hand under the newspaper with which it was carefully covered.

"What's this, my dear?" cried I, for the
black neck of a bottle had popped out of
the basket.

"A bottle of Kalydor, Mr. Bullfrog,"
said my wife, coolly taking the basket from
my hands and replacing it on the front seat.

There was no possibility of doubting my
wife's word, but I never knew genuine
Kalydor such as I use for my own complexion to smell so much like cherry brandy. I
was about to express my fears that the lotion
would injure her skin, when an accident occurred which threatened more than a skin-
deep injury. Our Jehu had carelessly driven
over a heap of gravel and fairly capsized
the coach, with the wheels in the air and
our heels where our heads should have been.
What became of my wits I cannot imagine:
they have always had a perverse trick of
deserting me just when they were most
needed ; but so it chanced that in the con-
fusion of our overthrow I quite forgot that
there was a Mrs. Bullfrog in the world.
Like many men's wives, the good lady
served her husband as a stepping-stone. I
had scrambled out of the coach and was
instinctively settling my cravat, when somebody brushed roughly by me, and I heard a
smart thwack upon the coachman's ear.

"Take that, you villain!" cried a strange, hoarse voice. "You have ruined me, you blackguard! I shall never be the woman I have been."

And then came a second thwack, aimed at the driver's other ear, but which missed it and hit him on the nose, causing a terrible effusion of blood. Now, who or what fearful apparition was inflicting this punishment on the poor fellow remained an impenetrable mystery to me. The blows were given by a person of grisly aspect, with a head almost bald, and sunken cheeks, apparently of the feminine gender, though hardly to be classed in the gentler sex. There being no teeth to modulate the voice, it had a mumbled fierceness—not passionate, but stern—which absolutely made me quiver like calves-foot jelly. Who could the phantom be? The most awful circumstance of the affair is yet to be told, for this ogre—or whatever it was—had a riding-habit like Mrs. Bullfrog's, and also a green silk calash dangling down her back by the strings. In my terror and turmoil of mind I could imagine nothing less than that the Old Nick at the moment of our overturn had annihilated my wife and jumped into her petticoats. This idea seemed the more probable since I could nowhere perceive Mrs. Bullfrog alive, nor, though I looked very sharp about the coach, could I detect any traces of that beloved woman's dead body. There would have been a comfort in giving her Christian burial.

"Come, sir! bestir yourself! Help this rascal to set up the coach," said the hobgoblin to me; then with a terrific screech to three countrymen at a distance, "Here, you fellows! Ain't you ashamed to stand off when a poor woman is in distress?"

The countrymen, instead of fleeing for their lives, came running at full speed, and laid hold of the topsy-turvy coach. I also, though a small-sized man, went to work like a son of Anak. The coachman, too, with the blood still streaming from his nose, tugged and toiled most manfully, dreading, doubtless, that the next blow might break his head. And yet, bemauled as the poor fellow had been, he seemed to glance at me with an eye of pity, as if my case were more deplorable than his. But I cherished a hope that all would turn out a dream, and seized the opportunity, as we raised the coach, to jam two of my fingers under the wheel, trusting that the pain would waken me.

"Why, here we are all right again!" exclaimed a sweet voice, behind,—"Thank you for your assistance, gentlemen.—My dear Mr. Bullfrog, how you perspire! Do let me wipe your face.—Don't take this little accident too much to heart, good driver. We ought to be thankful that none of our necks are broken!"

"We might have spared one neck out
of the three," muttered the driver, rubbing
his ear and pulling his nose, to ascertain
whether he had been cuffed or not. "Why,
the woman's a witch!"

I fear that the reader will not believe, yet
it is positively a fact, that there stood Mrs.
Bullfrog with her glossy ringlets curling
on her brow and two rows of Orient pearls
gleaming between her parted lips, which
wore a most angelic smile. She had re-
gained her riding-habit and calash from the
grisly phantom, and was in all respects the
lovely woman who had been sitting by my
side at the instant of our overturn. How
she had happened to disappear, and who
had supplied her place, and whence she did
now return, were problems too knotty for
me to solve. There stood my wife: that
was the one thing certain among a heap of
mysteries. Nothing remained but to help
her into the coach and plod on through the
journey of the day and the journey of life
as comfortably as we could. As the driver
closed the door upon us I heard him whisper
to the three countrymen :

" How do you suppose a fellow feels shut
up in the cage with a she-tiger?"

Of course this query could have no reference to my situation ; yet, unreasonable as
it may appear, I confess that my feelings
were not altogether so ecstatic as when I
first called Mrs. Bullfrog mine. True, she

' was a sweet woman and an angel of a wife ;
but what if a gorgon should return amid
the transports of our connubial bliss and take
the angel's place!   I recollected the tale of
a fairy who half the time was a beautiful
woman and half the time a hideous monster.
Had I taken that very fairy to be the wife
of my bosom?   While such whims and
chimeras were flitting across my fancy I began to look askance at Mrs. Bullfrog, almost
expecting that the transformation would be
wrought before my eyes.

To divert my mind I took up the newspaper which had covered the little basket
of refreshments, and which now lay at the
bottom of the coach blushing with a deep
red stain, and emitting a potent spirituous
fume from the contents of the broken bottle
of Kalydor.   The paper was two or three
years old, but contained an article of several
columns, in which I soon grew wonderfully
interested.   It was the report of a trial for
breach of promise of marriage, giving the
testimony in full, with fervid extracts from
both the gentleman's and lady's amatory
correspondence.   The deserted damsel had
personally appeared in court, and had borne
energetic evidence to her lover's perfidy and
the strength of her blighted affections.   On
the defendant's part, there had been an attempt, though insufficiently sustained, to
blast the plaintiff's character, and a plea, in
mitigation of damages, on account of her

unamiable temper. A horrible idea was
suggested by the lady's name.
"Madame," said I, holding the newspaper before Mrs. Bullfrog's eyes—and,
though a small, delicate and thin-visaged
man, I feel assured that I looked very terrific—"Madame," repeated I, through my
shut teeth, "were you the plaintiff in this
cause?"
"Oh, my dear Mr. Bullfrog!" replied
my wife, sweetly; "I thought all the world
knew that."
"Horror! horror!" exclaimed I, sinking
back on the seat.
Covering my face with both hands, I
emitted a deep and deathlike groan, as if
my tormented soul were rending me asunder.
I, the most exquisitely fastidious of men,
and whose wife was to have been the most
delicate and refined of women, with all the
fresh dewdrops glittering on her virgin rosebud of a heart! I thought of the glossy
ringlets and pearly teeth, I thought of the
Kalydor, I thought of the coachman's
bruised ear and bloody nose, I thought of
the tender love-secrets which she had whispered to the judge and jury, and a thousand
tittering auditors, and gave another groan.
"Mr. Bullfrog!" said my wife.
As I made no reply, she gently took my
hands within her own, removed them from
my face, and fixed her eyes steadfastly on
mine.

"Mr. Bullfrog," said she, not unkindly, yet with all the decision of her strong character, "let me advise you to overcome this foolish weakness, and prove yourself to the best of your ability as good a husband as I will be a wife. You have discovered, perhaps, some little imperfections in your bride. Well, what did you expect? Women are not angels; if they were, they would go to heaven for husbands—or, at least, be more difficult in their choice on earth."

"But why conceal those imperfections?" interposed I, tremulously.

"Now, my love, are not you a most unreasonable little man?" said Mrs. Bullfrog, patting me on the cheek. "Ought a woman to disclose her frailties earlier than the wedding-day? Few husbands, I assure you, make the discovery in such good season, and still fewer complain that these trifles are concealed too long. Well, what a strange man you are! Poh! you are joking."

"But the suit for breach of promise!" groaned I.

"Ah! and is that the rub?" exclaimed my wife. "Is it possible that you view that affair in an objectionable light? Mr. Bullfrog, I never could have dreamed it. Is it an objection that I have triumphantly defended myself against slander, and vindicated my name in a court of justice? Or do you complain because your wife has

shown [the proper spirit of a woman, and
punished the villain who trifled with her
affections?"

"But," persisted I, shrinking into a corner of the coach, however, for I did not
know precisely how much contradiction the
proper spirit of a woman would endure—
"but, my love, would it not have been more
dignified to treat the villain with the silent
contempt he merited?"

"That is all very well, Mr. Bullfrog,"
said my wife, slyly, "but in that case
where would have been the five thousand
dollars which are to stock your dry-goods
store?"

"Mrs. Bullfrog, upon your honor," demanded I, as if my life hung upon her
words, "is there no mistake about those
five thousand dollars?"

"Upon my word and honor there is none,"
replied she. "The jury gave me every cent
the rascal had, and I have kept it all for my
dear Bullfrog."

"Then, thou dear woman," cried I, with
an overwhelming gush of tenderness, "let
me fold thee to my heart! The basis of
matrimonial bliss is secure, and all thy little
defects and frailties are forgiven. Nay,
since the result has been so fortunate, I
rejoice at the wrongs which drove thee to
this blessed lawsuit, happy Bullfrog that I
am!"

"WIPED OUT."

BY A. A. HAYES.

I.

Any one who has seen an outward bound clipper ship getting under way and heard the "shanty-songs" sung by the sailors as they toiled at capstan and halyards, will probably remember that rhymeless but melodious refrain—

> "I'm bound to see its muddy waters
> Yeo ho! that rolling river;
> Bound to see its muddy waters
> Yeo ho! the wild Missouri."

Only a happy inspiration could have impelled Jack to apply the adjective "wild" to that ill-behaved and disreputable river which, tipsily bearing its enormous burden of mud from the far Northwest, totters, reels, runs its tortuous course for hundreds on hundreds of miles; and which, encountering the lordly and thus far well-behaved Mississippi at Alton, and forcing its company upon this splendid river (as if some drunken fellow should lock arms with a dignified pedestrian) contaminates it all the way to the Gulf of Mexico.

At a certain point on the banks of this river, or rather—as it has the habit of abandoning and destroying said banks—at a safe distance therefrom, there is a town from which a railroad takes its departure for its long climb up the natural incline of the Great Plains, to the base of the mountains; hence the importance to this town of the large but somewhat shabby building serving as terminal station. In its smoky interior, late in the evening and not very long ago, a train was nearly ready to start. It was a train possessing a certain consideration. For the benefit of a public easily gulled and enamored of grandiloquent terms, it was advertised as the " Denver Fast Express ; " sometimes, with strange unfitness, as the " Lightning Express ; " " elegant " and " palatial " cars were declared to be included therein ; and its departure was one of the great events of the twenty-four hours, in the country round about. A local poet de-scribed it in the "live" paper of the town, cribbing from an old Eastern magazine and passing off as original, the lines—

> " Again we stepped into the street,
> A train came thundering by,
> Drawn by the snorting iron steed
> Swifter than eagles fly.
> Rumbled the wheels, the whistle shrieked,
> Far rolled the smoky cloud,
> Echoed the hills, the valley shook,
> The flying forests bowed."

The trainmen, on the other hand, used no fine phrases. They called it simply " Num-ber Seventeen ; " and, when it started, said it had "pulled out."

On the evening in question, there it stood, nearly ready. Just behind the great hissing locomotive, with its parabolic headlight and its coal-laden tender, came the baggage, mail and express cars; then the passenger coaches, in which the social condition of the occupants seemed to be in inverse ratio to their distance from the engine. First came emigrants, "honest miners," "cowboys" and laborers; Irishmen, Germans, Welshmen, Mennonites from Russia, quaint of garb and speech, and Chinamen. Then came long cars full of people of better station, and last the great Pullman "sleepers," in which the busy black porters were making up the berths for well-to-do travelers of diverse nationalities and occupations.

It was a curious study for a thoughtful observer, this motley crowd of human beings sinking all differences of race, creed, and habits in the common purpose to move Westward,—to the mountain fastnesses, the sage-brush deserts, the Golden Gate.

The warning bell had sounded, and the fireman leaned far out for the signal. The gong struck sharply, the conductor shouted, "All aboard" and raised his hand; the tired ticket-seller shut his window, and the train moved out of the station, gathered way as it cleared the outskirts of the town, rounded a curve, entered on an absolutely straight line, and, with one long whistle from the engine, settled down to its work.

Through the night hours it sped on, past lonely ranches and infrequent stations, by and across shallow streams, fringed with cottonwood trees, over the greenish-yellow buffalo grass; near the old trail where many a poor emigrant, many a bold frontiersman, many a brave soldier, had laid his bones but a short time before.

Familiar as they may be, there is something strangely impressive about all night journeys by rail; and those forming part of an American transcontinental trip are almost weird. From the windows of a night-express in Europe, or the older portions of the United States, one looks on houses and lights, cultivated fields, fences and hedges; and, hurled as he may be through the darkness, he has a sense of companionship and semi-security. Far different is it when the long train is running over those two rails which, seen before night set in, seemed to meet on the horizon. Within, all is as if between two great seaboard cities;—the neatly dressed people, the uniformed officials, the handsome fittings, the various appliances for comfort. Without are now long, dreary levels, now deep and wild cañons, now an environment of strange and grotesque rock-formations, castles, battlements, churches, statues. The antelope fleetly runs, and the coyote skulks away from the track, and the gray wolf howls afar off. It is for all the world, to

one's fancy, as if a bit of civilization, a
family or community, its belongings and
surroundings complete, were flying through
regions barbarous and inhospitable.

From the cab of Engine No. 32, the
driver of the Denver Express saw, showing
faintly in the early morning, the buildings
grouped about the little station ten miles
ahead, where breakfast awaited his passengers. He looked at his watch ; he had just
twenty minutes in which to run the distance, as he had run it often before. Something, however, traveled faster than he.
From the smoky station out of which the
train passed the night before, along the
slender wire stretched on rough poles at the
side of the track, a spark of that mysterious
something which we call electricity flashed
at the moment he returned the watch to his
pocket ; and in five minutes time, the
station-master came out on the platform, a
little more thoughtful than his wont, and
looked eastward for the smoke of the train.
With but three of the passengers in that
train has this tale specially to do, and they
were all in the new and comfortable Pullman '' City of Cheyenne.''   One was a tall,
well-made man of about thirty,—blonde,
blue-eyed, bearded, straight, sinewy, alert.
Of all in the train he seemed the most thoroughly at home, and the respectful greeting
of the conductor, as he passed through the
car, marked him as an officer of the road.

Such was he—Henry Sinclair, assistant
engineer, quite famed on the line, high in
favor with the directors, and a rising man in
all ways. It was known on the road that
he was expected in Denver, and there were
rumors that he was to organize the parties
for the survey of an important "extension."
Beside him sat his pretty young wife. She
was a New Yorker—one could tell at first
glance—from the feather of her little bon-
net, matching the gray traveling dress, to
the tips of her dainty boots ; and one, too,
at whom old Fifth Avenue promenaders
would have turned to look. She had a
charming figure, brown hair, hazel eyes,
and an expression at once kind, intelligent
and spirited. She had cheerfully left a
luxurious home to follow the young engineer's fortunes ; and it was well known that
those fortunes had been materially advanced
by her tact and cleverness.

The third passenger in question had just
been in conversation with Sinclair, and the
latter was telling his wife of their curious
meeting. Entering the toilet room at the
rear of the car, he said, he had begun his
ablutions by the side of another man, and it
was as they were sluicing their faces with
water that he heard the cry :

" Why, Major, is that you ? Just to think
of meeting you here ! "

A man of about twenty-eight years of age,
slight, muscular, wiry, had seized his wet

hand and was wringing it. He had black
eyes, keen and bright, swarthy complexion,
black hair and mustache. A keen observer
might have seen about him some signs of a
jeunesse orageuse, but his manner was frank
and pleasing. Sinclair looked him in the
face, puzzled for a moment.

"Don't you remember Foster?" asked
the man.

"Of course I do," replied Sinclair. "For
a moment I could not place you. Where
have you been and what have you been
doing?"

"Oh," replied Foster, laughing, "I've
braced up and turned over a new leaf. I'm
a respectable member of society, have a
place in the express company and am going
to Denver to take charge."

"I am very glad to hear it, and you must
tell me your story, when we have had our
breakfast."

The pretty young woman was just about
to ask who Foster was, when the speed of
the train slackened, and the brakeman
opened the door of the car and cried out in
stentorian tones:

"Pawnee Junction; twenty minutes for
refreshments!"

II.

When the celebrated Rocky Mountain
gold excitement broke out, more than

twenty years ago, and people painted "PIKE'S PEAK OR BUST" on the canvas covers of their wagons and started for the diggings, they established a "trail" or "trace" leading in a southwesterly direction from the old one to California.

At a certain point on this trail a frontiersman named Barker built a forlorn ranchhouse and *corral* and offered what is conventionally called "entertainment for man and beast."

For years he lived there, dividing his time between fighting the Indians and feeding the passing emigrants and their stock. Then the first railroad to Denver was built, taking another route from the Missouri, and Barker's occupation was gone. He retired with his gains to St. Louis and lived in comfort.

Years passed on, and the "extension" over which our train is to pass was planned. The old pioneers were excellent natural engineers, and their successors could find no better route than they had chosen. Thus it was that "Barker's" became, during the construction period, an important point, and the frontiersman's name came to figure on time-tables. Meanwhile the place passed through a process of evolution which would have delighted Darwin. In the party of engineers which first camped there was Sinclair, and it was by his advice that the contractors selected it for division head-quarters. Then came drinking "saloons" and gambling houses—alike the inevitable concomitant and the bane of western settlements ; then scattered houses and shops, and a shabby so-called hotel, in which the letting of miserable rooms (divided from each other by canvas partitions) was wholly subordinated to the business of the bar. Before long Barker's had acquired a worse reputation than even other towns of its type, the abnormal and uncanny aggregations of squalor and vice which dotted the plains in those days ; and it was at its worst when Sinclair returned thither and took up his quarters in the engineers' building. The passion for gambling was raging, and to pander thereto were collected as choice a lot of desperadoes as ever "stocked" cards or loaded dice. It came to be noticed that they were on excellent terms with a man called "Jeff" Johnson, who was lessee of the hotel ; and to be suspected that said Johnson, in local parlance, "stood in with" them. With this man had come to Barker's his daughter Sarah, commonly known as "Sally," a handsome girl with a straight, lithe figure, fine features, reddish auburn hair and dark blue eyes. It is but fair to say that even the "toughs" of a place like Barker's show some respect for the other sex, and Miss Sally's case was no exception to the rule. The male population admired her ; they said she "put on heaps of style;"

but none of them had seemed to make any progress in her good graces.

On a pleasant afternoon, just after the track had been laid some miles west of Barker's, and construction trains were running with some regularity to and from the end thereof, Sinclair sat on the rude veranda of the engineers' quarters, smoking his well-colored meerschaum and looking at the sunset. The atmosphere had been so clear during the day that glimpses were had of Long's and Pike's Peaks, and as the young engineer gazed at the gorgeous cloud display he was thinking of the miners' quaint and pathetic idea that the dead '' go over the Range.''

'' Nice looking, ain't it, Major?'' asked a voice at his elbow, and he turned to see one of the contractors' officials taking a seat near him.

'' More than nice looking to my mind, Sam,'' he replied. '' What is the news to-day ? ''

'' Nothin' much. There's a sight of talk about the doin's of them faro an' keno sharps. The boys is gittin' kind o' riled, fur they allow the game ain't on the square wuth a cent. Some of 'em down to the tie-camp wuz a-talkin' about a vigilance committee, an' I wouldn't be surprised ef they meant business. Hev yer heard about the young feller that come in a week ago from Laramie an' set up a new faro-bank ? ''

"No. What about him ? "

"Wa'al, yer see he's a feller thet's got a
lot of sand an' ain't afeared of nobody, an'
he's allowed to hev the deal to his place on
the square every time. Accordin' to my
idee, gamblin's about the wust racket a
feller kin work, but it takes all sorts of men
to make a world, an' ef the boys is bound
to hev a game, I calkilate they'd like to
patronize his bank. Thet's made the old
crowd mighty mad, an' they're a-talkin'
about puttin' up a job of cheatin' on him
an' then stringin' him up. Besides, I kind
o' think there's some cussed jealousy on
another lay as comes in. Yer see the young
feller—Cyrus Foster's his name—is sweet
on thet gal of Jeff Johnson's. Jeff wuz to
Laramie before he come here, an' Foster
knowed Sally up thar. I allow he moved
here to see her. Hello ! If thar they ain't
a-comin' now."

Down a path leading from the town, past
the railroad buildings, and well on the prai-
rie, Sinclair saw the girl walking with the
" young feller." He was talking earnestly
to her, and her eyes were cast down. She
looked pretty and, in a way, graceful ; and
there was in her attire a noticeable attempt
at neatness, and a faint reminiscence of by-
gone fashions. A smile came to Sinclair's
lips as he thought of a couple walking up
Fifth Avenue during his leave of absence
not many months before, and of a letter,

many times read, lying at that moment in
his breast-pocket.

"Papa's bark is worse than his bite," ran
one of its sentences. "Of course he does
not like the idea of my leaving him and going away to such dreadful and remote places
as Denver and Omaha, and I don't know
what else ; but he will not oppose me in the
end, and when you come on again—"

"By thunder !" exclaimed Sam ; "ef
thar ain't one of them there sharps a-
watchin' 'em."

Sure enough, a rough-looking fellow, his
hat pulled over his eyes, half-concealed
behind a pile of lumber, was casting a sin-
ister glance toward the pair.

"The gal's well enough," continued Sam;
"but I don't take a cent's wuth of stock in
thet thar father of her'n. He's in with them
sharps, sure pop, an' it don't suit his book
to hev Foster hangin' round. It's ten to
one he sent that cuss to watch 'em. Wa'al,
they're a queer lot, an' I'm afeared thar's
plenty of trouble ahead among 'em. Good
luck to you, Major," and he pushed back
his chair and walked away.

After breakfast next morning, when Sinclair was sitting at the table in his office,
busy with maps and plans, the door was
thrown open and Foster, panting for breath,
ran in.

"Major Sinclair," he said, speaking with
difficulty, "I've no claim on you, but I ask

you to protect me. The other gamblers are going to hang me. They are more than ten to one. They will track me here, and unless you harbor me, I'm a dead man."

Sinclair rose from his chair in a second and walked to the window. A party of men were approaching the building. He turned to Foster :

"I do not like your trade," said he ; "but I will not see you murdered if I can help it. You are welcome here." Foster said "Thank you," stood still a moment, and then began to pace the room, rapidly clenching his hands, his whole frame quivering, his eyes flashing fire—"for all the world," Sinclair said, in telling the story afterward, "like a fierce caged tiger."

"Trapped !" he muttered, with concentrated intensity, "to be *trapped*, TRAPPED, like this ! "

Sinclair stepped quickly to the door of his bed-room and motioned Foster to enter. Then there came a knock at the outer door, and he opened it and stood on the threshold, erect and firm. Half-a-dozen "toughs" faced him.

"Major," said their spokesman, "we want that man."

"You cannot have him, boys."

"Major, we're a-goin' to take him."

"You had better not try," said Sinclair, with perfect ease and self-possession, and in a pleasant voice. "I have given him shelter, and you can only get him over my dead body. Of course you can kill me, but you won't do even that without one or two of you going down ; and then you know perfectly well, boys, what will happen. You *know* that if you lay your finger on a railroad man it's all up with you. There are five hundred men in the graders' camp, not five miles away, and you don't need to be told that in less than one hour after they get word there won't be a piece of one of you big enough to bury."

The men made no reply. They looked him straight in the eyes for a moment. Had they seen a sign of flinching they might have risked the issue, but there was none. With muttered curses, they slunk away. Sinclair shut and bolted the door, then opened the one leading to the bed-room.

"Foster," he said, "the train will pass here in half an hour. Have you money enough ? "

"Plenty, Major."

"Very well ; keep perfectly quiet, and I will try to get you safely off." He went to an adjoining room and called Sam, the contractors' man. He took in the situation at a glance.

"Wa'al, Foster," said he, "kind 'o ' close call ' for yer, warn't it ? Guess yer'd better be gittin' up an' gittin' pretty lively. The train boys will take yer through, an' yer kin come back when this racket's worked out."

Sinclair glanced at his watch, then he walked to the window and looked out. On a small *mesa*, or elevated plateau, commanding the path to the railroad, he saw a number of men with rifles.

"Just as I expected," said he. "Sam, ask one of the boys to go down to the track and, when the train arrives, tell the conductor to come here."

In a few minutes the whistle was heard, and the conductor entered the building. Receiving his instructions, he returned, and immediately on engine, tender and platform appeared the trainmen, with *their* rifles covering the group on the bluff. Sinclair put on his hat.

"Now, Foster," said he, "we have no time to lose. Take Sam's arm and mine, and walk between us."

The trio left the building and walked deliberately to the railroad. Not a word was spoken. Besides the men in sight on the train, two behind the window blinds of one of the passenger coaches, and unseen, kept their fingers on the triggers of their repeating carbines. It seemed a long time, counted by anxious seconds, until Foster was safe in the coach.

"All ready, conductor," said Sinclair. "Now, Foster, good-bye. I am not good at lecturing, but if I were you, I would make this the turning point in my life."

Foster was much moved.

"I will do it, Major," said he ; "and I shall never forget what you have done for me to-day. I am sure we shall meet again."

With another shriek from the whistle the train started. Sinclair and Sam saw the men quietly returning the firearms to their places as it gathered way. Then they walked back to their quarters. The men on the *mesa*, balked of their purpose, had withdrawn.

Sam accompanied Sinclair to his door and then sententiously remarked : "Major, I think I'll light out and find some of the boys. You ain't got no call to know anything about it, but I allow it's about time them games was bounced."

Three nights after this a powerful party of *Vigilantes*, stern and inexorable, made a raid on all the gambling dens, broke the tables and apparatus, and conducted the men to a distance from the town, where they left them with an emphatic and concise warning as to the consequences of any attempt to return. An exception was made in Jeff Johnson's case—but only for the sake of his daughter—for it was found that many games of chance had been carried on in his house.

Ere long he found it convenient to sell his business and retire to a town some miles to the eastward, where the railroad influence was not as strong as it was at Barker's. At about this time, Sinclair made his arrangements to go to New York, with the pleasant prospect of marrying the young lady in Fifth Avenue. In due time he arrived at Barker's with his young and charming wife and remained for some days. The changes were astounding. Commonplace respectability had replaced abnormal lawlessness. A neat station stood where had been the rough contractors' buildings. At a new "Windsor" (or was it "Brunswick?") the performance of the kitchen contrasted sadly (alas! how common is such contrast in these regions!) with the promise of the *menu*. There was a tawdry theatre yclept "Academy of Music," and there was not much to choose in the way of ugliness between two "meeting-houses."

"Upon my word, my dear," said Sinclair to his wife, "I ought to be ashamed to say it, but I prefer Barker's *au naturel.*"

One evening, just before the young people left the town, and as Mrs. Sinclair sat alone in her room, the frowsy waitress announced "a lady," and was requested to bid her enter. A woman came with timid mien into the room, sat down, as invited, and removed her veil. Of course the young bride had never known Sally Johnson, the whilom belle of Barker's, but her husband would have noticed at a glance how greatly she was changed from the girl who walked with Foster past the engineer's quarters.

It would be hard to find a more striking contrast than was presented by the two women as they sat facing each other ; the one in the flush of health and beauty, calm, sweet, self-possessed ; the other still retaining some of the shabby finery of old days, but pale and haggard, with black rings under her eyes, and a pathetic air of humiliation.

"Mrs. Sinclair," she hurriedly began, "you do not know me, or the like of me. I've got no right to speak to you, but I couldn't help it. Oh ! please believe me, I am not real downright bad. I'm Sally Johnson, daughter of a man whom they drove out of the town. My mother died when I was little, and I *never* had a show ; and folks think because I live with my father, and he makes me know the crowd he travels with, that I must be in with them, and be of their sort. I never had a woman speak a kind word to me, and I've had so much trouble that I'm just drove wild, and like to kill myself ; and then I was at the station when you came in and I saw your sweet face and the kind look in your eyes, and it came in my heart that I'd speak to you if I died for it." She leaned eagerly forward, her hands nervously closing on the back of a chair. "I suppose your husband never told you of me ; like enough he never knew me ; but I'll never forget him as long as I live. When he was here before, there was

a young man "—here a faint color came in
the wan cheeks—"who was fond of me, and
I thought the world of him, and my father
was down on him, and the men that father
was in with wanted to kill him ; and Mr.
Sinclair saved his life. He's gone away,
and I've waited and waited for him to come
back—and perhaps I'll never see him again.
But oh ! dear lady, I'll never forget what
your husband did. He's a good man and
he deserves the love of a dear good woman
like you, and if I dared, I'd pray for you
both, night and day."

She stopped suddenly, and sank back in
her seat, pale as before and as if frightened
by her own emotion. Mrs. Sinclair had listened with sympathy and increasing interest.

" My poor girl," she said, speaking tenderly (she had a lovely, soft voice) and with
slightly heightened color, "I am delighted
that you came to see me, and that my husband was able to help you. Tell me, can
we not do more for you ? I do not for one
moment believe you can be happy with your
present surroundings. Can we not assist
you to leave them ?"

The girl rose, sadly shaking her head.
" I thank you for your words," she said.
" I don't suppose I'll ever see you again,
but I'll say God bless you !"

She caught Mrs. Sinclair's hand, pressed
it to her lips and was gone.

Sinclair found his wife very thoughtful

when he came home, and he listened with
much interest to her story.

"Poor girl!" said he; "Foster is the
man to help her. I wonder where he is? I
must inquire about him."

The next day, they proceeded on their
way to San Francisco, and matters drifted
on at Barker's much as before. Johnson
had, after an absence of some months, come
back and lived without molestation, amid
the shifting population. Now and then,
too, some of the older residents fancied they
recognized, under slouched sombreros, the
faces of some of his former "crowd" about
the "Ranchman's Home," as his gaudy
place was called.

On the very evening on which this story
opens, and they were "making up" the
Denver Express in the train-house on the
Missouri, "Jim" Watkins, agent and teleg-
rapher at Barker's, was sitting in his little
office, communicating with the station rooms
by the ticket window. Jim was a cool,
silent, efficient man, and not much given to
talk about such episodes in his past life as
the "wiping out" by Indians of the construction party to which he belonged, and
his own rescue by the scouts. He was smoking an old and favorite pipe, and talking with
one of "the boys" whose head appeared at
the wicket. On a seat in the station sat a
woman in a black dress and veil, apparently
waiting for a train.

''Got a heap of letters and telegrams there, ain't yer, Jim?'' remarked the man at the window.

''Yes,'' replied Jim; ''they're for Engineer Sinclair, to be delivered to him when he passes through here. He leaves on No. 17, to-night.'' The inquirer did not notice the sharp start of the woman near him.

''Is that good-lookin' wife of his'n a comin' with him?'' asked he.

''Yes, there's letters for her, too.''

''Well, good-night, Jim. See yer later,'' and he went out. The woman suddenly rose and ran to the window.

''Mr. Watkins,'' cried she, ''can I see you for a few moments, where no one can interrupt us?'' She clutched the sill with her thin hands and her voice trembled. Watkins recognized Sally Johnson in a moment. He unbolted a door, motioned her to enter, closed and again bolted it, and also closed the ticket window. Then he pointed to a chair, and the girl sat down and leaned eagerly forward.

''If they knew I was here,'' she said in a hoarse whisper, ''my life wouldn't be safe five minutes. I was waiting to tell you a terrible story, and then I heard who was on the train due here to-morrow night. Mr. Watkins, don't for God's sake, ask me how I found out, but I hope to die if I ain't telling you the living truth! They're going to wreck that train—No. 17—at Dead Man's

Crossing, fifteen miles east, and rob the
passengers and the express car. It's the
worst gang in the country, *Perry's.* They're
going to throw the train off the track, the
passengers will be maimed and killed,—and
Mr. Sinclair and his wife on the cars!
Oh ! I pray ! Mr. Watkins, send them warning.

She stood upright, her face deadly pale,
her hands clasped. Watkins walked deliberately to the railroad map which hung on
the wall and scanned it. Then he resumed
his seat, laid his pipe down, fixed his eyes
on the girl's face, and began to question her.
At the same time his right hand, with which
he had held the pipe, found its way to the
telegraph key. None but an expert could
have distinguished any change in the *click-
ing* of the instrument, which had been
almost incessant; but Watkins had
"called" the head office of the Missouri.
In two minutes the "sounder" rattled out
"All right ! What is it?"

Watkins went on with his questions, his
eyes still fixed on the poor girl's face and all
the time his fingers, as it were, playing
with the key. If he were imperturbable, so
was *not* a man sitting at a receiving intru-
ment nearly five hundred miles away. He
had "taken" but a few words when he
jumped from his chair and cried :

"Shut that door, and call the superintendent and be quick ! Charley, brace up—

lively— and come and write this out!''
With his wonderful electric pen, the handle
several hundreds of miles long, Watkins,
unknown to his interlocutor, was printing
in the Morse alphabet this startling message :

"*Inform'n rec'd. Perry gang going to
throw No. 17 off track near —xth mile post,
this division, about nine to-morrow (Thursday) night, kill passengers, and rob express
and mail. Am alone here. No chance to
verify story, but believe it to be on square.
Better make arrangements from your end to
block game. No sheriff here now. Answer.*"

The superintendent, responding to the
hasty summons, heard the message before
the clerk had time to write it out.   His lips
were closely compressed as he put his own
hand on the key and sent these laconic
sentences :   "*O. K.   Keep perfectly dark.
Will manage from this end.*"

Watkins, at Barker's, rose from his seat,
opened the door a little way, saw that the
station was empty, and then said to the
girl, brusquely, but kindly :

"Sally, you've done the square thing,
and saved that train.   I'll take care that
you don't suffer and that you get well paid.
Now come home with me, and my wife will
look out for you."

"Oh ! no," cried the girl, shrinking back,
"I must run away.   You're mighty kind,

but I daren't go with you." Detecting a shade of doubt in his eye, she added : "Don't be afeared ; I'll die before they'll know I've given them away to you !" and she disappeared in the darkness.

At the other end of the wire, the superintendent had quietly impressed secrecy on his operator and clerk, ordered his fast mare harnessed, and gone to his private office.

"Read that!" said he to his secretary. "It was about time for some trouble of this kind, and now I'm going to let Uncle Sam take care of his mails. If I don't get to the reservation before the General's turned in, I shall have to wake him up. Wait for me, please."

The gray mare made the six miles to the military reservation in just half an hour. The General was smoking his last cigar, and and was alert in an instant ; and before the superintendent had finished the cup of hot coffee hospitably tended, the orders had gone by wire to the commanding officer at Fort——, some distance east of Barker's, and been duly acknowledged.

Returning to the station, the superintendent remarked to the waiting secretary :

"The General's all right. Of course we can't tell that this is not a sell ; but if those Perry hounds mean business they'll get all the fight they want ; and if they've got any souls,—which I doubt,—may the Lord have mercy on them !"

He prepared several dispatches, two of which were as follows:

"MR. HENRY SINCLAIR:

"*On No. 17, Pawnee Junction :*

This telegrams your authority to take charge of train on which you are and demand obedience of all officials and trainmen on road. Please do so, and act in accordance with information wired station agent at Pawnee Junction."

To the Station Agent:

"*Reported Perry gang will try wreck and rob No. 17 near—xth mile post, Denver Division, about nine Thursday night. Troops will await train at Fort——. Car ordered ready for them. Keep everything secret, and act in accordance with orders of Mr. Sinclair.*"

"It's worth about ten thousand dollars," sententiously remarked he, "that Sinclair's on that train. He's got both sand and brains. Good-night," and he went to bed and slept the sleep of the just.

III.

The sun never shone more brightly and the air was never more clear and bracing than when Sinclair helped his wife off the train at Pawnee Junction. The station-master's face fell as he saw the lady, but he

saluted the engineer with as easy an air as
he could assume, and watched for an opportunity to speak to him alone. Sinclair read
the dispatches with an unmoved countenance, and after a few minutes' reflection,
simply said : "All right. Be sure to keep
the matter perfectly quiet." At breakfast
he was *distrait*—so much so that his wife
asked him what was the matter. Taking
her aside, he at once showed her the telegrams.

"You see my duty," he said. " My only
thought is about you, my dear child. Will
you stay here ? "

She simply replied, looking into his face
without a tremor :

" My place is with you." Then the conductor called " All aboard," and the train
once more started.

Sinclair asked Foster to join him in the
smoking-compartment and tell him the
promised story, which the latter did. His
rescue at Barker's, he frankly and grate-
fully said, *had* been the turning-point in his
life. In brief, he had "sworn off" from
gambling and drinking, had found honest
employment, and was doing well.

" I've two things to do now, Major," he
added : "first, I must show my gratitude ;
to you ; and next—" he hesitated a little—
" I want to find that poor girl that I left behind at Barker's. She was engaged to
marry me, and when I come to think of it,

and what a life I'd have made her lead, I
hadn't the heart till now to look for her ;
but, seeing I'm on the right track, I'm going
to find her, and get her to come with me.
her father is a bad old scoundrel, but that
ain't her fault, and I ain't going to marry
him."

"Foster," quietly asked Sinclair, "do you
know the Perry gang ? "

The man's brow darkened.

"Know them ? " said he. " I know them
much too well.   Perry is as ungodly a cut-
throat as ever killed an emigrant in cold
blood, and he's got in his gang nearly all
those hounds that tried to hang me.   Why
do you ask, Major ? "

Sinclair handed   him   the   dispatches.
" You are the only man on the train to whom
I have shown them," said he.

Foster read them slowly, his eyes lighting
up as he did so.   " Looks as if it was true,"
said he.   " Let me see ! Fort ——.   Yes,
that's the —th infantry.   Two of their boys
were killed at Sidney last summer by some
of the same gang, and the regiment's sworn
vengeance.   Major, if this story's on the
square, that crowd's goose is cooked, and
don't you forget it ! I say, you must give me
a hand in."

"Foster," said Sinclair, " I am going to
put responsibility on your shoulders. I have
no doubt that, if we be attacked, the soldiers
will dispose of the gang ; but I must take

all possible precautions for the safety of the
passengers. We must not alarm them. They
can be made to think that the troops are
going on a scout, and only a certain number
of resolute men need be told of what we expect. Can you, late this afternoon, go
through the cars, and pick them out ? I will
then put you in charge of the passenger cars,
and you can post your men on the platforms
to act in case of need. My place will be
ahead."

"Major, you can depend on me," was
Foster's reply. "I'll go through the train
and have my eye on some boys of the right
sort, and that's got their shooting-irons with
them."

Through the hours of that day on rolled
the train, still over the crisp buffalo grass,
across the well-worn buffalo trails, past the
prairie-dog villages. The passengers chatted,
dozed, read newspapers, all unconscious,
with the exception of three, of the coming
conflict between the good and the evil forces
bearing on their fate ; of the fell preparations making for their disaster ; of the grim
preparations making to avert such disaster ;
of all of which the little wires alongside of
them had been talking back and forth.
Watkins had telegraphed that he still saw
no reason to doubt the good faith of his
warning, and Sinclair had reported his receipt of authority and his acceptance thereof.
Meanwhile, also, there had been set in

motion a measure of that power to which appeal is so reluctantly made in time of peace. At Fort ——, a lonely post on the plains, the orders had that morning been issued for twenty men under Lieutenant Halsey to parade at 4 p. m., with overcoats, two days' rations, and ball cartridges; also for Assistant Surgeon Kesler to report for duty with the party. Orders as to destination were communicated direct to the lieutenant from the post commander, and on the minute the little column moved, taking the road to the station. The regiment from which it came had been in active service among the Indians on the frontier for a long time, and the officers and men were tried and seasoned fighters. Lieutenant Halsey had been well known at West Point. From there he had gone straight to the field, and three years had given him an enviable reputation for *sang froid* and determined bravery. He looked every inch the soldier as he walked along the trail, his cloak thrown back and his sword tucked under his arm. The doctor, who carried a Modoc bullet in some inaccessible part of his scarred body, growled good-naturedly at the need of walking, and the men, enveloped in their army-blue overcoats, marched easily by fours. Reaching the station, the lieutenant called the agent aside, and with him inspected, on a siding, a long platform car on which benches had been placed and secured. Then he took his seat in the station and quietly waited, occasionally twisting his long blonde mustache. The doctor took a cigar with the agent and the men walked about or sat on the edge of the platform. One of them, who obtained a surreptitious glance at his silent commander, told his companions that there was trouble ahead for somebody.

"That's just the way the leftenant looked, boys," said he, "when we was laying for them Apaches that raided Jones' Ranch and killed the women and little children."

In a short time the officer looked at his watch, formed his men, and directed them to take their places on the seats of the car. They had hardly done so, when the whistle of the approaching train was heard. When it came up, the conductor, who had his instructions from Sinclair, had the engine detached and backed on the siding for the soldiers' car, which thus came between it and the foremost baggage-car, when the train was again made up. As arranged, it was announced that the troops were to be taken a certain distance to join a scouting party, and the curiosity of the passengers was but slightly excited. The soldiers sat quietly in their seats, their repeating rifles held between their knees, and the officer in front. Sinclair joined the latter and had a few words with him as the train moved on. A little later, when the stars were shining brightly overhead, they passed into the express car, and sent for the conductor and other trainmen, and for Foster. In a few words Sinclair explained the position of affairs. His statement was received with perfect coolness, and the men only asked what they were to do.

"I hope, boys," said Sinclair, "that we are going to put this gang to-night where they will make no more trouble. Lieutenant Halsey will bear the brunt of the fight, and it only remains for you to stand by the interests committed to your care. Mr. Express Agent, what help do you want?" The person addressed, a good-natured giant, girded with a cartridge belt, smiled as he replied:

"Well, sir, I'm wearing a watch which the company gave me for standing off the James gang in Missouri for half an hour, when we hadn't a ghost of a soldier about. I'll take the contract, and welcome, to hold *this* fort alone."

"Very well," said Sinclair. "Foster, what progress have you made?"

"Major, I've got ten or fifteen as good men as ever drawed a bead, and just red-hot for a fight."

"That will do very well. Conductor, give the trainmen the rifles from the baggage car and let them act under Mr. Foster. Now, boys, I am sure you will do your duty. That is all."

From the next station Sinclair telegraphed "All ready" to the superintendent,
who was pacing his office in much suspense.
Then he said a few words to his brave but
anxious wife, and walked to the rear platform. On it were several armed men, who
bade him good-evening, and asked "when
the fun was going to begin." Walking
through the train, he found each platform
similarly occupied, and Foster going from
one to the other. The latter whispered as
he passed him :

" Major, I found Arizona Joe the scout,
in the smokin' car, and he's on the front
platform. That let's me out, and although
I know as well as you that there ain't no
danger about that rear sleeper where the
madam is, I ain't a-goin' to be far off from
her." Sinclair shook him by the hand ;
then he looked at his watch. It was half-
past eight. He passed through the baggage
and express cars, finding in the latter the
agent sitting behind his safe, on which lay
two large revolvers. On the platform car
he found the soldiers and their commander,
sitting silent and unconcerned as before.
When Sinclair reached the latter and nodded,
he rose and faced the men, and his fine voice
was clearly heard above the rattle of the
train.

" Company, 'ten*tion !* " The soldiers
straightened themselves in a second.

" With ball cartridge, *load !* " It was done

with the precision of a machine. Then the lieutenant spoke, in the same clear, crisp tones that the troops had heard in more than one fierce battle.

"Men," said he, "in a few minutes the Perry gang, which you will remember, are going to try to run this train off the track, wound and kill the passengers, and rob the cars and the United States mail. It is our business to prevent them. Sergeant Wilson" (a gray-bearded non-commissioned officer stood up and saluted), "I am going on the engine. See that my orders are repeated. Now men, aim low, and don't waste any shots." He and Sinclair climbed over the tender and spoke to the engine driver, who received the news with great nonchalance.

"How are the air-brakes working?" asked Sinclair.

"First-rate."

"Then, if you slow down now, you could stop the train in a third of her length, couldn't you?"

"Easy, if you don't mind being shaken up a bit."

"That is good. How is the country about the —xth mile-post."

"Dead level, and smooth."

"Good again. Now, Lieutenant Halsey, this is a splendid headlight, and we can see a long way with my night-glass, I will have a ——"

"—8th mile-post just passed," interrupted the engine driver.

"Only one more to pass, then, before we ought to strike them. Now, Lieutenant, I undertake to stop the train within a very short distance of the gang. They will be on both sides of the track, no doubt ; and the ground, as you hear, is quite level. You will best know what to do."

The officer stepped back. "Sergeant," called he, " do you hear me plainly ? "

" Yes, sir."

" Have the men fix bayonets. When the train stops, and I wave my sword, let half jump off each side, run up quickly, and form line *abreast of the engine*—not ahead."

"Jack," said Sinclair to the engine driver, " is your hand steady ? " The man held it up with a smile. "Good. Now, stand by your throttle and your air-brake. Lieutenant, better warn the men to hold on tight, and tell the sergeant to pass the word to the boys on the platforms, or they will be knocked off by the sudden stop. Now for a look ahead ! " and he brought the binocular to his eyes.

The great parabolic head-light illuminated the track a long way in advance, all behind it being of course in darkness. Suddenly Sinclair cried out :

" The fools have a light there, as I am a living man ; and there is a little red one near us. What can that be? All ready,

Jack? By heavens! they have taken up two rails. Now, *hold on, all!* STOP HER!!"

The engine-driver shut his throttle-valve with a jerk. Then, holding hard by it, he sharply turned a brass handle. There was a fearful jolt—a grating—and the train's way was checked. The lieutenant, standing sidewise, had drawn his sword. He waved it, and almost before he could get off the engine, the soldiers were up and forming, still in shadow, while the bright light was thrown on a body of men ahead.

"Surrender, or you are dead men!" roared the officer. Curses and several shots were the reply. Then came the orders, quick and sharp:

"*Forward! Close up! Double-quick! Halt!* FIRE!"

* * * It was speedily over. Left on the car with the men, the old sergeant had said: "Boys, you hear. It's that old Perry gang. Now don't forget Larry and Charley that they murdered last year," and there had come from the soldiers a sort of fierce, subdued *growl.* The volley was followed by a bayonet charge, and it required all the officer's authority to save the lives of even those who "threw up their hands." Large as the gang was (outnumbering the troops), well-armed and desperate as they were, every one was dead, wounded, or a prisoner when the men who guarded the train platforms ran up. The surgeon, with

professional coolness, walked up to the robbers, his instrument case under his arm.

"Not much for me to do here, Lieutenant," said he. "That practice for Creedmoor is telling on the shooting. Good thing for the gang, too. Bullets are better than rope, and a Colorado jury will give them plenty of that."

Sinclair had sent a man to tell his wife that all was over. Then he ordered a fire lighted, and the rails relaid. The flames lit a strange scene as the passengers flocked up. The lieutenant posted men to keep them back.

"Is there a telegraph station not far ahead, Sinclair?" asked he. "Yes? All right." He drew a pad from his pocket, and wrote a dispatch to the post commander.

"Be good enough to send that for me," said he, "and leave orders at Barker's for the night express eastward to stop for us, and to bring a posse to take care of the wounded and prisoners. And now, my dear Sinclair, I suggest that you get the passengers into the cars, and go on as soon as those rails are spiked.' When they realize the situation, some of them will feel precious ugly, and you know we can't have any lynching."

Sinclair glanced at the rails and gave the word at once to the conductor and brakeman, who began vociferating, "All aboard!" Just then Foster appeared, an expression of intense satisfaction showing clearly on his face, in the firelight.

"Major," said he, "I didn't use to take much stock in special Providence, or things being ordered; but I'm wrong if I don't believe in them from this day. I was bound to stay where you put me, but I was uneasy, and wild to be in the scrimmage; and, if I had been there, I wouldn't have taken notice of a little red light that wasn't much behind the rear platform when we stopped. When I saw there was no danger there, I ran back, and what do you think I found? There was a woman, in a dead faint, and just clutching a lantern that she had tied up in a red scarf, poor little thing! And, Major, it was Sally! It was the little girl that loved me out at Barker's, and has loved me and waited for me ever since! And when she came to, and knew me, she was so glad she 'most fainted away again; and she let on as it was her that gave away the job. And I took her into the sleeper, and the madam, God bless her!—she knew Sally before and was good to her—she took care of her, and is cheering her up. And now, Major, I'm going to take her straight to Denver, and send for a parson and get her married to me, and she'll brace up, sure pop."

The whistle sounded, and the train started. From the window of the "sleeper" Sinclair and his wife took their last look at the weird scene. The lieutenant, standing at the side of the track, wrapped in his cloak, caught a glimpse of Mrs. Sinclair's pretty face, and returned her bow. Then, as the car passed out of sight, he tugged at his moustache and hummed—

"Why, boys, why,
Should we be melancholy, boys,
Whose business 'tis to die?"'

In less than an hour, telegrams having in the mean time been sent in both directions, the train ran alongside the platform at Barker's ; and Watkins, imperturbable as usual, met Sinclair, and gave him his letters.

" Perry gang wiped out, I hear, Major," said he. " Good thing for the country. That's a lesson the ' toughs' in these parts won't forget for a long time. Plucky girl that give 'em away, wasn't she? Hope she's all right."

" She is all right," said Sinclair, with a smile.

" Glad of that. By-the-way, that father of her'n passed in his checks to-night. He'd got one warning from the Vigilantes, and yesterday they found out he was in with this gang, and they was a-going for him ; but when the telegram come, he put a pistol to his head and saved them all trouble. Good riddance to everybody, I say. The sheriff's here now, and is going east on the next train to get them fellows. He's got a big posse together, and I wouldn't wonder if they was hard to hold in, after the 'boys in blue' is gone.''

In a few minutes the train was off, with its living freight,—the just and the unjust, the reformed and the rescued, the happy and the anxious. With many of the passengers the episode of the night was already a thing of the past. Sinclair sat by the side of his wife, to whose cheeks the color had all come back ; and Sally Johnson lay in her berth, faint still, but able to give an occasional smile to Foster. In the station on the Missouri the reporters were gathered about the happy superintendent, filling their note-books with items. In Denver, their brethren would gladly have done the same, but Watkins failed to gratify them. He was a man of few words. When the train had gone, and a friend remarked :

''Hope they'll get through all right, now,'' he simply said :

''Yes, likely. Two shots don't most always go in the same hole.'' Then he went to the telegraph instrument. In a few minutes he could have told a story as wild as a Norse *saga*, but what he said, when Denver had responded, was only —

''*No.* 17, *fifty-five minutes late.*''

EPISTOLARY CRAZY-WORK.

BY FRED. C. VALENTINE.

I.

AUBURN, August 2d, '83.

MY OWN DEAR JENNIE.

It is very simple. All I did was to write to several dry-goods houses requesting samples of evening silks at from $2 to seven $ a yard. Lots of them came ; some mean people did not answer, others who were inexpressibly mean and sent their samples glued to stiff card-board, are not worth mentioning. My pieces are nearly used up, therefore I sent out a new batch of letters yesterday. My quilt will be finished before October. The work is very easy, and the material costs only postage. Cheap, eh ?—Any new conquests ?

With much love,

EULALIA.

II.

ROBERT ANDERSON.   JAMES DUDLEY.

ANDERSON & DUDLEY.

𝔇𝔯𝔶 𝔊𝔬𝔬𝔡𝔰,

8310 BROADWAY,

New York, Aug. 5 188 3.

MY DEAR JIM.

Your order 1404 rec'd. Really am glad you went on the road. Also glad your health has improved.

By the way, am awfully bothered by girls writing for samples. Three days ago rec'd enclosed letter from Miss Eulalia Eccles, Auburn, N. Y. Sent samples. As you see by it, she is daughter of Hon. Jeremiah Eccles. When you go to Auburn see if you cannot make an example of her.

Your partner and friend,

BOB.

III.

MY OWN DEAR EULALIA :—

You are a genius. I have not "booked the idea" but put it into immediate execution. I will inform you what success I have.

Your devoted

JENNIE.

BRIDGEPORT, Saturday, Aug. 4, '83.

IV.

ANDERSON & DUDLEY.   8310 Broadway.

New York. Aug. 6th, '83.

Dear Jim,

Just this postal-card to tell you that since writing you yesterday, have received another request for "samples." This one is from Miss Jennie Reron, Bridgeport. Will the nuisance ever stop?—I will send pieces, but hope that you will make it your biz. to look her up and do what you can.

Yours,

Bob.

V.

ON THE ROAD, Aug. 8, '83.

DEAR BOB :—

Yours of 5th and 6th rec'd. Will look up the sample young ladies. Expect large orders next week. Regards to all. Write me to Auburn.

Yours,

JIM.

VI.

OFFICE OF

JEREMIAH ECCLES,

ATTORNEY AND COUNSELLOR-AT-LAW.

In answer to yours of.......................

Auburn, N. Y., ...*188*

OH JENNIE——

Did you ever feel like a murderer, or a thief, or a dynamiter or some other wicked thing? And know you were guilty? Oh, what *shall* I do? You know, even if Papa *is* a lawyer and was a judge, of course he can't keep me out of prison if I am guilty, can he? This is terrible. Let me tell you all about it.

I wanted just three skeins more of shaded floss for that awful crazy quilt, and went to Bodenheimer's to get it. When I went in, there was, what I then thought, rather a handsome man talking with Mr. Bodenheimer.

Young Jimpson, that ugly thing with freckles all over his face, waited on me, and was as affably obtrusive and as disagreeably polite as only such an article can be. And then the stupid thing said: " Miss Eccles, shall I send them ? Anything else, Miss Eccles ? Is your crazy-work quilt finished, Miss Eccles ?"

I did not answer him, could not move, for I saw the man who was talking with Mr. Bodenheimer look at me, take a letter from his pocket (just as somebody in Esmeralda did) and ask Mr. Bodenheimer something.

Mr. Bodenheimer glanced at me and said: "Yes, Mr. Dudley."

Now I am sure that that horrible Mr. Dudley is something to Anderson and Dudley, and that the letter he had, was my letter asking for samples.

I am frightened to death ; he looks like a man who would stop at nothing,—still I cannot tell, you see, my dear Jennie, I am not as good a judge of the *genus homo* as you are.

I stood in the store, looking at the show-cases as a person who is about to be hung might be looking at the gallows, I presume. I soon felt that I was making a

show of myself, so I exercised our preroga-
tive, pricing, or do you spell it priceing?
—somehow neither of them looks exactly
right to me.

I woke to consciousness through an exclamation of surprise from that stupid Jimpson,
whose freckles disappeared for once under
intense blushes—his red neck-tie looked
pale compared to his face. I do not know
what I asked for, cavalry boots it may have
been, or pistols, or, perhaps, even pantaloons.

All I know is that I am here, at Papa's
office, and have not the remotest idea of
what brought me. Fortunately Papa is out
—oh, if he discovers the matter I am ruined
—he'll make me pay for the samples or—
horrors—he may compel me to apologize!

Do you think that that Mr. Dudley—he
has very large brown eyes and is somewhat
pale—I just hate pale men—do you think
that Mr. Dudley will have me arrested?
Would not that be dreadful!

Jennie, I wish you were here. Write to
me immediately and tell me what I shall do.
You are three months older than I, and
have more knowledge of the world. Help
your distressed

EULALIA.

P. S. I will not return the pieces of
silk, would you? I think I am feverish.
I will go home and have Ma send for
Dr. Brinner.

VII.

𝕰. 𝕵. 𝕭𝖗𝖎𝖓𝖓𝖊𝖗, 𝕸. 𝕯.,

Physician and Surgeon.

OFFICE HOURS:
8 TO 10 A. M.
4 TO 6 P. M.   *Auburn, N.Y.,* 10. viii *1883*

℞

Tr. Valerian . . f ℥ j
" *Asafœtid* . . . f ʒ iij
Spts. aeth. comp. . . f ʒ v
Elix. simpl. . . . . f ℥ ij

M.D.S.

Teaspoonful every half hour.

Brinner.

For

Miss Eulalia Eccles.

EAGLE PHARMACY,
AUBURN, N. Y.
No. 78,055. — $1.35.

VIII.

The Daily Nutmeg.

THIS PAPER HAS THE LARGEST CIRCULATION OF ANY PAPER
IN THE NEW ENGLAND STATES.

SEE ADVERTISING
RATES ON BACK OF
THIS SHEET.

JOHN Q. RERON,
EDITOR AND PROPRIETOR.

Bridgeport, Conn., ... *1883*

Saturday night.

MY POOR, DEAR EULALIA :

Your yesterday's letter was evidently written under great excitement, or
else you would not have forgotten yourself
so far as to say that I am three months older
than you.   I did not like to tell you so
before, but when we were in N. Y. last
winter, everybody thought that you looked
fully two years my senior.   But I will forgive you, owing to your trouble.

Of course I want to advise you as to the
best course to be pursued, and, therefore, I
took your letter to Mrs. Bradely, whom I
like, although she *does* dress better than I,
and I laid the whole matter before her.

After mature deliberation, we have concluded that the pale Mr. Dudley, with the
large, brown eyes, may not have thought of
the samples, and that his glance at you,
which your conscience misconstrued, was
nothing but—ah, well, Eulalia dear, you
are not accustomed to being admired.

However, supposing that he really is insane enough to annoy you about such a trifle, there are several ways for you to checkmate him. One you might try first— have your Papa swear out a warrant, or a *habeas corpus* or a *caveat*—he will know what is best—and then have Mr. Dudley locked up as a dangerous lunatic. If you do not like the publicity, although I do not see why a lawyer's daughter should fear anything, then try to buy him off, and if that cannot be done, there will be but one way left to get rid of him—marry him. The latter is an extreme measure, to be adopted only when all else fails, and providing that he presents no serious obstacle, such as a wife or other encumbrance, a hunch or a crooked nose, or some kindred variance from the ordinary run of mortals.

Hoping, my dearest Eulalia, that I will receive immediately a recital of how you got rid of the horrid nightmare, I am, with much love, your true and devoted friend,

JENNIE.

P.S. If they should bother *me* about the samples, I will give them a very extensive piece of my mind. How can they expect to do business if they will not be obliging? I will get Papa to abuse them terribly .n the *Nutmeg*.

J.

IX.

Monday eve.

DEAR JENNIE :

I hardly know how to designate your letter of Saturday. I have often deplored your tendency to frivolity, but *this* letter exceeds anything you have ever perpetrated. Only delicacy on my part has prevented my telling you that when we were out together last, everybody commented upon your good appearance by remarking how young you looked to have a daughter as old as myself.

Your showing my letter to Mrs. Bradely is nothing less than a breach of trust, a very serious charge, which only my affection for you prevents me from pressing. The idea ! *that* Mrs. Bradely, who has nothing in her favor except her pretty face and a very fair taste in dressing, and a sweet baby, that dear little honey-bug Ethel. I wonder how in the world Mr. Bradely ever married *her !* I know *him* very well ; Papa foreclosed a mortgage for him at Mount Vernon last year and I went with him.

But Jennie, I am more than surprised at the disrespectful manner in which you speak of Mr. Dudley of Anderson and

Dudley. I know that he is a gentleman and, if I can forgive your disagreeable reflections upon me, I can only say that I am very sorry that you should make sport of poor Mr. Dudley's pale complexion. He is quite ill and I have induced him to spend his summer vacation here, which he will do.

He is out with Papa now, attending to some important law-matters, and as I expect them in to late tea, I will close, hoping you will be very careful in the future how you express yourself about a gentleman you have never seen.

Your friend,
EULALIA.

X.

MEMORANDUM.

FROM	TO
ANDERSON & DUDLEY	Miss Jennie Reron
𝔇𝔯𝔶 𝔊𝔬𝔬𝔡𝔰,	Bridgeport,
8310 BROADWAY,	Conn.

New York, Aug. 15, *1883*

DEAR MISS :—

If you have determined to make no selection from the samples of silk mailed you Aug. 6th, will you please return them to

Yours, very repectfully,
ANDERSON & DUDLEY.

XI.

Bridgeport, Aug. 17, '83

Messrs. Anderson & Dudley.

Gentlemen : If you will send me your bill for the samples of silk kindly sent me on the sixth, I will take pleasure in sending you a money-order for the amount, as I wish to keep the samples.

Yours, etc.,

Jennie Reron.

XII.

MEMORANDUM.

FROM

ANDERSON & DUDLEY

𝔇𝔯𝔶 𝔊𝔬𝔬𝔡𝔰,

8310 BROADWAY,

To Mr. James Dudley

Auburn,

N. Y.

New York Aug. 19, *1888*

DEAR JIM :

Have heard nothing from you since your telegram of the 9th. What is the matter? If you are dead say so, but break it to me gently. Joking aside, I hardly think it is quite the thing to leave me in ignorance. Do not, my dear fellow, imagine for a moment that I am displeased at receiving no orders from you, but I am anxious about your health.

Please to answer on receipt.

Yours aff.,

BOB.

XIII.

Aug. 21, *1883.*

Auburn, N. Y.

Telegram *to Anderson & Dudley,*

8310 Broadway.

Memorandum nineteenth received. Am perfectly well. Busy making example of sample fiend. Particulars by mail.

15 Paid. *James Dudley.*

XIV.

QUICK SALES AND SMALL PROFITS.

BODENHEIMER & CO.,

(*No connection with any house of a similar name.*)

Dry Goods, Fancy Goods, Boots and Shoes, Cutlery.

AGENTS FOR DEMOREST'S PATTERNS.

Auburn, N. Y.,

Aug. 23, *1883.*

MESSRS. ANDERSON & DUDLEY, N. Y.

GENTLEMEN:—Enclosed please find order sheets 1405, 1406, 1407 and 1408, to which you will give immediate attention.

Yours, &c., JAMES DUDLEY.

MY DEAR BOB :

I really do not know how to begin
this letter ; for the first time since our boyhood do I feel hesitancy in expressing myself to you—you who have always been my
confidant. Yet I presume that the only way
to do a thing is to do it, therefore I will attempt to be as succinct as possible.

I arrived here on the 10th and, of course,
looked up Bodenheimer first. Order 1405
shows what I did with him. While I was
talking to him, I heard one of his clerks
mention Miss Eccles ; I looked up and saw
—well I will not attempt a description.
Bodenheimer told me that this vision was
Miss Eulalia, our fair sampler.

For the first time in my life did I feel annoyed at being seen in traveling garb ; yet
I determined that I would allow no foolish
idea to interfere with business, and I agreed
with you . thoroughly, that though this
sampling is a small matter in itself, in the
aggregate it amounts to something. Therefore, I set aside all considerations, and after
making myself as presentable as possible,
called on the young lady.

I was deeply pained to hear that she was
ill, could not receive visitors—and Bob, had
you seen her, you would have agreed with
me that though she might steal samples,
she would not lie. I left my address, c/o
Bodenheimer ; why I did so I do not know.

But Bob, it is better to tell the whole truth, and, therefore, I will confess to you that I wrote on the card : '' Hope that Miss Eccles will soon recover." This, of course, was wrong in me, both as a business man and as a man of society. But one will sometimes do absurd things, especially when dealing with a thief so very pretty as my thief.

How little I have attended to biz. is shown by the very few orders I send—I will not attempt to say how I have spent my time.

On the following Monday (13th) I received a note, which, being from a lady, it would be wrong for me to show even you. The result was that at 2 p. m. I called on Miss Eccles.

She came into the parlor, and was so filled with the fear that I came to do terrible things to her, that I forgot all about the object of my visit and went vigorously to work consoling her.

To cut the matter short, I have concluded that Miss Eulalia Eccles is a consummate thief, for she has stolen

Your partner,

JIM.

By the way, Bob, the above conclusion is somewhat premature. I confess that I am captivated—that does not mean that she is —I wish she were. Now you will understand my silence. I expect a derisive letter

from you ; pitch in, old fellow, I will bear
your abuse calmly—no, I will take it to Miss
Eccles, perhaps she will console me.

J.

XV.

ROBERT ANDERSON.   JAMES DUDLEY.

ANDERSON & DUDLEY,
Dry Goods,
8310 BROADWAY,

New York, Aug. 26, 188 3:

MR. JAMES DUDLEY,
           AUBURN.
   DEAR SIR :
           We are in receipt of your favor
of the 23d, enclosing order sheets Nos. 1405,
1406, 1407 and 1408, which will receive our
immediate attention.   While we cannot but
deplore the paucity of business in Auburn,
we fully appreciate the circumstances which
have prevented it, as will be seen in private
note to you by our Mr. R. Anderson, which
is enclosed with this, and we are,
           Yours, etc.,
                ANDERSON & DUDLEY.

[PERSONAL TO JAMES DUDLEY.]

MY DEAR JIM :
           The intense heat which prevails
would prevent my answering your private

note of 23d were it not that it contains a matter of surpassing importance.

And therefore I take off my collar, which is as wilted as yesterday's flower, look at the ice-cooler (what an asinine name —as if it were destined to cool ice), plant myself before my desk and answer you at length.

1. This is a serious matter and requires time, therefore, if you will send back your samples (except such as Miss Eccles may wish) and will take your summering at Auburn, it will do you much good, and you will return here a new man.

2. I will, if you so desire, express you your other clothes—shall I send your ulster?

3. You need not go to Bridgeport; delicate matters, such as fair sample-pirates, will be looked after by the senior partner of Messrs. A. & D.

4. No biz. here. You need not hurry back.

5. Bradstreet reports your future father-in-law at $1,800,000.

6. Bye-bye.

BOB.

I received an impudent little note from Bridgeport. I will show you how *business-men* manage these matters.

XVI.

ANDERSON & DUDLEY. 8310 Broadway.

New York, Aug. 26, '83.

Miss Reron,

Bridgeport.

Our Mr. Anderson will call on you personally in ans. to your favor of the 17th inst.

Resp'ly,

Anderson & Dudley.

XVII.

FOR SADDLES GO TO BODENHEIMER'S.
6m

PUBLIC WEAL.
T. XENOPHON SIBBRY, ... EDITOR.

AUBURN, N. Y., AUGUST 29th, 1883.

A BRAVE MAN.

We spare our readers an editorial repetition of the details of the accident which threatened to rob our fair city of one of its fairest daughters yesterday afternoon, but take great pleasure in signalizing the unexampled bravery of Mr. James Dudley, junior partner of the well-known New York dry-goods merchants, Anderson & Dudley, whose advertisement appears on our last page.

From the news columns of PUBLIC WEAL our readers will learn that as Mr. Dudley was leaving the house of the Hon. J. Eccles, in a buggy in which he and Miss Eulalia Eccles were to take a drive, a youth rushed towards the horse, which became frightened and ran off. With rare skill, Mr. Dudley directed the unmanageable animal towards a tree on Main street and in such a manner as to throw the weight of the left side of the buggy, on which he sat, against the tree.

The vehicle was demolished, but Mr. Dudley grasped Miss Eccles and shielded her from harm, while he received some very severe bruises on the left side of his head, his left arm and side. He was carried to Mr. Eccles' house and is being carefully nursed there. Dr. Brinner assures us that none of Mr. Dudley's bones are broken, and that he will be able to enjoy all of the diversions which our city offers within a week or ten days.

The unfortunate youth who was the cause of the accident is Morris Jimpson, one of the clerks of Messrs. Bodenheimer & Co., who seems, from his record, to have a special genius for getting himself and others into trouble. It appears that he noticed that a rein had become detached from the horse's bit and blustered up to replace it.

We hope that our comment on young Jimpson's erratic conduct will not be attributed to the fact that he is the son of the editor of an alleged daily paper, which we believe is published in this city; but as we never stoop to personalities we feel safe in informing all that we shall take no notice of any vulgar attacks made on us because of the truthful manner in which we publish the news.

Yet it might be *pro bono publico* if the aforesaid editor were to tie up his scion with a short rope, and thus prevent him from frightening horses and endangering the lives of respectable and respected people.

XVIII.

BRIDGEPORT, Friday.

MY DEAR EULALIA.

I was too angry with you to answer your last letter, but now that a misfortune has befallen you, as I see by the *Public Weal* of the 29th, I feel that I can do nothing less than go to help you nurse poor Mr. Dudley. I give you my word, my dear Eulalia, that I am very glad that Mr. Dudley is not severely injured.

Were it not my duty to go to you now, I would remain at home, for I received a postal card from Mr. Anderson a few days ago, in which he threatened to call on me about those samples. His writing is so pretty that I am quite anxious to see him.

Expect me by the afternoon train.

Your true friend,

JENNIE.

P.S.—If Mr. Anderson *should* go to Auburn to look after his injured partner, would it not be just *too* peculiar?

XIX.

AUBURN, Sept. 3, '83.

MY DEAR BOB:

I am a bruised man (for details see *Public Weal* which I send with this) and ——let me tell you the whole story.

When the buggy struck the tree, or shortly thereafter, I lost consciousness and came to myself in this room in Mr. Eccles' house; Eulalia was holding my head in her arms and weeping. I heard her sweet voice say : "You must not die, my darling. Oh, my love," and I did not—to oblige her. I did not become conscious, that is to say, I allowed no one to discover that I knew what was going on, until that wretch, Dr. Brinner, lifted my eyelids and after staring at me a moment, winked in a most atrocious manner.

I then endeavored to take Eulalia's hand, but found that I could barely move—I did not care to move.

Eulalia, my angel, says she will report me to the doctor if I continue writing, therefore I will leave the rest to her.

Yours,

JIM.

————

DEAR MR. ANDERSON :

James insists that I shall call you "Bob," or at least Robert, but I cannot do that——yet. It would not be at all proper, would it?

Will you forgive me, Mr. Anderson? I did not think what I was doing when I defrauded you and James of a few samples, but I am neither ashamed nor repentant for having stolen your partner. For the latter I can make restitution. My dear friend Miss Jennie Reron is here, helping me nurse

James, the poor darling ; I am sure you will like her.

We want you to come here. James says there is no reason for your remaining in New York during the hot weather, and you promised him to make an example of the other sample thief. She is here.

My dear James says that Dr. Brinner deserves to be caned for divulging that he was conscious when I thought that he was dying, and therefore wishes you to get the finest gold-headed walking-stick you can and have it engraved

Dr. E. J. Brinner

FROM HIS GRATEFUL

Eulalia and James Dudley.

We will present it to him on our wedding-day. Please to bring it with you—the cane, I mean.

Papa sends you his compliments, and says that you must come directly to our house and remain with us until your return to New York.

James says that you can rely upon Mr. Collins to conduct the business, and that you are to be here by next Saturday. We expect no answer from you otherwise than in person.

Your happy friend,

EULALIA ECCLES.

XX.

ECCLES—DUDLEY.—At the residence of the bride's father, on Thursday, Sept. 20th, 1883, by the Rev. P. R. Day of New York, Mr. James Dudley of New York to Miss Eulalia Eccles, daughter of the Hon. Jeremiah Eccles of Auburn, N. Y.

𝔄.𝔍ℜ.

Jennie Reron

Robert Anderson

Thursday, Oct. fourth, 1883.
Bridgeport, Conn

XXI.

DR. HEIDEGGER'S EXPERIMENT.

BY NATHANIEL HAWTHORNE.

That very singular man, old Dr. Heidegger, once invited four venerable friends to meet him in his study. There were three white-bearded gentlemen—Mr. Medbourne, Colonel Killigrew and Mr. Gascoigne—and a withered gentlewoman whose name was the widow Wycherly. They were all melancholy old creatures who had been unfortunate in life, and whose greatest misfortune it was that they were not long ago in their graves. Mr. Medbourne, in the vigor of his age, had been a prosperous merchant, but had lost his all by a frantic speculation, and was now little better than a mendicant. Colonel Killigrew had wasted his best years and his health and substance in the pursuit of sinful pleasures which had given birth to a brood of pains, such as the gout and divers other torments of soul and body. Mr. Gascoigne was a ruined politician, a man of evil fame—or, at least, had been so till time had buried him from the knowledge of the present generation and made him obscure instead of infamous. As for the widow Wycherly, tradition tells us that she was a great beauty in her day, but for a long while past she had lived in deep seclusion on account of certain scandalous stories which had prejudiced the gentry of the

town against her. It is a circumstance
worth mentioning that each of these three
old gentlemen—Mr. Medbourne, Colonel
Killigrew and Mr. Gascoigne—were early
lovers of the widow Wycherly, and had
once been on the point of cutting each
other's throats for her sake. And before
proceeding farther I will merely hint that
Dr. Heidegger and all his four guests were
sometimes thought to be a little beside
themselves, as is not infrequently the case
with old people when worried either by
present troubles or woful recollections.

"My dear old friends," said Dr. Heidegger, motioning them to be seated, "I am
desirous of your assistance in one of those
little experiments with which I amuse myself here in my study."

If all stories were true, Dr. Heidegger's
study must have been a very curious place.
It was a dim, old-fashioned chamber fes-
tooned with cobwebs and besprinkled with
antique dust. Around the walls stood several oaken bookcases, the lower shelves of
which were filled with rows of gigantic
folios and black-letter quartos, and the
upper with little parchment-covered duo-
decimos. Over the central bookcase was a
bronze bust of Hippocrates, with which,
according to some authorities, Dr. Heidegger was accustomed to hold consultations in
all difficult cases of his practice. In the
obscurest corner of the room stood a tall and

narrow oaken closet with its door ajar, within which doubtfully appeared a skeleton. Between two of the bookcases hung a looking-glass, presenting its high and dusty plate within a tarnished gilt frame. Among many wonderful stories related of this mirror, it was fabled that the spirits of all the doctor's deceased patients dwelt within its verge and would stare him in the face whenever he looked thitherward. The opposite side of the chamber was ornamented with the full-length portrait of a young lady arrayed in the faded magnificence of silk, satin and brocade, and with a visage as faded as her dress. Above half a century ago Dr. Heidegger had been on the point of marriage with this young lady, but, being affected with some slight disorder, she had swallowed one of her lover's prescriptions and died on the bridal evening. The greatest curiosity of the study remains to be mentioned: it was a ponderous folio volume bound in black leather, with massive silver clasps. There were no letters on the back, and nobody could tell the title of the book. But it was well known to be a book of magic, and once, when a chambermaid had lifted it merely to brush away the dust, the skeleton had rattled in its closet, the picture of the young lady had stepped one foot upon the floor and several ghastly faces had peeped forth from the mirror, while the brazen head of Hippocrates frowned and said, " Forbear ! "

Such was Dr. Heidegger's study. On the summer afternoon of our tale a small round table as black as ebony stood in the centre of the room, sustaining a cut-glass vase of beautiful form and elaborate workmanship. The sunshine came through the window between the heavy festoons of two faded damask curtains and fell directly across this vase ; so that a mild splendor was reflected from it on the ashen visages of the five old people who sat around. Four goblets were also on the table.

"My dear old friends," repeated Dr. Heidegger, "may I reckon on your aid in performing an exceeding curious experiment?"

Now, Dr. Heidegger was a very strange old gentleman whose eccentricity had become the nucleus for a thousand fantastic stories. Some of these fables—to my shame be it spoken—might possibly be traced back to mine own veracious self; and if any passages of the present tale should startle the reader's faith, I must be content to bear the stigma of a fiction-monger.

When the doctor's four guests heard him talk of his proposed experiment, they anticipated nothing more wonderful than the murder of a mouse in an air-pump or the examination of a cobweb by the microscope, or some similar nonsense with which he was constantly in the habit of pestering his inmates. But without waiting for a reply Dr·

Heidegger hobbled across the chamber and returned with the same ponderous folio bound in black leather which common report affirmed to be a book of magic. Undoing the silver clasp, he opened the volume and took from among its black-letter pages a rose, or what was once a rose, though now the green leaves and crimson petals had assumed one brownish hue and the ancient flower seemed ready to crumble to dust in the doctor's hands.

"This rose," said Dr. Heidegger, with a sigh—"this same withered and crumbling flower—blossomed five and fifty years ago. It was given me by Sylvia Ward, whose portrait hangs yonder, and I meant to wear it in my bosom at our wedding. Five and fifty years it has been treasured between the leaves of this old volume. Now, would you deem it possible that this rose of half a century could ever bloom again?"

"Nonsense!" said the widow Wycherly, with a peevish toss of her head. "You might as well ask whether an old woman's wrinkled face could ever bloom again."

"See!" answered Dr. Heidegger. He uncovered the vase and threw the faded rose into the water which it contained. At first it lay lightly on the surface of the fluid, appearing to imbibe none of its moisture. Soon, however, a singular change began to be visible. The crushed and dried petals stirred and assumed a deepening tinge of crimson, as if the flower were reviving from a deathlike slumber, the slender stalk and twigs of foliage became green, and there was the rose of half a century, looking as fresh as when Sylvia Ward had first given it to her lover. It was scarcely full-blown, for some of its delicate red leaves curled modestly around its moist bosom, within which two or three dewdrops were sparkling.

"That is certainly a very pretty deception," said the doctor's friends—carelessly, however, for they had witnessed greater miracles at a conjurer's show. "Pray, how was it effected?"

"Did you never hear of the Fountain of Youth?" asked Dr. Heidegger, "which Ponce de Leon, the Spanish adventurer, went in search of two or three centuries ago?"

"But did Ponce de Leon ever find it?" said the widow Wycherly.

"No," answered Dr. Heidegger, "for he never sought it in the right place. The famous Fountain of Youth, if I am rightly informed, is situated in the southern part of the Floridian peninsula, not far from Lake Macaco. Its source is overshadowed by several gigantic magnolias which, though numberless centuries old, have been kept as fresh as violets by the virtues of this wonderful water. An acquaintance of mine, knowing my curiosity in such matters, has sent me what you see in the vase."

"Ahem!" said Colonel Killigrew, who believed not a word of the doctor's story; "and what may be the effect of this fluid on the human frame?"

"You shall judge for yourself, my dear colonel," replied Dr. Heidegger. "And all of you, my respected friends, are welcome to so much of this admirable fluid as may restore to you the bloom of youth. For my own part, having had much trouble in growing old, I am in no hurry to grow young again. With your permission, therefore, I will merely watch the progress of the experiment."

While he spoke Dr. Heidegger had been filling the four goblets with the water of the Fountain of Youth. It was apparently impregnated with an effervescent gas, for little bubbles were continually ascending from the depths of the glasses, and bursting in silvery spray at the surface. As the liquor diffused a pleasant perfume the old people doubted not that it possessed cordial and comfortable properties, and though utter skeptics as to its rejuvenescent power, they were inclined to swallow it at once. But Dr. Heidegger besought them to stay a moment.

"Before you drink, my respectable old friends," said he, "it would be well that, with the experience of a life-time to direct you, you should draw up a few general rules for your guidance in passing a second time

through the perils of youth. Think what
a sin and shame it would be if, with your
peculiar advantages, you should not become
patterns of virtue and wisdom to all the
young people of the age!"

The doctor's four venerable friends made
him no answer except by a feeble and tremulous laugh, so very ridiculous was the idea
that, knowing how closely Repentance
treads behind the steps of Error, they should
ever go astray again.

"Drink, then," said the doctor, bowing;
"I rejoice that I have so well selected the
subjects of my experiment."

With palsied hands they raised the glasses
to their lips. The liquid, if it really possessed such virtues as Dr. Heidegger im-
puted to it, could not have been bestowed
on four human beings who needed it more
wofully. They looked as if they had never
known what youth or pleasure was, but had
been the offspring of Nature's dotage, and
always the gray, decrepit, sapless, miserable
creatures who now sat stooping round the
doctor's table without life enough in their
souls or bodies to be animated even by the
prospect of growing young again. They
drank off the water and replaced their goblets on the table.

Assuredly, there was an almost immediate
improvement in the aspect of the party,
together with a sudden glow of cheerful
sunshine, brightening over all their visages

at once. There was a healthful suffusion on their cheeks instead of the ashen hue that had made them look so corpse-like. They gazed at one another, and fancied that some magic power had really begun to smooth away the deep and sad inscriptions which Father Time had been so long engraving on their brows. The widow Wycherly adjusted her cap, for she felt almost like a woman again.

"Give us more of this wondrous water," cried they, eagerly. "We are younger, but we are still too old. Quick! give us more!"

"Patience, patience!" quoth Dr. Heidegger, who sat watching the experiment with philosophic coolness. "You have been a long time growing old; surely you might be content to grow young in half an hour. But the water is at your service." Again he filled their goblets with the liquor of youth, enough of which still remained in the vase to turn half the old people in the city to the age of their own grandchildren.

While the bubbles were yet sparkling on the brim, the doctor's four guests snatched their goblets from the table and swallowed the contents at a single gulp. Was it delusion? Even while the draught was passing down their throats it seemed to have wrought a change on their whole systems. Their eyes grew clear and bright; a dark shade deepened among their silvery locks;

they sat around the table, three gentlemen
of middle age and a woman hardly beyond
her buxom prime.

" My dear widow, you are charming ! "
cried Colonel Killigrew, whose eyes had
been fixed upon her face while the shadows
of age were flitting from it like darkness
from the crimson daybreak.

The fair widow knew of old that Colonel
Killigrew's compliments were not always
measured by sober truth ; so she started up
and ran to the mirror, still dreading that the
ugly visage of an old woman would meet
her gaze.

Meanwhile, the three gentlemen behaved
in such a manner as proved that the water
of the Fountain of Youth possessed some
peculiar qualities—unless, indeed, their ex-
hilaration of spirits were merely a lightsome
dizziness caused by the sudden removal of
the weight of years. Mr. Gascoigne's mind
seemed to run on political topics, but
whether relating to the past, present or
future could not easily be determined, since
the same ideas and phrases have been in
vogue these fifty years. Now he rattled
forth full-throated sentences about patriot-
ism, national glory and the people's right ;
and now, again, he spoke in measured accents and a deeply deferential tone, as if a
royal ear were listening to his well-turned
periods. On the other side of the table,
Mr. Medbourne was involved in a calcula-

tion of dollars and cents with which was strangely intermingled a project for supplying the East Indies with ice by harnessing a team of whales to the polar icebergs. As for the widow Wycherly, she stood before the mirror courtesying and simpering to her own image and greeting it as the friend whom she loved better than all the world besides. She thrust her face close to the glass to see whether some long-remembered wrinkle or crows-foot had indeed vanished; she examined whether the snow had so entirely melted from her hair that the venerable cap could be safely thrown aside. At last, turning briskly away, she came with a sort of dancing step to the table.

"My dear old doctor," cried she, "pray favor me with another goblet."

"Certainly, my dear madam—certainly," replied the complaisant doctor. "See! I have already filled the goblets."

There, in fact, stood the four goblets brimful of this wonderful water, the delicate spray of which, as it effervesced from the surface, resembled the tremulous glitter of diamonds.

It was now so nearly sunset that the chamber had grown duskier than ever, but a mild and moonlike splendor gleamed from within the vase and rested alike on the four guests and on the doctor's venerable figure. He sat in a high-backed, elaborately carved oaken arm-chair with a gray dignity of aspect that might have well befitted that very Father Time whose power had never been disputed save by this fortunate company. Even while quaffing the third draught of the Fountain of Youth, they were almost awed by the expression of his mysterious visage. But the next moment the exhilarating gush of young life shot through their veins. They were now in the happy prime of youth. Age, with its miserable train of cares and sorrows and diseases, was remembered only as the trouble of a dream from which they had joyously awoke. The fresh gloss of the soul, so early lost and without which the world's successive scenes had been but a gallery of faded pictures, again threw its enchantment over all their prospects. They felt like new-created beings in a new-created universe.

"We are young ! We are young !" they cried, exultingly.

Youth, like the extremity of age, had effaced the strongly-marked characteristics of middle life and mutually assimilated them all. They were a group of merry youngsters almost maddened with the exuberant frolicsomeness of their years. The most singular effect of their gayety was an impulse to mock the infirmity and decrepitude of which they had so lately been the victims. They laughed loudly at their old-fashioned attire—the wide-skirted coats and flapped waistcoats of the young men and the ancient cap and gown of the blooming girl. One limped across the floor like a gouty grandfather; one set a pair of spectacles astride of his nose and pretended to pore over the black-letter pages of the book of magic; a third seated himself in an armchair and strove to imitate the venerable dignity of Dr. Heidegger. Then all shouted mirthfully and leaped about the room.

Never was there a livelier picture. Yet, by a strange deception, owing to the duskiness of the chamber and the antique dresses which they still wore, the tall mirror is said to have reflected the figures of the three old, gray, withered grandsires and the skinny ugliness of a shriveled grandma.

As they gamboled to and fro the table was overturned and the vase dashed into a thousand fragments. The precious Water of Youth flowed in a bright stream across the floor, moistening the wings of a butterfly which, grown old in the decline of summer, had alighted there to die. The insect fluttered lightly through the chamber and settled on the snowy head of Dr. Heidegger.

"Come, come, gentlemen! Come, Madam Wycherly!" exclaimed the doctor.

They stood still and shivered, for it seemed as if gray Time were calling them back from their sunny youth far down into the chill and darksome vale of years. They looked at old Dr. Heidegger, who sat in his carved arm-chair holding the rose of half a century, which he had rescued from among the fragments of the shattered vase. At the motion of his hand the four rioters resumed their seats—the more readily because their violent exertions had wearied them, youthful though they were.

"My poor Sylvia's rose!" ejaculated Dr. Heidegger, holding it in the light of the sunset clouds. "It appears to be fading again."

And so it was. Even while the party were looking at it the flower continued to shrivel up, until it became as dry and fragile as when the doctor had first thrown it into the vase. He shook off the few drops of moisture which clung to its petals.

"I love it as well thus as in its dewy freshness," observed he, pressing the withered rose to his withered lips.

While he spoke the butterfly fluttered down from the doctor's snowy head and fell upon the floor. His guests shivered again. A strange chillness—whether of the body or spirit they could not tell—was creeping gradually over them all. They gazed at one another, and fancied that each fleeting moment snatched away a charm and left a deepening furrow where none had been before. Was it an illusion? Had the changes of a life-time been crowded into so brief a space, and were they now four aged people sitting with their old friend Dr. Heidegger?

"Are we grown old again so soon?" cried they, dolefully.

In truth, they had. The Water of Youth possessed merely a virtue more transient than that of wine; the delirium which it created had effervesced away. Yes, they were old again. With a shuddering impulse that showed her a woman still, the widow clasped her skinny hands before her face and wished that the coffin-lid were over it, since it could be no longer beautiful.

"Yes, friends, ye are old again," said Dr. Heidegger, "and lo! the Water of Youth is all lavished on the ground. Well, I bemoan it not; for if the fountain gushed at my very doorstep, I would not stoop to bathe my lips in it—no, though its delirium were for years instead of moments. Such is the lesson ye have taught me."

But the doctor's four friends had taught no such lesson to themselves. They resolved forthwith to make a pilgrimage to Florida and quaff at morning, noon and night from the Fountain of Youth.

——

A MODERN KNIGHT.

BY JOHN HABBERTON.

"There's your shop," remarked the driver of the very shabby carryall in which Miss Eve Lansome, recently engaged as teacher of the Redtuft District School, was being conveyed from a railway station to the house of Farmer Raygin, where she was to board for the six months which at Redtuft constituted the school year.

"Shop?" echoed Miss Lansome, leaning a little forward, as if she had not rightly heard.

"Yes," replied the driver, and then, after a pause, continued in a lower tone, "school-house, I s'pose I ought 'o hev said."

"My school-house!" gasped the young lady clutching the back of the seat as if to support herself. "Is that the building in which School Number One of the Redtuft District is held?"

"Cert'nly; Number Two is way over on t'other side of the township. An' there's yer boardin' place, right up there at the bend of the road; ye can see the top of the barn ef ye look sharp acrost the ridge of the rise; the house ain't so high, so you don't sight that till ye git on higher ground."

"Dear me!" murmured Miss Lansome. She opened her eyes and regarded the school-house so intently that the driver stopped his horse, and said:

"'Taint exactly like school-houses down in York, I s'pose?"

"No," replied Miss Lansome, slowly, "I can hardly say it is."

"Not quite so big, p'raps?"

The teacher's doleful face lapsed into a curious smile as she answered, "Not quite."

" Waal," said the driver, " taint so big as some I've seen in this very country, but it'll hold a lot of folks when it's put to it. I've knowed the time when a spellin' school of more'n sixty folks on each side has stood up in that old school-house, an' yit ther' was room for all them as wuz spelled down to do their sparkin' along the walls an' in the seats. Mebbe some of 'em went outside, but 'twasn't 'cause there wasn't room fur 'em in-doors."

" Does it look inside as it does outside? " asked Miss Lansome, her gaze still fixed on the reddish-brown walls.

" Waal, I don't hardly know 'bout that," said the driver ; then he turned sidewise in his seat, threw his right leg over the left, shifted the contents of one protuberant cheek to the other side of his face, and dropped into reverie, from which he wakened, a moment or two later, to say—

" No, I don't know ez it does, any more'n the inside of any house looks like the outside. Both sides kind o' look ez if they might b'long to each other, an' yit, when you come to think about it, they kind o' don't. I wish I could tell you 'xack'ly how they're alike and how they ain't, but——"

As the driver paused he suddenly rose to his feet, and his homely countenance was radiant with intelligence as he exclaimed :

" By ginger ! Ye ken make it all clear to yourself in a minute by jest gittin' out an' walkin' in. The door ain't locked—nobody hain't seen the key for so long that I'll bet there's some that believes there never wasn't no key."

" I think I will avail myself of your suggestion," said the new teacher, getting out of the carryall ; then, seeing the driver also about to alight, she continued : " I'm sure I will have no trouble in finding my way about the building alone, so I will feel obliged if you will drive on to Squire Raygin's, leave my trunk, and say I will be there in a few minutes. I can easily walk the distance."

" Hev it yer own way, ma'am ; but I'd just as lief wait, if you say so. Time ain't worth nothin' to me."

" You're very kind," said the teacher, " but I'd rather walk. I must learn the way sooner or later, you know." She said this with a pleasant smile, but the smile vanished as soon as she turned her face again toward the school-house. A moment later she heard the driver's whip descend upon the anatomical antique that drew the vehicle, but before this the breeze had wafted to her the sound of one word—low-toned as when one does not want to be heard ; soft as is always the way with words spoken to one's self, yet, for all that, long-drawn and distinct, as if the speaker fully meant all he said—it was the monosyllable—

" Gosh ! "

The longer the teacher looked at her new post of duty, the longer grew her countenance. Redtuft District School-house Number One was certainly not what she had expected it to be. She had selected it, in preference to another school that had been offered her at the "agency" in New York, because of its name, which seemed to her to have a certain quaint attractiveness about it. It suggested color, and natural color, too, which is always delightful to a city born girl—a girl with yearnings toward æsthetic culture. She had wondered what the name meant; perhaps a clump of blazing maples, near the site of the school-house, or a thicket of wild roses, or a knoll covered with the red clover that looked so pretty in the flower pictures that found their way to the water color exhibitions every winter.

But none of these things could she see. Neither tree, bush, nor knoll was near the building; the school-house had been built on the edge of a bog, in which were indications that in rainy weather a stream had flowed near the house and across the road; now, however, in a dry October week, the ground was merely damp, and from the mud arose many tufts of marsh grass of which the inner leaves showed traces of green, but the outer ones, which were dry and dead, were a dirty yellowish red.

The building itself was a simple parallelogram, one story high, and with a roof so low that the new teacher wondered if any of the youngest pupils could stand erect against the walls. Its foundations were slender brick pillars, not very high, but still high enough to display, under the building, a mixed débris of slates, books, baskets, straw hats, tin pails, sleds, hand-carts, and other articles, that had been worn out in the cause of popular education ; there was also a sober-looking family of pigs, whose mother came cautiously to the front to see who it was that dared invade the solitude of her kindergarten.

Miss Lansome felt that a "hard cry" was imminent, and as soon as she entered the door the tears burst forth. It was true as the man had said, that the inside and the outside of the house "kind o' looked as 'ef they might b'long to each other." The walls had once been white, and to be sure this color was still present as a background; but lead-pencils, charcoal, red chalk, poke-berry-juice, and the purplish blue extract of the native huckleberry had been so freely used by the amateur artists of different classes that the general color effect greatly resembled the curious medley of a Turkish rug. Miss Lansome had long been enamored of Oriental art, but the likeness of what she had admired to what she now saw did not at first occur to her.

On the wall behind the platform where

the teacher's desk—a plain pine table—stood
was a map of the United States, as this
country used to be depicted when Michigan
and Minnesota were territories, and all of
the country west of Missouri was "The
Great American Desert." Centred on the opposite wall was an enormous picture of an ele-
phant, evidently cut from a circus poster, but
as the low ceiling had made it impossible to
present the beast in his full proportions, the
legs and trunk had been carefully ampu-
tated. The color, originally rather monot-
onous, had, by some critical rural hand,
been relieved with red chalk, and the great
brute provided with a red eye as big as a
boy's head. The desks bore witness of
countless hours consumed in wood carving
—an art on which Miss Lansome had been
wont to vent much enthusiasm—enthusiasm now forgotten. Indeed, she forgot
everything, except her day-dreams of what
her first school was to be ; so she dropped
into the teacher's chair, which, in spite of
her grief, she observed was uncompromis-
ingly hard, placed her arms on the table
and her head on her arms and moistened the
dingy top of the table with a great many
tears.

In the meantime there was great excitement at Squire Raygin's, where Miss Lansome was to board, for the driver, as he un-
loaded the truck, informed the lady of the
house and her two daughters that the new

teacher was "ez pretty ez a peach, ez trim ez a cherry saplin', an' ez sweet ez a dough-nut." Mrs. Raygin was "doing up" quinces, and she and her daughters were appropriately dressed for the work, but she exclaimed:

"Here gals, drop that fruit right away, an' get into your Sunday things; first, though, one of you blow the horn for your father an' the boys. I'm not goin' to have any such gal comin' here an, thinkin' we're common folks." Then Mrs. Raygin proceeded to put on her own "Sunday things," and she did this with such alacrity that by the time her husband reached the house she stood resplendent in a brick-red dress with a blue waist, and a white lace cap with green bow and yellow strings.

"Sakes alive, Marthy!" exclaimed the astonished farmer, "why didn't you let on this mornin' that you'd invited the preacher to supper?"

The old man was somewhat indignant when he was informed of the cause of the excitement, but he was nevertheless prevailed upon to shave and change his shirt; he resolutely refused to put on his coat, however. "What's good enough fur my own gals to see me in is good enough fur any city piece to see me in," he declared, " even ef she *hez* turned the head of that there harum-scarum Nosmo King. Hello! —she's a-comin'."

Every member of the family looked down the road from one window or another.

"She *don't* look just like the gals about here," remarked Mrs. Raygin.

" It's the city way of cuttin' dresses that makes the difference," said the elder Miss Raygin.

" Or the city way of wearin' the hair," said the younger sister. The head of the family ventured no comments, but as the teacher neared the house and the fingers of the ladies began to fidget about their own hair and apparel, the farmer remarked :

" 'Pears to me it's gettin' kind o' chilly as the sun drops low. Guess I'll have to put somethin' warmer on me." And he hastily disappeared as the ladies went to the door to receive the new-comer.

* * * The evening meal at the Raygin mansion was nearly ended when a shadow was cast on the table from one of the dining-room windows.

" Wonder who's out there ? " mumbled the lady of the house. The old farmer arose, went to the door, looked out, turned his head again toward the family, and remarked :

" It's only Nosmo, ma."

" Sho ! " exclaimed Mrs. Raygin, " I b'lieve there never was the like of that feller for turnin' up when ye least expect him."

" Perhaps he forgot to put out something

of Miss Lansome's, and has come back to bring it," suggested the elder Miss Raygin.

"Or perhaps," said the younger sister with a sly smile, "he didn't forget Miss Lansome herself."

The teacher looked up wonderingly, and the hostess hastened to explain :

"The gals are talkin' about Nosmo—the young feller that druv ye over from the depot. It's him that's outside."

"I've not missed anything, I'm sure," said Miss Lansome. Whatever any one else may have intended to say was stopped by the spectacle of the head of the family endeavoring to coax the young man to enter the house and partake of the evening meal, and the latter's desperate efforts to keep out of sight of the ladies, yet look into the room. Miss Lansome was amused, in a quiet way, and on looking toward her new hosts she saw that they too were smiling, but apparently at her rather than with her. What had she done to excite merriment? As she wondered, the younger man succeeded in getting out of range of the four pairs of eyes inside, but all heard Squire Raygin say :

"Well, Nosmo, hev it yer own way ; stay outside ef ye don't want to go in ; but 'pears to me that if I was gone, all of a sudden, on a city gal, an' was tuk so bad ez to walk a mile to look at her, I wouldn't let the thickness of a wall stan' between me an her."

Then the ladies of the Raygin family

laughed, and Miss Lansome blushed, hurriedly left the table, and went to her room.
For her to gain admiration at short notice
was not unusual; she had been adored by
all sorts of chance acquaintances; should
she, therefore, be astonished that the young
farmer who had been her coachman during
the afternoon had deemed her attractive?
No! Still, there were men—and men—and
she had some preference as to the sort of
person who should admire her.

By and by she descended to the "best
room," in which she had first been received.
It was empty. So she passed to the piazza,
where she found the source of her mortifica-
tion—young Nosmo King—alone. She did
not recognize him at first, for he also had
invested himself with "Sunday things,"
and his loose reddish-brown locks had been
reduced to exceeding propriety. The air
was redolent of bergamot; there was also
perceptible a strong odor of tobacco, although Nosmo King, who was struggling
with one of his trousers pockets, was not
smoking.

The young man arose, bowed profoundly,
and might have appeared quite dignified
but for an occasional half-suppressed
wriggle.

"Mr. King, I believe?" said the young
lady with a smile. "I learned your name,
accidentally, from my kind entertainers
here."

"Yes,—oh,—yes," said the youth, in the midst of his contortions ; "that's my name ; it's—it's—why, of course it's my name," he continued, in an excitable manner, as he seized the sides of his trousers legs and spread them as zouaves used to do in the early days of the war, when bagginess of apparel was something for a soldier to be proud of.

Miss Lansome took a chair, arranged her drapery as carefully as if she was in the presence of a prince, and said :

"Won't you be seated, Mr. King?"

"Oh—yes—certainly—thank you," ejaculated the young man, still comporting himself like a victim of St. Vitus' dance. "I would, if——"

"If what?" asked the teacher, whose curiosity had been slowly aroused by the young farmer's peculiar antics.

"If—if this darned pipe of mine wasn't burning a hole in me," said the ex-coachman. "I put it in my pocket just as you came out, not wantin' to smoke before a lady, an' I never knew before that the outside of a pipe could be so hot."

Miss Lansome was taken by surprise, and laughed heartily. Then she recovered herself enough to say :

"Might it not be well to take it from your pocket and put it aside?"

"Gosh !" exclaimed the youth, rising to his feet ; "I never thought of that."

A second later the offending source of consolation had been withdrawn and cast as far into the orchard as a strong arm could throw it; and when Mr. King ejaculated "Thar!" and sank again into his chair, it was with the air of a martyr who had overcome the bitterness of death.

"Your baptismal name," said the teacher, anxious to change the subject of conversation, "has a foreign sound; is it Italian?"

"Waal, not as I knows on," said the youth. "Kinder funny, the way I came to be called Nosmo. Ye see, when I wuz a baby, the mother didn't know what to name me. She'd hev liked to give me dad's name, but that was John, and ther' wuz so many John Kings in the county already, that when the war broke out an' they raised a company nigh Redtuft, ther' wuz such a lot of Johns among the Kings that enlisted that the captain had to number 'em. Well, I wuzn't christened for such an awful spell that folks began to say they reckoned our family wuz a-gettin' to be backsliders. But all the time the mother wuz a-lookin' fur a new name, an' at last she got it. She wuz on a little steamboat one day, an' on a door of the back room of that there boat was the name 'King.' Then the mother was dead bent to know what wuz the first name of the puttik'lar King that had that room. So she edged around an' around till she saw it on the other door. It wuz Nosmo, an'

Nosmo I wuz baptized the very next Sunday, though 'twuz a rainy day an' folks
said 'twuz a sin to bring a young one out
in such weather.''

'' How strange !'' said Miss Lansome.

'' Yes, but that wuzn't the strangest,''
continued the young man. '' 'Bout a year
after that the mother wuz on the same boat
agin. Both doors of that back room wuz
shut, an' how do ye s'pose the name read?
Why, '*No Smoking.*' Don't ye see? —
N-o-s-m-o k-i-n-g.''

Miss Lansome was overcome by laughter,
which pleased her admirer greatly, for this
was his one joke, and he had not been able
to tell it to a new listener for at least a year.
He lingered over it affectionately, ejacula-
ting '' No smoking—Nosmo King ''—alternately, until, through sheer exhaustion, his
sole hearer could laugh no longer. The
subject of conversation was finally changed
by Miss Lansome, who said :

'' Mr. King, I wonder if you can tell me
anything about the pupils I am to have.
Are there many of them ? Are they old or
young ? What do they study ?''

'' That's just what I wuz comin' to talk
to ye 'bout,'' said Nosmo, becoming sober
at once. '' Some of 'em ain't so little an'
some ain't so big ; but the biggest of 'em,
I s'pose, is me.''

'' You ? '' Miss Lansome was really surprised.

"Yes," said Nosmo, rapidly. " I'll tell
ye how 'tis : brother Bill's out in the mines
and brother Sam went to sea, so I've ben
the only one at home to help the father
these five years, so I've missed my schoolin'.
Sam went to the bottom in a gale, an' Bill
hez made a pile for himself, so the old man,
who's old an' can't last much longer, is
goin' to leave me the farm. It's wuth a
lot of money, an' whoever hez owned it hez
been expected to be a good deal of a feller,
an' I ain't fit to keep up the repitation of
the family ef I don't pick up some idees.
Now, seein' I'm not quite twenty-one, I'm
of school age and I've made up my mind
I'll go to school an' do my level best to
make the right sort of a man of myself;
but——"

There was silence for a moment ; it was
finally broken by Miss Lansome saying :

" But what?"

" Why, I'm afraid any teacher'd make
fun of such a big gawk comin' into a school-
house."

Miss Lansome arose, stepped to where
the young man sat, with his elbows on
his knees and his face in both his hands,
and said :

" Mr. King, you are a noble fellow, and
and if you come to my school I'll teach
you everything I can."

" Reely?" said the would-be student,
springing to his feet.

" Really," replied the little teacher, with great earnestness. " Here's my hand on it."
" Bless ye !" exclaimed the big fellow, taking the soft little hand. " But I'm 'fraid you'll find me dull an' stupid most of the time. I ken break the wildest colts that travels, an' ther's no man that ken beat me harvestin' ; but when it comes to stowin' books inside of my head, I ain't much to speak of."
" Never mind," said the teacher, encouragingly. " I will help you to the best of my ability."
" Will ye, though? That settles it, then," said Nosmo, with a great sigh as if a load had been taken off his mind. " I wish I knowed how to thank ye, but I don't." As he spoke he squeezed Miss Lansome's hand tightly to express his gratitude. Then Mr. King picked up his hat from the piazza floor, and abruptly started to go, but he stopped at the step, turned round irresolutely, caressed the brim of the hat a moment, and said :
" Ef I make mistakes, ez I guess I'll do by the cartload, ye won't laugh at me, will ye? The young ones in school will, of course ; I don't mind *them*, but ef you wuz to do it I'd—I'd—why I'd kind o' lose my grip."
" Don't fear," replied the teacher kindly.
" All right," said the pupil, and departed suddenly without even saying " good-bye."

As he walked away Miss Lansome saw him thrust his hands into his coat pockets, throw back his head, and assume a gait which, although not fashionable, was certainly very unlike the shambling walk of countrymen in general. Then the new teacher resumed her chair and informed herself that at last she had a mission.

Once again before school opened, Miss Lansome saw Nosmo King; it was at the little church which every one at Redtuft attended, and he gave her a look of recognition and a slight toss of the head that seemed intended for an assurance that he had not changed his mind, but was determined to absorb all the information that the stated course of study could supply.

When the teacher reached her schoolroom on Monday morning, which she did at an early hour, so as to encounter her pupils singly and not be obliged to endure a general stare of scrutiny, she found some enormous pears on her desk and Nosmo King at one end of the back seat looking as if he was trying to shrink his habitual dimensions to schoolboy size. The teacher bowed and smiled pleasantly, at which the young man seemed suddenly to lengthen several inches as he remarked :

"Come early, so's not to be grinned at? So did I."

No conversation ensued, for other early arrivals greeted the teacher, who chatted pleasantly with one group after another, as they sidled into favorite seats ; she was thus enabled to interrogate Nosmo without making him as conspicuous as he would have been had she called him alone to her desk. She looked at the books he had brought, and suggested that he examine each one during the day, and make sure how far he had studied when a lad, and how much he remembered.

The remainder of the school-day was spent in enrolling the children and classifying them. The largest pupil faded entirely from the teacher's mind, except for a moment at noon when she ate the pears he had brought. When she started for home she was too tired to think of anything in particular, but as she passed a group of children a little girl brought the newly discovered mission to Miss Lansome's mind by remarking, in the teacher's hearing :

'' That great big Nosmo King didn't do nothin' all day but just gawp at the teacher.''

The child's companions giggled, and then one hissed '' Sh-h-h ! '' which had the effect of making the teacher's cheeks burn more hotly than they had at first promised to do. She wished there was some place in school where the young farmer could sit without seeing her and occasioning remarks. How could that child have known what Nosmo was doing, when the fellow sat on the last seat? Miss Lansome determined to enforce, in future, the normal custom of "eyes front;" and yet she did not see but that would make it necessary for Nosmo King to stare at her when he was not looking at his books.

There were plums instead of pears on the teacher's desk next morning, and a small boy, who was hungrily contemplating them, volunteered the information that "Nosmo King brung 'em"—a fact that Miss Lansome already guessed, for she saw that her largest pupil, although bent almost double over his desk, was trying hard to see her from under the edges of his eyebrows. The experiment did not succeed very well; so the fellow boldly picked up his books and came to her desk to report progress. When told that he was fully entitled to a place among the most advanced pupils, he seemed greatly relieved in his feelings; he looked contemplative for a moment, and then asked, with a most pathetic expression of countenance, and in a low, appealing tone:

"Say; I don't look such an *awful* lot bigger than some of the biggest boys and gals, do I?"

"No, indeed," replied the teacher. "Why, some of the pupils are much taller than I."

"Waal," said Nosmo, meditatively, as his eye passed over the teacher's figure, "there's a good deal of difference 'tween you an' me, you know—a good deal." He turned and shook his head doubtfully as he went back to his seat; Miss Lansome thought she understood him, and she was sure she was sorry for him. In spite of his awkwardness, Nosmo seemed a manly fellow, which was more than the teacher could say of most of her male acquaintances. If he were only a gentleman—if, although ignorant of books, he knew anything of the manners of society, how romantic it would be to teach him ! It might even happen that— At this point the teacher discovered, by looking at her watch, that the school should have been opened five minutes before.

Out-of-doors, the children teased Nosmo unceasingly; and no amount of discipline could prevent them laughing derisively whenever he made a mistake in school, but the big fellow not only kept up with his classes, but even found time to read some books which Miss Lansome had suggested would be useful to him. Every day, too, he managed to get something to lay on the teacher's desk. Tokens of regard, from pupils to teacher, were not unusual at Red-tuft, but Miss Lansome imagined she could always distinguish Nosmo's offerings from the others. They were more abundant in quantity ; their quality was generally better, and there was about them a variety that the presents of the younger pupils lacked, so when she thanked the supposed giver, which she never failed to do, she never found

herself mistaken.   If she ventured to admire,
in Nosmo's hearing, any flower, or fruit, or
colored leaf that was to be seen in the local-
ity, she found a material reminder of it on
her desk in the morning, and when one day
she went into raptures over a large maple
that began early to make of itself a dazzling
mass of color, nothing but the limits of the
school-house prevented Nosmo from bringing his teacher the entire tree.

Later, when opportunity allowed, the
largest pupil began to follow his teacher to
her home. His chances were infrequent, for
Miss Lansome generally had several juvenile retainers, but when she happened to remain at the desk a few minutes later than
usual, she could depend upon seeing Nosmo
somewhere near the roadside as she walked
homeward.   On such occasions the young
man always explained ; he had either seen
a fox and was looking for its reappearance,
or was wondering whether Farmer Raygin's
tobacco crop was far enough advanced to be
cut before frost, or he had been "sampling" apples in the Raygin orchard, or test-
ing fences to see what would be best for a
bit of his own land that needed a new en-
closure.   But his special occupation always
ended as the teacher approached : He would
allow her to pass him ; then he would follow, at a few steps' distance, and begin a
conversation that compelled Miss Lansome
to turn her head whenever she spoke.

Sometimes she would stop ; then he would stand by her side and talk till again she moved forward, when he would lag behind at his original distance.

The autumn was almost rainless, and Miss Lansome enjoyed the pure air and pleasing alternations of field, meadow, orchard and woodland so much that she had become almost reconciled to her lot, when one morning she awoke to find rain pouring in torrents. The entire landscape was dismal and the now familiar road a sheet of mud. Miss Lansome ate a late breakfast in silence ; she was wishing for either New York sidewalks or a pair of rubber boots, neither of which were within reach, when Mr. Raygin exclaimed :

"Sakes alive ! if there ain't Nosmo Kings's fast colt an' the city buggy he don't take out four times a year ! And now to bring it out in this mud and rain ! Well, I never ! "

Meanwhile the owner of the horse and buggy had alighted, tied his spirited animal, thrown robes and rubber cloth over the seat of the buggy, and entered the house.

" Good morning, ev'rybody," said he. Although his address was general, he looked at but one, and to her he said :

" I thought I'd drive ye down to school, so's you wouldn't git wet. Umbrells ain't no good in a downpour like this."

" Nosmo," said Miss Lansome, " your intention is as commendable as your grammar is bad. I will be ready in a moment."

The young man drove to the front door, and when the teacher appeared he was at the step to shelter her with an umbrella— not one of your tiny combinations of silk and steel, but an immense blue parachute— a family heirloom that looked as if it had been made for the purpose of shielding a haystack. He placed the lady in the carriage, threw a blanket and rubber cloth over and about her, and then seated himself and drove off, covering his knees as he went, with the still open umbrella.

" What a handsome carriage ! " exclaimed the teacher, anxious to please the young man who had been so thoughtful of her comfort. " But what a shame to use it in all this rain and mud ! Why didn't you use an older one in such weather ? "

" Waal," said Nosmo, wondering whether Miss Lansome could be made to understand that only the best was good enough for her, " the old rockaway's got two seats ! you'd hev picked the back one ; then you wouldn't have seen the storm."

The excuse was painfully idiotic, but Miss Lansome did not seem to realize it, for she exclaimed :

" Do *you* enjoy storms ? "

" Waal," said Nosmo, " I do, an' then

ag'in I don't. Them as comes all of a sudden, an' spiles crops, don't suit me wuth a
cent, an' I don't mind sayin that I'd ez lief
see a hunk of Jedgment Day ez a storm at
the end of a day's mowin'. But when it
comes to a hard, solid, come-in-the-mornin'-
an'-stay-all-day kind of a rain, that gives
me the chance to git out the best that's in
the barn and ride to school alongside o' the
best-lookin' young woman in the country,
why—gosh, let her pour, *I* say."

This view of storms was entirely new to
Miss Lansome, and somewhat startling,
too, particularly as Nosmo, after saying it,
looked straight ahead with the blank look
of a child who has said something hastily,
and wonders if punishment is coming. Miss
Lansome began to feel so much embarrassment that she was glad when the school-
house door was reached. Nosmo sprang to
the ground, raised the great blue umbrella
once more, and helped the teacher to alight.

It was the work of only a second or two,
but while the umbrella shielded both, Nosmo found time to whisper :

"Ye ain't mad at me, air ye?"

Miss Lansome looked up quickly at the
appealing face, and answered, with a smile :
" Not in the least, Nosmo ; I am very,
very much obliged." Why she extended a
hand as she said this, when she needed both
hands to keep her skirts from the muddy
steps, she did not know, but evidently

Nosmo had anticipated the act, for one of his own hands was disengaged, and as the teacher entered the school she said to herself that the oldest pupil's palm was less hard and more warm than it was the only other time it had ever before touched her own.

A few moments later, as she looked through the window commanding the road, she beheld an immense blue umbrella, apparently a relative of the King family's faithful parachute; it was so broad and convex that beneath it little was visible but a pair of boots that seemed too enormous to belong to any school child. A pair of boots carrying an umbrella was funny enough to laugh at, and Miss Lansome, seizing a pencil, began to sketch it; but looking up from her paper and at her subject, the relative positions of boots and umbrella had changed enough to disclose the face of Nosmo between them. What could it mean? Had she not left him at the door only two or three minutes before? How had he—why, certainly; how stupid of her not to have thought of it!—the poor fellow had been obliged to take his horse to shelter—probably in Squire Raygin's barn, there being no nearer place—and was now trudging back through the rain and mud! She just did not care, she told herself in unteacherlike language, what other folks might think about it; *she* would always feel that Nosmo

had extended the most thoughtful and gen-
tlemanly courtesy she had ever received.
She was about to tear the half-completed
sketch, but changing her mind she dashed
in several dots and lines where the face
should be, scrawled underneath, "A Modern Knight," and hurriedly placed the
sketch under the school register just as her
late escort entered the room. He looked at
the teacher rather sheepishly and she returned a glance that somehow made Nosmo,
when the first class in arithmetic was called,
look wonderfully unlike the great, awkward
fellow who usually stood at the head of the
line.

When the noon intermission was announced, Nosmo started hurriedly to leave
the room ; but Miss Lansome held up her
little forefinger warningly, and the tall fellow stopped, saying :

"I'll git ye to the dinner-table in less'n
ten minutes."

"You must not ; I positively forbid it ;
I'm not a bit hungry," said the teacher,
swallowing a fib in lieu of better food.

Nosmo seemed disappointed ; he fingered
his hat brim irresolutely for a moment, and
then said :

"Waal, the hoss'll be hungry, anyhow ;
I guess I'll go up an' give him a bite."
Again the teacher saw the blue cotton umbrella against the reddish-yellow background of the muddy road ; she mused a

moment, took the sketch from its hiding-
place, retouched and elaborated the face,
and might have worked upon it during the
entire noon hour, so careful and deliberate
was she, had not the original of her picture
stalked into the room, his heavy boots
making noise enough to attract general attention. He saw that the eyes of all the
lounging, dinner-munching children were
upon him and the teacher, but he kept an
impassive face as he placed a small basket
on the table, and said, in a loud tone.

"Missis Raygin told me to give ye this."

"How very kind of her!" exclaimed
Miss Lansome, as she took from the basket
a napkin filled with buttered biscuits, sliced
ham and cake. "Nosmo!" continued the
teacher, calling back the young man, who
had started for his seat, and was already
extracting his own dinner from his capacious
pockets. "I hope," she said, in a very low
tone, as the youth approached her, "that
you did not *ask* Mrs. Raygin to put herself
to this trouble."

"No—oh, no, ma'am—of course not,"
said Nosmo, quickly, but Miss Lansome,
who had studied juvenile faces long enough
to know the simpler signs of untruthfulness,
shook her head sadly as the big pupil hurried back to his seat.

When school was finally dismissed the
rain still poured in torrents, so when Nosmo
informed the teacher that he would "hev

the colt here purty soon,'' he got a grateful
smile in payment. The children straggled
off home in little parties, and the teacher
found herself alone. She was half inclined
to feel impatient, for the school-room, shabby
enough by sunlight, seemed on this dull
day a dungeon of a place. She had spoken
to the directors about it, but all she got for
her pains was the information that a dozen
different ladies, beside one man, had taught
there, and that not one of them had ever
complained. She declared that she would
renovate the room at her own expense ; she
did not know how, but she would ask Nosmo. Why was it, she asked herself, that
young men in the country and those in town
differed so strangely ? Nosmo had scarcely
reached his twenty-first birthday, yet he
was tall, strong, manly, self-reliant, court-
eous and trustworthy, while her city acquaintances of similar age were the reverse
of all this. If Nosmo did not butcher the
English language with almost every breath,
if he wore clothing of modern cut, and
shaved regularly, and read something beside the *Farmer's Companion*, and knew an
etching from a poster cut, he might make—
some girl—a very acceptable husband. Not
that *she* could be satisfied with such a mate ;
that is, not if—indeed, she did not see what
could induce her to think for a moment of
being a farmer's wife. Nevertheless, she
was heartily sorry for Nosmo ; he was

probably doomed to marry some good-
natured, stupid country girl, like one of
Mrs. Raygin's daughters, who thought that
dress brought refinement; his unselfishness
would be accepted as a matter of course.
Poor fellow! How did this world come to
be such a dreadful place for men—and
women?

Her reverie was abruptly shortened by
the sound of wheels at the door; she must
have been deeply absorbed in thought for
him to have approached without her knowing it.

"I will be ready in an instant, Nosmo,"
she said, turning toward the nails on which
hung her hat, cloak, and water-proof wrap.
"I have been very busy" (the little sin-
ner!), "or I should not have to keep you
waiting."

"My time's yourn," responded Nosmo,
leaning against the table, and, like a great
child, trifling with everything his fingers
could reach. He examined the ruler, studied
the cover of the inkstand, tried the teacher's
pen on his thumb nail, and picked up the register, when his eye was caught by the sketch
the teacher had made of him and his umbrella. In a second Miss Lansome heard
again the soft, long-drawn "Gosh," and
turning around she saw Nosmo with her
drawing in his hand and an expression of
countenance that she never could have
imagined possible. She wanted to laugh at

him ; then she wanted to cry at him, but
before she succeeded in doing either, the
subject looked slowly from the sketch to the
artist, and did it so earnestly that Miss
Lansome, silly thing (she said to herself),
blushed, and dropped her eyes. Why could
not the stupid fellow say something, instead
of staring at her in that strange way ?
Well, if *he* would not, *she* would.

"That is a sketch I made hastily this
morning," she said. "I suppose you don't
understand it, but you mustn't think I was
making fun of you. A knight is—he is—"

"I know all about knights," interrupted
Nosmo, gravely ; "there's a book about
'em in our Sunday School library. An' I'm
more obliged to ye than I ever wuz to any
human bein'."

"I'm so glad I haven't offended you,"
said the teacher, her composure returning.
She stepped to the desk, hastily put it in
order, and then took hold of the sketch, but
Nosmo did not relinquish his possession
of it.

"I must put it away," said Miss Lansome, smiling pleasantly. "It will always
remind me of a very thoughtful courtesy."

"I don't want to rob ye," said Nosmo,
still holding the sketch, "but I'll tell you
what I'll do. I'll give ye the hull farm,
when its mine, fur that little pictur'."

The teacher laughed, shook her head, and
tugged playfully at the bit of paper.

"Ye won't?" said Nosmo. "Then—though I s'pose it's no use—I'll put it another way." He looked out of the window for a moment, as if for some one to come and help him; then he turned his head and said:

"I'll give ye the old place, an' the young man that runs it, an' ye can do jest what ye please with both of 'em forever and ever, ef ye'll give me a half-interest in this pictur' fur life!"

What should she say? She did not feel equal to rebuking the youth—at least not while he stood there with that look in his eyes. So with a pleasant smile she answered:

"You must give me time to think about it, Nosmo. I've made many sketches, but this is the first one anybody has thought worth having. I may have to raise the price, if it's really valuable. Oh—see, the sun is shining again! Let us get out of this dingy room." And the teacher put the sketch between the leaves of a magazine and hurried out to the carriage. Nosmo followed her; she pretended not to look at him, nevertheless she saw that his face was very gloomy. She began at once to talk rapturously of the scenery under the sunlight.

"Oh, Nosmo, see how fresh and beautiful all the wild flowers are after their bath! And Squire Raygin's tobacco-plants are covered with diamonds—don't you see them sparkling? And that flaming maple away off yonder in the swamp—oh, oh, oh!—when the ground dries I'll walk over there, some Saturday morning, and feast my eyes on it as long as I like."

"Walk?—you?—over thar?—through that bog?" said Nosmo. And in a second he had turned his horse's head toward the school-house.

"Have you forgotten something?" asked Miss Lansome.

"Not a thing," said Nosmo; "but ef ye want to see that maple, I'm goin' to drive ye thar, an' save yer shoe-leather, *an'* yer clothes, *an'* yer breath, *an'* yer temper ef ye happen to hev one. Why, I wouldn't go thar myself, acrost lots, fur the price of a new pair of boots. There's a wood road goes roun' behind the fields an' it comes within twenty rod of that very tree."

"What a handsome horse you have! Is he fast?"

"Is he?—Joe?—fast?—waal, ef he hed just a-heard you say that, he'd hev showed ye whether he wuz fast or not; but I'll just let him out a minute and give you a hint of what he can do."

At a touch of the whip Joe gave a mighty bound that nearly threw Miss Lansome out of the carriage; then he dashed down the slightly inclined road and past the school-house. It seemed to Miss Lansome that the

colt must be running away, but a glance at
Nosmo reassured her, for the big pupil sat
erect, with tightly compressed lips, dis-
tended nostrils, eyes wide open, and a slight
wrinkle between his brows.   At the end of
the field, beyond the school-house, a narrow
road divided the fenced ground from the
woods, and into this Nosmo guided the
horse.   The turn was made so abruptly that
the carriage swayed dangerously, and Miss
Lansome screamed.

"Don't be afeard, little woman," said
Nosmo, "I'll soon make him know who's
master.   But these wood-roads *air* narrer,
an' they *air* rough."

And Nosmo was right.   A farm-wagon
might be safely dragged over and between
the roots, stumps, logs, and mud holes, of
which the narrow roadway was full, but a
light buggy, drawn by a runaway horse,
was manifestly out of place amid such ob-
structions.   And Nosmo's colt, smarting
under the indignity of the whip, evidently
cared neither for the condition of the road
nor the feelings of the occupants of the
carriage.   The buggy rocked as if on rubber
springs, and the teacher found herself resting alternately upon the driver and the side
of the carriage.

"Hold on—tight!" said Nosmo suddenly, as the wheels on his side neared a
projecting log.   Miss Lansome grasped the
ribs of the buggy top.

"Not there!" exclaimed Nosmo; "hold on to *me*—quick!" The teacher obeyed; as she did so Nosmo's side of the carriage rose, the driver leaned to the right; the wheels crossed the log, and Nosmo leaned slowly back in the other direction to restore the equilibrium. As he did so he said :

"Don't let go; the brute has took the bit in his teeth."

"Oh, Nosmo!" exclaimed Miss Lansome, "aren't you afraid?"

"'Fraid?" echoed the young farmer. "Gosh! why I wouldn't be 'fraid—not *now* —ef I wuz a-drivin' a span of royal Bengal tigers!"

But tigers were not necessary to test Nosmo's courage. Nosmo's colt seemed to lay his course maliciously, for one wheel or other was in air most of the time.

"Durn him!" growled Nosmo, as the wheel on one side went over a stump and the teacher tightened her grasp of the brawny figure beside her, "ef he c'ud turn his head fur a second an' see who wus behind him he'd stop makin' a fool of himself."

"Yes, Nosmo, so he would if he could look into your face."

"I didn't mean *me*," said the driver. "Gosh! The rain hez floated the bridge off o' the crick! Hold fast, now!"

The "crick" was a tiny brook, only two feet wide, that crossed the road, and the

bridge consisted merely of three boards laid
crosswise of the road, on two beams. The
smallest pupil at Redtuft school could jump
the stream at any time, but as an obstruction to a light buggy moving at the rate of
a mile in three minutes or less it was serious.
The colt Joe, as he reached it, gave an
enormous leap; as the animal sprang,
Nosmo took both reins in his right hand,
and put his left arm around the teacher.
There was a crash, Miss Lansome felt herself flying through space, and then—she
found herself leaning helplessly upon Nosmo
and crying as if her heart would break ;
Nosmo was supporting her quite effectively
with one arm, and the colt was contemplating both, with his face very close to
them, and Nosmo was addressing his companions alternately :

   " Poor little thing, it *wuz* an awful skeer,
wuzn't it ? Joe, durn yer unmannerly hoofs,
I'll sell ye to a clam peddler 'fore ye'r a day
older. Well, well, she *shell* cry ef it does
her good, God bless her. Joe, ye ort to be
tied out in the brush an' chawed to death
by woodticks. I wish, ma'am, I c'ud hev
got all the skeer an' you c'ud hev seen all
the fun, but somehow I *can't* skeer at a
hoss."

   Then Miss Lansome laughed hysterically,
and disengaged herself, without much assistance from Nosmo, and blamed herself, in
the most penitent manner imaginable for the

whole trouble, for had she not asked Nosmo if his horse was fast? As Nosmo looked about at the wreck he saw the magazine Miss Lansome had brought from the school-house. He picked it up and the sketch fell from it. He stooped again, the teacher also attempted to recover her property, so, once more, two hands held the sketch. Both figures arose at the same time, and their eyes met. The silence that followed was broken by Nosmo :

"About that half interest I was speakin' of, in this pictur'——"

"You—you may have it, Nosmo," said Miss Lansome ; upon which, although the teacher was quite able to stand alone, Nosmo hastened to support her with two arms instead of one.

———

THE LIGHTNING-ROD MAN.

BY HERMAN MELVILLE.

What grand irregular thunder, thought I, standing on my hearthstone among the Acroceraunian hills, as the scattered bolts boomed overhead, and crashed down among the valleys, every bolt followed by zigzag irradiations, and swift slants of sharp rain, which audibly rang, like a charge of spear-points, on my low shingled roof. I suppose, though, that the mountains hereabout break and churn up the thunder, so that it is far more glorious here than on the plain. Hark!—some one at the door. Who is this that chooses a time of thunder for making calls? And why don't he, man-fashion, use the knocker, instead of making that doleful undertaker's clatter with his fist against the hollow panel? But let him in. Ah, here he comes. "Good day, sir:" an entire stranger. "Pray be seated." What is that strange-looking walking-stick he carries? "A fine thunder-storm, sir!"

"Fine?—Awful!"

"You are wet. Stand here on the hearth before the fire."

"Not for worlds!"

The stranger still stood in the exact middle of the cottage, where he had first planted himself. His singularity impelled a closer scrutiny. A lean, gloomy figure. Hair dark and lank, mattedly streaked over his brow. His sunken pitfalls of eyes were ringed by indigo halos, and played with an innocuous sort of lightning; the gleam without the bolt. The whole man was dripping. He stood in a puddle on the bare oak floor; his strange walking-stick vertically resting at his side.

It was a polished copper rod, four feet long, lengthwise attached to a neat wooden staff, by insertion into two balls of greenish glass, ringed with copper bands. The metal rod terminated at the top tripodwise, in three keen tines, brightly gilt. He held the thing by the wooden part alone.

"Sir," said I, bowing politely, "have I the honor of a visit from that illustrious god, Jupiter Tonans? So stood he in the Greek statue of old, grasping the lightning bolt. If you be he, or his viceroy, I have to thank you for this noble storm you have brewed among our mountains. Listen : That was a glorious peal. Ah, to a lover of the majestic, it is a good thing to have the Thunderer himself in one's cottage. The thunder grows finer for that. But pray be seated. This old rush-bottomed arm-chair, I grant, is a poor substitute for your ever-green throne on Olympus ; but, condescend to be seated."

While I thus pleasantly spoke, the stranger eyed me, half in wonder, and half in a strange sort of horror, but did not move a foot.

"Do, sir, be seated ; you need to be dried ere going forth again."

I planted the chair invitingly on the broad hearth, where a little fire had been kindled that afternoon to dissipate the dampness, not the cold ; for it was early in the month of September.

But without heeding my solicitations, and still standing in the middle of the floor, the stranger gazed at me portentously and spoke.

"Sir," said he, "excuse me ; but instead of my accepting your invitation to be seated on the hearth there, I solemnly warn *you*, that you had best accept *mine*, and stand with me in the middle of the room. Good heavens!" he cried, starting—"there is another of those awful crashes. I warn you, sir, quit the hearth."

"Mr. Jupiter Tonans," said I, quietly rolling my body on the stone, " I stand very well here."

" Are you so horridly ignorant, then," he cried, " as not to know that by far the most dangerous part of the house, during such a terrific tempest as this, is the fireplace ? "

"Nay, I did not know that," involuntarily stepping upon the first board next to the stone.

The stranger now assumed such an unpleasant air of successful admonition that— quite involuntarily again—I stepped back upon the hearth, and threw myself into the erectest, proudest posture I could command. But I said nothing.

" For Heaven's sake," he cried, with a strange mixture of alarm and intimidation— "for Heaven's sake, get off the hearth! Know you not that the heated air and soot are conductors ;—to say nothing of those immense iron fire-dogs ? Quit the spot—I conjure—I command you."

" Mr. Jupiter Tonans, I am not accustomed to be commanded in my own house."

"Call me not by that pagan name. You are profane in this time of terror."

"Sir, will you be so good as to tell me your business? If you seek shelter from the storm, you are welcome, so long as you be civil; but if you come on business, open it forthwith. Who are you?"

"I am a dealer in lightning-rods," said the stranger, softening his tone; "my special business is ———. Merciful heaven! what a crash!—Have you ever been struck—your premises, I mean? No? It's best to be provided;"—significantly rattling his metallic staff on the floor;—"by nature, there are no castles in thunder-storms; yet, say but the word, and of this cottage I can make a Gibraltar by a few waves of this wand. Hark, what Himalayas of concussions!"

"You interrupted yourself; your special business you were about to speak of."

"My special business is to travel the country for orders for lightning-rods. This is my specimen-rod;" tapping his staff; "I have the best of references"—fumbling in his pockets. "In Criggan last month, I put up three-and-twenty rods on only five buildings."

"Let me see. Was it not at Criggan last week, about midnight on Saturday, that the steeple, the big elm, and the assembly-room cupola were struck? Any of your rods there?"

"Not on the tree and cupola, but the steeple."

"Of what use is your rod, then?"

"Of life-and-death use. But my work-man was heedless. In fitting the rod at top to the steeple, he allowed a part of the metal to graze the tin sheeting. Hence the accident. Not my fault, but his. Hark!"

"Never mind. That clap burst quite loud enough to be heard without finger-pointing. Did you hear of the event at Montreal last year? A servant girl struck at her bed-side with a rosary in her hand; the beads being metal. Does your beat extend into the Canadas?"

"No. And I hear that there, iron rods only are in use. They should have *mine*, which are copper. Iron is easily fused. Then they draw out the rod so slender, that it has not body enough to conduct the full electric current. The metal melts; the building is destroyed. My copper rods never act so. Those Canadians are fools. Some of them knob the rod at the top, which risks a deadly explosion, instead of imperceptibly carrying down the current into the earth, as this sort of rod does. *Mine* is the only true rod. Look at it. Only one dollar a foot."

"This abuse of your own calling in an-other might make one distrustful with re-spect to yourself."

"Hark! The thunder becomes less mut-tering. It is nearing us, and nearing the

earth, too. Hark! One crammed crash!
All the vibrations made one by nearness
Another flash. Hold!"

"What do you?" I said, seeing him
now, instantaneously relinquishing his staff,
lean intently forward toward the window,
with his right fore and middle fingers on his
left wrist.

But ere the words had well escaped me,
another exclamation escaped him.

"Crash! only three pulses—less than a
third of a mile off—yonder, somewhere in
that wood. I passed three stricken oaks
there, ripped out new and glittering. The
oak draws lightning more than other tim-
ber, having iron in solution in its sap. Your
floor here seems oak."

"Heart-of-oak. From the peculiar time
of your call upon me, I suppose you pur-
posely select stormy weather for your journeys. When the thunder is roaring, you
deem it an hour peculiarly advantageous for
producing impressions favorable to your
trade."

"Hark!—awful!"

"For one who would arm others with
fearlessness, you seem unbeseemingly tim-
erous yourself. Common men choose fair
weather for their travels: you choose thunder storms; and yet——"

"That I travel in thunder-storms, I
grant; but not without particular precautions, such as only a lightning-rod man may

know. Hark! Quick—look at my specimen rod. Only one dollar a foot."

"A very fine rod, I dare say. But what
are these particular precautions of yours?
Yet first let me close yonder shutters; the
slanting rain is beating through the sash.
I will bar up."

"Are you mad? Know you not that yon
iron bar is a swift conductor? Desist."

"I will simply close the shutters, then,
and call my boy to bring me a wooden bar.
Pray, touch the bell-pull there."

"Are you frantic? That bell-wire might
blast you. Never touch bell-wire in a
thunder-storm, nor ring a bell of any sort."

"Nor those in belfries? Pray, will you
tell me where and how one may be safe in
a time like this? Is there any part of
my house I may touch with hopes of my
life?"

"There is; but not where you now stand.
Come away from the wall. The current
will sometimes run down a wall, and—a
man being a better conductor than a wall—
it would leave the wall and run into him.
Swoop! *That* must have fallen very nigh.
That must have been globular lightning."

"Very probably. Tell me at once, which
is, in your opinion, the safest part of this
house?"

"This room, and this one spot in it where
I stand. Come hither."

"The reasons first."

"Hark !—after the flash the gust—the sashes shiver—the house, the house !—Come hither to me !"

"The reasons, if you please."

"Come hither to me !"

"Thank you again, I think I will try my old stand—the hearth. And now, Mr. Lightning-rod man, in the pauses of the thunder, be so good as to tell me your reasons for esteeming this one room of the house the safest, and your own one standpoint there the safest spot in it."

There was now a little cessation of the storm for a while. The lightning-rod man seemed relieved, and replied :

"Your house is a one-story house, with an attic and a cellar ; this room is between. Hence its comparative safety. Because lightning sometimes passes from the clouds to the earth, and sometimes from the earth to the clouds. Do you comprehend?—and I choose the middle of the room, because, if the lightning should strike the house at all, it would come down the chimney or walls ; so, obviously, the further you are from them, the better. Come hither to me, now."

"Presently. Something you just said, instead of alarming me, has strangely inspired confidence."

"What have I said?"

"You said that sometimes lightning flashes from the earth to the clouds."

"Aye, the returning-stroke, as it is called; when the earth, being overcharged with the fluid, flashes its surplus upward."

"The returning-stroke; that is, from earth to sky. Better and better. But come here on the hearth and dry yourself."

"I am better here, and better wet."

"'How?'"

"It is the safest thing you can do — Hark, again !—to get yourself thoroughly drenched in a thunder-storm. Wet clothes are better conductors than the body ; and so, if the lightning strike, it might pass down the wet clothes without touching the body. The storm deepens again. Have you a rug in the house ? Rugs are non-conductors. Get one, that I may stand on it here, and you too. The skies blacken—it is dusk at noon. Hark !—the rug, the rug !"

I gave him one ; while the hooded mountains seemed closing and tumbling in the cottage.

"And now, since our being dumb will not help us," said I, resuming my place, "let me hear your precautions in traveling during thunder-storms."

"Wait till this one is passed."

"Nay, proceed with the precautions. You stand in the safest possible place according to your account. Go on."

"Briefly, then. I avoid pine trees, high houses, lonely barns, upland pastures, running water, flocks of cattle and sheep, a

crowd of men. If I travel on foot—as to-
day—I do not walk fast ; if in my buggy, I
touch not its back or sides ; if on horseback,
I dismount and lead the horse. But of all
things, I avoid tall men."

"Do I dream? Man avoid man? and in
danger-time, too."

"Tall men in a thunder-storm I avoid.
Are you so grossly ignorant as not to know
that the height of a six-footer is sufficient to
discharge an electric cloud upon him? Are
not lonely Kentuckians, plowing, smit in
the unfinished furrow? Nay, if the six-
footer stand by running water, the cloud
will sometimes *select* him as its conductor to
that running water. Hark! Sure, yon
black pinnacle is split. Yes, a man is a
good conductor. The lightning goes
through and through a man, but only peels
a tree. But sir, you have kept me so long
answering your questions, that I have not
yet come to business. Will you order one
of my rods? Look at this specimen one.
See : it is of the best of copper. Copper's
the best conductor. Your house is low ;
but being upon the mountains, that lowness
does not one whit depress it. You moun-
taineers are most exposed. In mountainous
countries, the lightning-rod man should
have most business. Look at the specimen,
sir. One rod will answer for a house so
small as this. Look over these recom-
mendations. Only one rod, sir ; cost, only

twenty dollars. Hark! There go all the
granite Taconics and Hoosics dashed together like pebbles. By the sound, that
must have struck something. An elevation
of five feet above the house will protect
twenty feet radius all about the rod. Only
twenty dollars, sir—a dollar a foot. Hark?
—Dreadful!—Will you order? Will you
buy? Shall I put down your name? Think
of being a heap of charred offal, like a
haltered horse burnt in its stall; and all in
one flash!"

"You pretended envoy extraordinary and
minister plenipotentiary to and from Jupiter
Tonans," laughed I; "you mere man who
come here to put you and your pipestem
between clay and sky, do you think that
because you can strike a bit of green light
from the Leyden jar, that you can thoroughly
avert the supernal bolt? Your rod rusts,
or breaks, and where are you? Who has
empowered you, you Tetzel, to peddle round
your indulgences from divine ordinations?
The hairs of our heads are numbered, and
the days of our lives. In thunder as in sunshine, I stand at ease in the hands of my
God. False negotiator, away! See, the
scroll of the storm is rolled back; the house
is unharmed; and in the blue heavens I
read in the rainbow, that the Deity will not,
of purpose, make war on man's earth."

"Impious wretch!" foamed the stranger,
blackening in the face as the rainbow

beamed, "I will publish your infidel notions."

The scowl grew blacker on his face; the indigo-circles enlarged round his eyes as the storm-rings round the midnight moon. He sprang upon me; his tri-forked thing at my heart.

I seized it; I snapped it; I dashed it; I trod it; and dragging the dark lightning-king out of my door, flung his elbowed, copper sceptre after him.

But spite of my treatment, and spite of my dissuasive talk of him to my neighbors, the Lightning-rod man still dwells in the land; still travels in storm time, and drives a brave trade with the fears of man.

RIP VAN WINKLE.

BY WASHINGTON IRVING.

Whoever has made a voyage up the Hudson must remember the Kaatskill Mountains. They are a dismembered branch of the great Appalachian family, and are seen away to the west of the river, swelling up to a noble height, and lording it over the surrounding country. Every change of season, every change of weather, indeed, every hour of the day, produces some change in the magical hues and shapes of these mountains, and they are regarded by all the good wives, far and near, as perfect barometers. When the weather is fair and settled, they are clothed in blue and purple, and print their bold outlines on the clear evening sky ; but sometimes, when the rest of the landscape is cloudless, they will gather a hood of gray vapors about their summits, which, in the last rays of the setting sun, will glow and light up like a crown of glory.

At the foot of these fairy mountains the voyager may have descried the light smoke curling up from a village, whose shingle roofs gleam among the trees, just where the blue tints of the upland melt away into the fresh green of the nearer landscape.   It is a little village of great antiquity, having been founded by some of the Dutch colonists in the early time of the province, just about the beginning of the government of the good Peter Stuyvesant (may he rest in peace !), and there were some of the houses of the original settlers standing within a few years, built of small yellow bricks brought from Holland, having latticed windows and gable fronts, surmounted with weather-cocks.

In that same village, and in one of these very houses (which, to tell the precise truth, was sadly time-worn and weather-beaten), there lived many years since, while the country was yet a province of Great Britain, a simple, good-natured fellow, of the name of Rip Van Winkle.   He was a descendant

of the Van Winkles who figured so gal-
lantly in the chivalrous days of Peter Stuyvesant, and accompanied him to the siege
of Fort Christina. He inherited, however,
but little of the martial character of his an-
cestors. I have observed that he was a simple, good-natured man ; he was, moreover,
a kind neighbor, and an obedient hen-
pecked husband. Indeed, to the latter circumstance might be owing that meekness
of spirit which gained him such universal
popularity ; for those men are most apt to
be obsequious and conciliating abroad, who
are under the discipline of shrews at home.
Their tempers, doubtless, are rendered
pliant and malleable in the fiery furnace of
domestic tribulation ; and a curtain lecture
is worth all the sermons in the world for
teaching the virtues of patience and long-
suffering. A termagant wife may, therefore, in some respects, be considered a tolerable blessing ; and if so, Rip Van Winkle
was thrice blessed.

Certain it is, that he was a great favorite
among all the good wives of the village,
who, as usual, with the amiable sex, took
his part in all family squabbles ; and never
failed, whenever they talked those matters
over in their evening gossipings, to lay all
the blame on Dame Van Winkle. The
children of the village, too, would shout
with joy whenever he approached. He assisted at their sports, made their playthings,

taught them to fly kites and shoot marbles,
and told them long stories of ghosts,
witches, and Indians. Whenever he went
dodging about the village, he was surrounded by a troop of them, hanging on his
skirts, clambering on his back, and playing
a thousand tricks on him with impunity ;
and not a dog would bark at him throughout the neighborhood.

The great error in Rip's composition was
an insuperable aversion to all kinds of pro-
fitable labor. It could not be from the want
of assiduity or perseverance ; for he would
sit on a wet rock, with a rod as long and
heavy as a Tartar's lance, and fish all
day without a murmur, even though he
should not be encouraged by a single nibble.
He would carry a fowling-piece on his
shoulder for hours together, trudging
through woods and swamps, and up hill and
down dale, to shoot a few squirrels or wild
pigeons. He would never refuse to assist
a neighbor, even in the roughest toil, and
was a foremost man at all country frolics
for husking Indian corn or building stone
fences ; the women of the village, too, used
to employ him to run their errands, and to
do such little odd jobs as their less obliging
husbands would not do for them. In a
word, Rip was ready to attend to anybody's
business but his own ; but as to doing
family duty, and keeping his farm in order,
he found it impossible.

In fact, he declared it was of no use to
work on his farm ; it was the most pestilent.
little piece of ground in the whole country ;
everything about it went wrong, and would
go wrong, in spite of him. His fences were
continually falling to pieces ; his cow would
either go astray or get among the cabbages ;
weeds were sure to grow quicker in his
fields than anywhere else ; the rain always
made a point of setting in just as he had
some out-door work to do ; so that, though
his patrimonial estate had dwindled away
under his management, acre by acre, until
there was little more left than a mere patch
of Indian-corn and potatoes, yet it was the
worst conditioned farm in the neighborhood.

His children, too, were as ragged and
wild as if they belonged to nobody. His
son Rip, an urchin begotten in his own likeness, promised to inherit the habits, with
the old clothes of his father. He was generally seen trooping like a colt at his mother's
heels, equipped in a pair of his father's cast-
off galli-gaskins, which he had much ado to
hold up with one hand, as a fine lady does
her train in bad weather.

Rip Van Winkle, however, was one of
those happy mortals, of foolish, well-oiled
dispositions, who take the world easy, eat
white bread or brown, whichever can be got
with least thought or trouble, and would
rather starve on a penny than work for a
pound. If left to himself, he would have

whistled life away in perfect contentment; but his wife kept continually dinning in his ears about his idleness, his carelessness, and the ruin he was bringing on his family. Morning, noon, and night her tongue was incessantly going, and everything he said or did was sure to produce a torrent of household eloquence. Rip had but one way of replying to all lectures of the kind, and that, by frequent use, had grown into a habit. He shrugged his shoulders, shook his head, cast up his eyes, but said nothing. This, however, always provoked a fresh volley from his wife; so that he was fain to draw off his forces, and take to the outside of the house—the only side which, in truth, belongs to a hen-pecked husband.

Rip's sole domestic adherent was his dog Wolf, who was as much hen-pecked as his master; for Dame Van Winkle regarded them as companions in idleness, and even looked upon Wolf with an evil eye, as the cause of his master's going so often astray. True it is, in all points of spirit befitting an honorable dog, he was as courageous an animal as ever scoured the woods—but what courage can withstand the ever-during and all-besetting terrors of a woman's tongue? The moment Wolf entered the house his crest fell, his tail drooped to the ground or curled between his legs, he sneaked about with a gallows air, casting many a sidelong glance at Dame Van Winkle, and at the least flourish of a broomstick or ladle he would fly to the door with yelping precipitation.

Times grew worse and worse with Rip Van Winkle as years of matrimony rolled on ; a tart temper never mellows with age, and a sharp tongue is the only edged tool that grows keener with constant use. For a long while he used to console himself, when driven from home, by frequenting a kind of perpetual club of the sages, philosophers, and other idle personages of the village ; which held its sessions on a bench before a small inn, designated by a rubicund portrait of His Majesty George the Third. Here they used to sit in the shade through a long lazy summer's day, talking listlessly over village gossip, or telling endless sleepy stories about nothing. But it would have been worth any statesman's money to have heard the profound discussions that sometimes took place, when by chance an old newspaper fell into their hands from some passing traveler. How solemnly they would listen to the contents, as drawled out by Derrick Van Bummel, the schoolmaster, a dapper learned little man, who was not to be daunted by the most gigantic word in the dictionary ; and how sagely they would deliberate upon public events some months after they had taken place.

The opinions of this junto were completely controlled by Nicholas Vedder, a patriarch of the village, and landlord of the inn, at the door of which he took his seat from morning till night, just moving sufficiently to avoid the sun and keep in the shade of a large tree; so that the neighbors could tell the hour by his movements as accurately as by a sun-dial. It is true he was rarely heard to speak, but smoked his pipe incessantly. His adherents, however (for every great man has his adherents), perfectly understood him, and knew how to gather his opinions. From even this stronghold the unlucky Rip was at length routed by his wife, who would suddenly break in upon the tranquillity of the assemblage and call the members all to naught; nor was that august personage, Nicholas Vedder himself, sacred from the daring tongue of this terrible virago, who charged him outright with encouraging her husband in habits of idleness.

Poor Rip was at last reduced almost to despair; and his only alternative, to escape from the labor of the farm and clamor of his wife, was to take gun in hand and stroll away into the woods. Here he would sometimes seat himself at the foot of a tree, and share the contents of his wallet with Wolf, with whom he sympathized as a fellow-sufferer in persecution. "Poor Wolf," he would say, "thy mistress leads thee a dog's life of it; but never mind, my lad, whilst I live thou shalt never want a friend to stand by thee ! " Wolf would wag his tail, look wistfully in his master's face, and if dogs can feel pity I verily believe he reciprocated the sentiment with all his heart.

In a long ramble of the kind on a fine autumnal day, Rip had unconsciously scrambled to one of the highest parts of the Kaatskill Mountains. He was after his favorite sport of squirrel shooting, and the still solitudes had echoed and re-echoed with the reports of his gun. Panting and fatigued, he threw himself, late in the afternoon, on a green knoll, covered with mountain herbage, that crowned the brow of a precipice. From an opening between the trees he could overlook all the lower country for many a mile of rich woodland. He saw at a distance the lordly Hudson, far, far below him, moving on its silent but majestic course, with the reflection of a purple cloud, or the sail of a lagging bark, here and there sleeping on its glassy bosom, and at last losing itself in the blue highlands.

On the other side he looked down into a deep mountain glen, wild, lonely, and shagged, the bottom filled with fragments from the impending cliffs, and scarcely lighted by the reflected rays of the setting sun. For some time Rip lay musing on this scene ; evening was gradually advancing ; the mountains began to throw their long blue shadows over the valleys ; he saw that it would be dark long before he could reach

the village, and he heaved a heavy sigh
when he thought of encountering the terrors
of Dame Van Winkle.

As he was about to descend, he heard a
voice from a distance, hallooing, " Rip Van
Winkle ! Rip Van Winkle ! " He looked
round, but could see nothing but a crow
winging its solitary flight across the mountain.   He thought his fancy must have de-
ceived him, and turned again to descend,
when he heard the same cry ring through
the still evening air : " Rip Van Winkle !
Rip Van Winkle ! "—at the same time Wolf
bristled up his back, and giving a low
growl, skulked to his master's side, looking
fearfully down into the glen.   Rip now felt
a vague apprehension stealing over him ; he
looked anxiously in the same direction, and
perceived a strange figure slowly toiling up
the rocks, and bending under the weight of
something he carried on his back.   He was
surprised to see any human being in this
lonely and unfrequented place ; but supposing it to be some one of the neighborhood in need of his assistance, he hastened
down to yield it.

On nearer approach he was still more surprised at the singularity of the stranger's
apperance.   He was a short, square-built
old fellow, with thick bushy hair, and a
grizzled beard.   His dress was of the antique Dutch fashion—a cloth jerkin strapped
round the waist—several pair of breeches,

the outer one of ample volume, decorated
with rows of buttons down the sides, and
bunches at the knees. He bore on his
shoulder a stout keg, and made signs for
Rip to approach and assist him with the load.
Though rather shy and distrustful of this
new acquaintance, Rip complied with his
usual alacrity ; and mutually relieving one
another, they clambered up a narrow gully,
apparently the dry bed of a mountain torrent. As they ascended, Rip every now and
then heard long rolling peals like distant
thunder, that seemed to issue out of a deep
ravine, or rather cleft, between lofty rocks,
toward which their rugged path conducted.
He paused for a moment, but supposing it
to be the muttering of one of those transient
thunder-showers which often take place in
mountain heights, he proceeded. Passing
through the ravine, they came to a hollow,
like a small amphitheatre, surrounded by
perpendicular precipices, over the brinks of
which impending trees shot their branches,
so that you only caught glimpses of the
azure sky and the bright evening cloud.
During the whole time Rip and his companion had labored on in silence ; for
though the former marveled greatly what
could be the object of carrying such a
burden up this wild mountain, yet there
was something strange and incomprehensible about the unknown, that inspired awe
and checked familiarity.

On entering the amphitheatre, new objects of wonder presented themselves. On a level spot in the centre was a company of odd-looking personages playing at ninepins. They were dressed in a quaint outlandish fashion ; some wore short doublets, others jerkins, with long knives in their belts, and most of them had enormous breeches of similar style with that of the guide's. Their visages, too, were peculiar ; one had a large beard, broad face, and small piggish eyes ; the face of another seemed to consist entirely of nose, and was surmounted by a white sugar-loaf hat, set off with a little red cock's tail. They all had beards, of various shapes and colors. There was one who seemed to be the commander. He was a stout old gentleman, with a weatherbeaten countenance ; he wore a laced doublet, broad belt and hanger, high crowned hat and feather, red stockings, and highheeled shoes, with roses in them. The whole group reminded Rip of the figures in an old Flemish painting in the parlor of Dominie Van Shaick, the village parson, which had been brought over from Holland at the time of the settlement.

What seemed particularly odd to Rip was, that though these folks were evidently amusing themselves, yet they maintained the gravest faces, the most mysterious silence, and were, withal, the most melancholy party of pleasure he had ever

witnessed. Nothing interrupted the stillness
of the scene but the noise of the balls,
which, whenever they were rolled, echoed
along the mountains like rumbling peals of
thunder.

As Rip and his companion approached
them, they suddenly desisted from their
play, and stared at him with such fixed,
statue-like gaze, and such strange, uncouth,
lack-lustre countenances, that his heart
turned within him, and his knees smote together. At length his senses were over-
powered, his eyes swam in his head, his
head gradually declined, and he fell into a
deep sleep.

On waking, he found himself on the green
knoll whence he had first seen the old man
of the glen. He rubbed his eyes—it was a
bright, sunny morning. The birds were
hopping and twittering among the bushes,
and the eagle was wheeling aloft, and
breasting the pure mountain breeze.
"Surely," thought Rip, "I have not slept
here all night." He recalled the occur-
rences before he fell asleep. The strange
man with the keg—the mountain ravine—
the wild retreat among the rocks—the woe-
begone party at nine-pins—the flagon—
"Oh! that flagon! that wicked flagon!"
thought Rip—"what excuse shall I make
to Dame Van Winkle?"

He looked round for his gun, but in place
of the clean, well-oiled fowling-piece, he

found an old firelock lying by him, the barrel incrusted with rust, the lock falling off, and the stock worm-eaten. He now suspected that the grave roisterers of the mountain had put a trick upon him, and, having dosed him, had robbed him of his gun. Wolf, too, had disappeared, but he might have strayed away after a squirrel or partridge. He whistled after him, and shouted his name, but all in vain; the echoes repeated his whistle and shout, but no dog was to be seen.

He determined to revisit the scene of the last evening's gambol, and if he met with any of the party, to demand his dog and gun. As he rose to walk, he found himself stiff in the joints, and wanting in his usual activity. "These mountain beds do not agree with me," thought Rip, "and if this frolic should lay me up with a fit of the rheumatism, I shall have a blessed time with Dame Van Winkle." With some difficulty he got down into the glen; he found the gully up which he and his companion had ascended the preceding evening; but to his astonishment a mountain stream was now foaming down it, leaping from rock to rock, and filling the glen with babbling murmurs. He, however, made shift to scramble up its sides, working his toilsome way through thickets of birch, sassafras, and witch-hazel, and sometimes tripped up or entangled by the wild grape-vines that twisted their coils

or tendrils from tree to tree, and spread a
kind of net-work in his path.

At length he reached to where the ravine
had opened through the cliffs to the amphitheatre : but no traces of such opening remained. The rocks presented a high, impenetrable wall, over which the torrent came
tumbling in a sheet of feathery foam, and
fell into a broad, deep basin, black from the
shadows of the surrounding forests. Here,
then, poor Rip was brought to a stand. He
again called and whistled after his dog ; he
was only answered by the cawing of a flock
of idle crows, sporting high in air about a
dry tree that overhung a sunny precipice,
and who, secure in their elevation, seemed
to look down and scoff at the poor man's
perplexities. What was to be done? The
morning was passing away, and Rip felt
famished for want of his breakfast. He
grieved to give up his dog and gun ; he
dreaded to meet his wife ; but it would not
do to starve among the mountains. He
shook his head, shouldered the rusty firelock, and, with a heart full of trouble and
anxiety, turned his steps homeward.

As he approached the village he met a
number of people, but none whom he knew,
which somewhat surprised him, for he had
thought himself acquainted with every one
in the country round. Their dress, too,
was of a different fashion from that to which
he was accustomed. They all stared at him

with equal marks of surprise, and whenever they cast their eyes upon him, invariably stroked their chins. The constant recurrence of this gesture induced Rip, involuntarily, to do the same, when, to his astonishment, he found his beard had grown a foot long !

He had now entered the skirts of the village. A troop of strange children ran at his heels, hooting after him, and pointing at his gray beard. The dogs, too, not one of which he recognized for an old acquaintance, barked at him as he passed. The very village was altered ; it was larger and more populous. There were rows of houses which he had never seen before, and those which had been his familiar haunts had disappeared. Strange names were over the doors—strange faces at the windows—everything was strange. His mind now misgave him ; he began to doubt whether both he and the world around him were not bewitched. Surely this was his native village, which he had left but the day before. There stood the Kaatskill Mountains—there ran the silver Hudson at a distance—there was every hill and dale precisely as it had always been. Rip was sorely perplexed. " The revel last night," thought he, " has addled my poor head sadly ! "

It was with some difficulty that he found the way to his own house, which he approached with silent awe, expecting every

moment to hear the shrill voice of Dame
Van Winkle. He found the house gone to
decay—the roof fallen in, the windows shattered, and the doors off the hinges. A half-
starved dog that looked like Wolf was
skulking about it. Rip called him by
name, but the cur snarled, showed his teeth
and passed on. This was an unkind cut
indeed. " My very dog," sighed poor Rip,
" has forgotten me ! "

He entered the house, which, to tell the
truth, Dame Van Winkle had always kept
in neat order. It was empty, forlorn, and
apparently abandoned. This desolateness
overcame all his connubial fears—he called
loudly for his wife and children—the lonely
chambers rang for a moment with his voice,
and then again all was silence.

He now hurried forth, and hastened to
his old resort, the village inn—but it, too
was gone. A large, rickety, wooden building stood in its place, with great gaping
windows, some of them broken and mended
with old hats and petticoats, and over the
door was painted, "The Union Hotel, by
Jonathan Doolittle." Instead of the great
tree that used to shelter the quiet little
Dutch inn of yore, there now was reared a
tall naked pole, with something on the top
that looked like a red nightcap, and from it
was fluttering a flag, on which was a singular assemblage of stars and stripes—all
this was strange and incomprehensible. He

recognized on the sign, however, the ruby
face of King George, but even this was singularly metamorphosed. The red coat was
changed for one of blue and buff, a sword
was held in the hand instead of a sceptre,
the head was decorated with a cocked hat,
and underneath was painted in large charac-
ters, GENERAL WASHINGTON.

There was, as usual, a crowd of folk
about the door, but none that Rip recollected. The very character of the people
seemed changed. There was a busy, bust-
ling, disputatious tone about it, instead of
the accustomed phlegm and drowsy tranquillity. He looked in vain for the sage
Nicholas Vedder, with his broad face,
double chin, and fair long pipe, uttering
clouds of tobacco smoke instead of idle
speeches ; or Van Bummel, the schoolmaster, doling forth the contents of an ancient
newspaper. In place of these, a lean, bil-
ious fellow, with his pockets full of hand-
bills, was haranguing vehemently about
rights of citizens—elections—members of
Congress—liberty—Bunker's Hill—heroes
of seventy-six—and other words, which
were a perfect Babylonish jargon to the bewildered Van Winkle.

The appearance of Rip, with his long
grizzled beard, his rusty fowling-piece, his
uncouth dress, and an army of women and
children at his heels, soon attracted the
attention of the tavern politicians. They

crowded round him, eyeing him from head
to foot with great curiosity. The orator
bustled up to him, and, drawing him partly
aside, inquired "on which side he voted?"
Rip stared in vacant stupidity. Another
short but busy little fellow pulled him by
the arm, and, rising on tiptoe, inquired in
his ear, "Whether he was Federal or Dem-
ocrat?" Rip was equally at a loss to comprehend the question; when a knowing,
self-important old gentleman, in a sharp
cocked hat, made his way through the
crowd, putting them to the right and left
with his elbows as he passed, and planting
himself before Van Winkle, with one arm
akimbo, the other resting on his cane, his
keen eyes and sharp hat penetrating as it
were, into his very soul, demanded in an
austere tone, "what brought him to the
election with a gun on his shoulder and a
mob at his heels, and whether he meant to
breed a riot in the village?—"Alas! gentlemen," cried Rip, somewhat dismayed, "I
am a poor quiet man, a native of the place
and a loyal subject of the King, God bless
him!"

Here a general shout burst from the bystanders—"A tory! a tory! a spy! a refu-
gee! hustle him! away with him!" It
was with great difficulty that the self-
important man in the cocked hat restored
order; and, having assumed a tenfold aus-
terity of brow, demanded again of the

unknown culprit, what he came there for, and whom he was seeking? The poor man humbly assured him that he meant no harm, but merely came there in search of some of his neighbors, who used to keep about the tavern.

"Well—who are they?—name them."

Rip bethought himself a moment, and inquired, "Where's Nicholas Vedder?"

There was silence for a little while, when an old man replied, in a thin, piping voice, "Nicholas Vedder! why, he is dead and gone these eighteen years! There was a wooden tombstone in the church-yard that used to tell all about him, but that's rotten and gone too."

"Where's Brom Dutcher?"

"Oh, he went off to the army in the beginning of the war; some say he was killed at the storming of Stony Point—others say he was drowned in a squall at the foot of Antony's Nose. I don't know—he never came back again."

"Where's Van Bummel, the schoolmaster?"

"He went off to the wars too, was a great militia general, and is now in Congress."

Rip's heart died away at hearing of these sad changes in his home and friends, and finding himself thus alone in the world. Every answer puzzled him, too, by treating of such enormous lapses of time, and of matters which he could not understand:

war—Congress—Stony Point ;—he had no courage to ask after any more friends, but cried out in despair, "Does nobody here know Rip Van Winkle?"

"Oh, Rip Van Winkle?" exclaimed two or three. "Oh, to be sure ! that's Rip Van Winkle yonder, leaning against the tree."

Rip looked, and beheld a precise counterpart of himself as he went up the mountain : apparently as lazy, and certainly as ragged. The poor fellow was now completely confounded. He doubted his own identity, and whether he was himself or another man. In the midst of his bewilderment, the man in the cocked hat demanded who he was, and what was his name?

"I'm not myself !" he exclaimed. "I'm somebody else—that's me yonder—no— that's somebody else got into my shoes—I was myself last night, but I fell asleep on the mountain, and they've changed my gun, and everything's changed, and I'm changed, and I can't tell what's my name, or who I am !"

The bystanders began now to look at each other, nod, wink significantly, and tap their fingers against their foreheads. There was a whisper, also, about securing the gun, and keeping the old fellow from doing mischief, at the very suggestion of which the self-important man in the cocked hat retired with some precipitation. At this critical moment a fresh, comely woman pressed through the throng to get a peep at the gray-bearded man. She had a chubby child in her arms, which, frightened at his looks, began to cry. "Hush, Rip," she cried, "hush, you little fool; the old man won't hurt you." The name of the child, the air of the mother, the tone of her voice, all awakened a train of recollections in his mind. "What is your name, my good woman?" asked he.

"Judith Gardenier."

"And your father's name?"

"Ah, poor man, Rip Van Winkle was his name, but it's twenty years since he went away from home with his gun, and never has been heard of since,—his dog came home without him; but whether he shot himself, or was carried away by the Indians, nobody can tell. I was then but a little girl."

Rip had but one question more to ask; and he put it with a faltering voice.

"Where's your mother?"

"Oh, she too has died but a short time since; she broke a blood-vessel in a fit of passion at a New England peddler."

The honest man could contain himself no longer. He caught his daughter and her child in his arms. "I am your father!" cried he—"Young Rip Van Winkle once—old Rip Van Winkle now! Does nobody know poor Rip Van Winkle?"

All stood amazed, until an old woman

tottering out from among the crowd, put
her hand to her brow, and peering under it
in his face for a moment, exclaimed, "Sure
enough ! it is Rip Van Winkle—it is himself ! Welcome home again, old neighbor—
Why, where have you been these twenty
long years ?"

Rip's story was soon told, for the whole
twenty years had been to him but as one
night. The neighbors stared when they
heard it ; some were seen to wink at each
other, and put their tongues in their cheeks ;
and the self-important man in the cocked
hat, who, when the alarm was over, had
returned to the field, screwed down the
corners of his mouth, and shook his head—
upon which there was a general shaking of
the head throughout the assemblage.

It was determined, however, to take the
opinion of old Peter Vanderdonk, who was
seen slowly advancing up the road. He
was a descendant of the historian of that
name, who wrote one of the earliest accounts
of the province. Peter was the most ancient
inhabitant of the village, and well versed
in all the wonderful events and traditions
of the neighborhood. He recollected Rip
at once, and corroborated his story in
the most satisfactory manner. He assured
the company that it was a fact, handed
down from his ancestor the historian,
that the Kaatskill Mountains had always
been haunted by strange beings. That

it was affirmed that the great Hendrick Hudson, the first discoverer of the river and country, kept a kind of vigil there every twenty years, with his crew of the *Half-Moon ;* being permitted in this way to revisit the scenes of his enterprise, and keep a guardian eye upon the river, and the great city called by his name. That his father had once seen them in their old Dutch dresses playing at nine-pins in a hollow of the mountain ; and that he himself had heard, one summer afternoon, the sound of their balls, like distant peals of thunder.

To make a long story short, the company broke up, and returned to the more important concerns of the election. Rip's daughter took him home to live with her ; she had a snug, well-furnished house, and a stout, cheery farmer for a husband whom Rip recollected for one of the urchins that used to climb upon his back. As to Rip's son and heir, who was the ditto of himself, seen leaning against a tree, he was employed to work on the farm ; but evinced a hereditary disposition to attend to anything else but his business.

Rip now resumed his old walks and habits ; he soon found many of his former cronies, though all rather the worse for the wear and tear of time ; and preferred making friends among the rising generation, with whom he soon grew into great favor.

Having nothing to do at home, and being arrived at that happy age when a man can be idle with impunity, he took his place once more on the bench at the inn door, and was reverenced as one of the patriarchs of the village, and a chronicle of the old times '' before the war.'' It was some time before he could get into the regular track of gossip, or could be made to comprehend the strange events that had taken place during his torpor. How that there had been a revolutionary war—that the country had thrown off the yoke of old England—and that, instead of being a subject of his Majesty George the Third, he was now a free citizen of the United States. Rip, in fact, was no politician; the changes of states and empires made but little impression on him; but there was one species of despotism under which he had long groaned, and that was— petticoat government. Happily that was at an end; he had got his neck out of the yoke of matrimony, and he could go in and out whenever he pleased, without dreading the tyranny of Dame Van Winkle. Whenever her name was mentioned, however, he shook his head, shrugged his shoulders, and cast up his eyes; which might pass either for an expression of resignation to his fate, or joy at his deliverance.

He used to tell his story to every stranger that arrived at Mr. Doolittle's hotel. He was observed at first to vary on some points every time he told it, which was, doubtless, owing to his having so recently awakened. It at last settled down precisely to the tale I have related, and not a man, woman or child in the neighborhood but knew it by heart. Some always pretended to doubt the reality of it, and insisted that Rip had been out of his head, and that this was one point on which he always remained flighty.

The old Dutch inhabitants, however, almost universally gave it full credit. Even to this day they never hear a thunderstorm of a summer afternoon about the Kaatskill, but they say Hendrick Hudson and his crew are at their game of nine-pins; and it is a common wish of all henpecked husbands in the neighborhood, when life hangs heavy on their hands that they might have a quieting draught out of Rip Van Winkle's flagon.

THE LAZY CROW.

BY GILMORE SIMMS.

We were on the Savannah river when the corn was coming up; at the residence of one of those planters of the middle country, the staid, sterling, old time gentlemen of the last century, the stock of which is so rapidly diminishing. The season was advanced and beautiful; the flowers every where in odor, and all things promised well for the crops of the planter. Hopes and seed, however, set out in March and April, have a long time to go before ripening, and when I congratulated Mr. Carrington on the prospect before him, he would shake his head, and smile and say, in a quizzical inquiring humor, ' ''wet or dry, cold or warm, which shall it be? what season shall we have? Tell me that, and I will hearken with more confidence to your congratulations. We can do more than plant the seed, scuffle with the grass, say our prayers, and leave the rest to Him without whose blessing no labor can avail.''

'' There is something more to be done, and of scarcely less importance it would seem, if I may judge from the movements of Scipio—kill or keep off the crows.''

Mr. Carrington turned as I spoke these words ; we had just left the breakfast table, where we had enjoyed all the warm comforts of hot rice-waffles, journey-cake, and glowing biscuit, not to speak of hominy and hoe-cake, without paying that passing acknowledgment to dyspeptic dangers upon which modern physicians so earnestly insist. Scipio, a sleek, well-fed negro, with a round, good-humored face, was busy in the corner of the apartment ; one hand employed in grasping a goodly fragment of bread, half-concealed in a similar slice of bacon, which he had just received from his young mistress ;— while the other carefully selected from the corner, one of half-a-dozen double-barrelled guns, which he was about to raise to his shoulder, when my remark turned the eye of his master upon him.

"How now, Scipio, what are you going to shoot?" was the inquiry of Mr. Carrington.

"Crow, sah; dere's a ugly crow dat's a-troubling me, and my heart's set for kill um."

"One only? why Scip, you're well off if you hav'n't a hundred. Do they trouble you very much in the pine land field?"

"Dare's a plenty, sah; but dis one I guine kill, sah, he's wuss more nor all de rest. You hab good load in bot' barrel, massa?"

"Yes, but small shot only. Draw the load, Scip, and put in some of the high duck; you'll find the bag in the closet. These crows will hardly let you get nigh enough, Scipio, to do them any mischief with small shot."

"Ha! but I will trouble dis black rascal, you see, once I set eye 'pon um. He's a ugly nigger, and he a'n't feared. I can git close 'nough, massa."

The expression of Scipio's face, while uttering the brief declaration of war against the innumerable and almost licensed pirates of the cornfield, or rather against one in particular, was full of the direst hostility. His accents were not less marked by malignity, and could not fail to command our attention.

"Why, you seem angry about it, Scipio ; this crow must be one of the most impudent of his tribe, and a distinguished character."

"I'll 'stinguish um, massa—you'll see. Jist as you say, he's a mos' impudent nigger. He no feared of me 't all. When I stan' and look 'pon him, he stan' and look 'pon me. I tak' up dirt and stick, and trow at um, but he no scare. When I chase um, he fly dis way, he fly dat, but he nebber gone so far, but he can turn round and cock he tail at me, jist when he see me stop. He's a mos' d—n sassy crow, as ebber walk in a cornfield."

"But, Scipio, you surprise me. You don't mean to say that it is one crow in particular that annoys you in this manner."

"De same one, ebbery day, massa ; de same one," was the reply.

"How long has this been?"

"Mos' a week now, massa ; ebber since las' Friday."

"Indeed ! but what makes you think this troublesome crow always the same one, Scipio? Do you think the crows never change their spies?"

"Golly, I know um, massa ; dis da same crow been trouble me ebber since las' Friday. He's a crow by hese'f, massa. I nebber see him wid t'oder crows ; he no hab complexion of t'oder crow, yet he's crow, all de same."

" Is he not black, like all his tribe ? "

" Yes, he black, but he ain't black like de oder ones. Dere's something like a gray dirt 'pon he wing. He's black, but he no gloss black—no jet ; he hab dirt, I tell you, massa, on he wing, jis' by de skirt ob de jacket—jis' here ; " and he lifted the lapel of his master's coat, as he concluded his description of the bird that troubled him.

" A strange sort of crow indeed, Scipio, if he answers your description. Should you kill him, be sure and bring him to me. I can scarcely think him a crow."

" How no crow, massa ? Golly, I know crow good as anybody. He's a crow, massa—a dirty, black nigger of a crow, and I'll shoot um through he head, sure as a gun. He trouble me too much ; look hard 'pon me as if you hab bin gib um wages for obersee. Nobody ax um for watch me, see wha' I do ! Who mak' him ober-seer ? "

" A useful crow, Scipio ; and now I think of it, it might be just as well that you shouldn't shoot him. If he does such good service in the cornfield as to see that you all do your work, I'll make him my overseer in my absence ! "

This speech almost astounded the negro. He dropped the butt of the gun upon the floor, suffered the muzzle to rest in the

hollow of his arm, and thus boldly expos-
tulated with his master against so strange a
decision.

''No shoot um, massa ; no shoot crow
dat's a-troubling you ? Dickens, massa, but
dat's too foolish now, I mus' tell you ; and
to tell you de blessed trut', if you don't
shoot dis lazy crow I tell you ob, or le' me
shoot um, one or t'oder, den you mus' take
Scip out of de cornfiel', and put 'n oder
nigger in he place. I can't work wid dat
ugly ting looking at me so sassy. When I
turn, he turn ; if I go to dis hand, why,
he's dere ; if I change 'bout, and go t'oder
hand, dere's de critter, jis' de same. He
nebber git out of de way till I run at um
wid a stick.''

'' Well, well, Scipio, kill your crow, but
be sure and bring him in when you do so.
You may go now.''

'' I hab um to-night for you, massa, ef
God spare me. Look 'a, young missus,
you hab any coffee lef' in de pot ; I tanks
you.''

Jane Carrington—a gentle and lovely girl
of seventeen—who did the honors of the
table, supplied Scipio's wants, and leaving
him to the enjoyment of his mug of coffee,
Mr. C. and myself walked forth into the
plantation.

The little dialogue just narrated had almost entirely passed out of my mind, when,
at evening, returning from his labors in the

cornfield, who should make his appearance
but Scipio. He came to place the gun in
the corner from which he had taken it ; but
he brought no trophies of victory. He had
failed to scalp his crow. The inquiry of his
master as to his failure drew my attention
to the negro, who had simply placed the
weapon in the rest, and was about to retire,
with a countenance, as I thought, rather
sullen and dissatisfied, and a hangdog,
sneaking manner, as if anxious to escape
observation. He had utterly lost that air
of confidence which he had worn in the
morning.

"What, Scipio! no crow?" demanded
his master.

"I no shoot, sah," replied the negro, moving off as he spoke, as if willing that the
examination should rest there. But Mr.
Carrington, who was something of a quiz,
and saw that the poor fellow labored under
a feeling of mortified self-conceit, was not
unwilling to worry him a little further.

"Ah, Scip, I always thought you a poor
shot, in spite of your bragging ; now I am
sure of it. A crow comes and stares you
out of countenance, walks round you, and
scarcely flies when you pelt him, and yet,
when the gun is in your hands, you do
nothing. . How's that?"

"I tell you, massa, I no bin shoot. Ef
I bin shoot, I bin hurt um in he head for
true ; but dere no use for shoot tel you can

get shot, inty? Wha' for trow 'way de
shot?—you buy 'em—becos' you money ;
well, you hab money for trow 'way? No !
Wha' den – Scip's a rascal for true, ef he
trow 'way you money. Dat's trow 'way
you money, wha's trow 'way you shot—
wha's trow you corn, you peas, you fodder,
you hog-meat, you chickens and eggs.
Scip nebber trow 'way you property, massa ;
nobody nebber say sich ting."

" Cunning dog—nobody accuses you,
Scipio. I believe you to be as honest as
the rest, Scipio, but haven't you been
throwing away time? Haven't you been
poking about after this crow to the neglect
of your duty? Come, in plain language,
did you get through your task to-day?"

" Task done, massa ; I finish um by three
o'clock."

" Well, what did you do with the rest of
your time? Have you been at your own
garden, Scipio?"

" No, sah ; I no touch de garden."

" Why not? what employed you from
three o'clock?"

" Dis same crow, massa ; I tell you,
massa, 'tis dis same nigger of a crow I bin
looking arter, ebber since I git over de task.
He's a ting da's too sassy, and aggrabates
me berry much. I follow um tel de sun
shut he eye, and nebber can git shot. Ef I
bin git shot, I nebber miss um, massa, I tell
you."

"But why did you not get a shot? You must have bungled monstrously, Scipio, not to succeed in getting a shot at a bird that is always about you. Does he bother you less than he did before, now that you have the gun?"

"I spec' he mus' know, massa, da's de reason; but he bodder me jis' de same. He nebber leff me all day I bin in de cornfield, but he nebber come so close for be shoot. He say to he sef, dat gun good at sixty yard, in Scip hand; I stan' sixty, I stan' a hundred; ef he shoot so far, I laf at 'em. Da's wha' he say."

"Well, even at seventy or eighty yards, you should have tried him, Scipio. The gun that tells at sixty, will be very apt to tell at seventy or eighty yards, if the nerves be good that hold it, and the eye close. Try him even at a hundred, Scipio, rather than lose your crow; but put in your biggest shot."

The conference ended with this counsel of the master. The fellow promised to obey, and the next morning he sallied forth with the gun as before. By this time, both Mr. Carrington and myself had begun to take some interest in the issue thus tacitly made up between the field negro and his annoying visitor. The anxiety which the former manifested, to destroy, in particular, one of a tribe, of which the corn-planter has an aversion so great as to prompt the

frequent desire of the Roman tyrant touching his enemies, and make him wish that they
had but one neck that a single blow might
dispatch them, was no less ridiculous than
strange ; and we both fell to our fancies to
account for a hostility, which could not
certainly be accounted for by any ordinary
anxiety of the good planter on such an
occasion. It was evident to both of us that
the imagination of Scipio was not inactive in
the strife, and knowing how exceeding
supertitious the negroes generally are, (and
indeed, all inferior people,) after canvassing
the subject in various lights, without coming
to any rational solution, we concluded that
the difficulty arose from some grotesque
fear or fancy, with which the fellow had
been inspired, probably by some other
negro, on a circumstance as casual as any one
of the thousand by which the Roman augur
divined, and the soothsayer gave forth his
oracular predictions. Scipio had good
authority for attaching no small importance to the flight or stoppage of a bird ;
and with this grave justification of his troubles, we resolved to let the matter rest, till
we could join the negro in the cornfield, and
look for ourselves into the condition of the
rival parties.

This we did that very morning. "Possum
Place"—for such had been the whimsical
name conferred upon his estate by the proprietor, in reference to the vast numbers of

the little animal nightly found upon it, the opossum, the meat of which a sagacious negro will always prefer to that of pig,—lay upon the Santee swamp, and consisted pretty evenly of reclaimed swamp-land, in which he raised his cotton, and fine high pine-land hammock, on which he made his corn. To one of the fields of the latter we made our way about mid-day, and were happy to find Scipio in actual controversy with the crow that troubled him. Controversy is scarce the word, but I can find no fitter, at this moment. The parties were some hundred yards asunder. The negro was busy with his hoe, and the gun leaned conveniently at hand on a contiguous and charred pine stump, one of a thousand that dotted the entire surface of the spacious field in which he labored. The crow leisurely passed to and fro along the alleys, now lost among the little hollows and hillocks, and now emerging into sight, sometimes at a less, sometimes at a greater distance, but always with a deportment of the most brass-like indifference to the world around him. His gait was certainly as lordly and as lazy as that of a Castilian the third remove from a king and the tenth from a shirt. We could discover in him no other singularity but this marked audacity; and both Mr. Carrington's eyes and mine were stretched beyond their orbits, but in vain, to discover that speck of "gray dirt upon he wing," which

Scipio had been very careful to describe
with the particularity of one who felt that
the duty would devolve on him to brush the
jacket of the intruder. We learned from
the negro that his sooty visitor had come
alone as usual,—for though there might
have been a sprinkling of some fifty crows
here and there about the field, we could not
perceive that any of them had approached
to any more familiarity with that one that
annoyed him, than with himself. He had
been able to get no shot as yet, though he
did not despair of better fortune through
the day ; and in order to the better assurance of his hopes, the poor fellow had borne
what he seemed to consider the taunting
swagger of the crow all around him, without so much as lifting weapon, or making a
single step toward him.

" Give me your gun," said Mr. Carrington. " If he walks no faster than now, I'll
give him greater weight to carry."

But the lazy crow treated the white man
with a degree of deference that made the
negro stare. He made off at full speed with
the first movement toward him, and disappeared from sight in a few seconds. We
lost him seemingly among the willows and
fern of a little bay that lay a few hundred
yards beyond us.

" What think you of that, Scip ? " demanded the master. " I've done more with
a single motion than you've done for days,

with all your poking and pelting. He'll hardly trouble you in a hurry again, though if he does, you know well enough now how, to get rid of him."

The negro's face brightened for an instant, but suddenly changed, while he replied,—

" Ah, massa, when you back turn, he will come gen—he dah watch you now."

Sure enough—we had not proceeded a hundred yards, before the calls of Scipio drew our attention to the scene we had left. The negro had his hands uplifted with an air of horror, while a finger guided us to the spot where the lazy crow was taking his rounds, almost in the very place from whence the hostile advance of Mr. Carrington had driven him ; and with a listless, lounging strut of aristocratic composure, that provoked our wonder quite as much as the negro's indignation.

" Let us see it out," said Mr. C., returning to the scene of action. "At him, Scipio; take your gun and do your best."

But this did not seem necessary. Our return to the scene of action had the effect of sending the sooty intruder to a distance, and after lingering some time to see if he would re-appear while we were present, but without success, we concluded to retire from the ground.

Some days passed by, and I saw nothing of Scipio. It appears, however, that his singular conflict with the lazy crow was

carried on with such pertinacity on the one
side, and as little patience on the other, as
before. Still, daily did he provide himself
with the weapon and munitions of war,
making as much fuss in loading it, and
putting in shot as large as if he proposed
warfare on some of the more imposing occupants of the forest, rather than a simple
bird, so innocent in all respects, except the
single one of corn stealing, as the crow. A
fact, of which we obtained possession some
time after, and from the other negroes, enlightened us somewhat on the subject of
Scipio's own faith as to the true character
of his enemy. In loading his gun he
counted out his shot, being careful to get an
odd number. In using big buck, he numbered two sevens for a load ; the small buck,
three ; and seven times seven duck shot,
when he used the latter, were counted out
as a charge, with the studious nicety of the
jeweler at his pearls and diamonds. Then
followed the mystic process of depositing the
load within the tube, from which it was to
issue forth in death and devastation. His
face was turned from the sunlight ; the
blaze was not suffered to rest upon the bore
or barrel ; and when the weapon was
charged, it was carried into the field only
on his left shoulder. In spite of all these
preparations, the lazy crow came and went
as before. He betrayed no change of demeanor ; he showed no more consciousness

of danger ; he submitted to pursuit quietly,
never seeming to hurry himself in escaping,
and was quite as close an overseer of
Scipio's conduct, as he had shown himself
from the first. Not a day passed that the
negro failed to shoot at him ; always, however, by his own account, at disadvantage,
and never, it appears, with any success.
The consequence of all this was, that Scipio
fell sick. What with the constant annoy-
ance of the thing, and a too excitable imagination, Scipio, a stout fellow nearly six feet
high, and half as many broad, laid himself
at length in his cabin, at the end of the
week, and was placed on the sick list accordingly. But as a negro will never take
physic, if he can help it, however ready he
may be to complain, it was not till Sunday
afternoon, that Jane Carrington, taking her
customary stroll on that day to the negro
quarters, ascertained the fact. She at once
apprised her father, who was something of
a physician (as every planter should be),
and who immediately proceeded to visit the
invalid. He found him without any of the
customary signs of sickness. His pulse was
low and feeble, rather than full or fast ; his
tongue tolerably clean ; his skin not unpleasant, and in all ordinary respects Scipio
would have been pronounced in very good
condition for his daily task, and his hog
and hominy. The more the master observed him, the more difficult it became to

utter an opinion ; and he was finally compelled to leave him for the night, without
medicine, judging it wiser to let nature take
the subject in hand, until he could properly
determine in what respect he suffered. But
the morrow brought no alleviation of
Scipio's sufferings. He was still sick as
before—incapable of work—indeed, as he
alleged, unable to leave his bed, though his
pulse was a little exaggerated from the night
previous, and exhibited only that degree of
energy and fullness, which might be supposed natural to one moved by sudden
physical excitement.

Mr. C. was puzzled, and concluded to
avoid the responsibility of such a case, by
sending for the neighboring physician. Dr.
C——, a very clever and well-read man,
soon made his appearance, and was regularly introduced to the patient. His replies
to the physician were as little satisfactory
as those which he had made to us ; and after
a long and tedious cross-examination by
doctor and master, the conclusion was still
the same. Some few things, however,
transpired in the inquiry, which led us all
to the same inference with the doctor, who
ascribed Scipio's condition to some mental
hallucination. While the conversation had
been going on in his cabin—a dwelling like
most negro houses, made with poles, and
the chinks stopped with clay—he turned abruptly from the physician to a negro girl

that brought him soup, and asked the following question :

" Who bin tell Gullah Sam for come in yer yisserday ? "

The girl looked confused and made no answer.

" Answer him," said the master.

" Da's him—why you no talk, nigger ? " said the patient authoritatively. " I ax you, who bin tell Gullah Sam for come in yer yisserday ? "

" He bin come ? " responded the girl with another inquiry.

" Sure, he bin come—enty I see um wid he dirty gray jacket, like dirt on a crow wing ? He tink I no see um—he 'tan der in dis corner, close de chimney, and look wha's a cook in de pot. Oh, how my ear bu'n—somebody's a talking bad tings about Scipio now."

There was a good deal in this speech to interest Mr. Carrington and myself; we could trace something of illness to his strife with the crow ; but who was Gullah Sam ? This was a question put both by the doctor and myself at the same moment.

" Yoo no know Gullah Sam, enty ? Ha ! better you don't know um—he's a nigger da's more dan nigger—wish he mind he own business."

With these words the patient turned his face to the wall of his habitation, and seemed unwilling to vouchsafe us any

further speech. It was thought unnecessary
to annoy poor Scipio with further inquiries,
and leaving the cabin, we obtained the desired information from his master.

" Gullah Sam," said he, " is a native
born African from the Gold Coast, who belongs to my neighbor, Mr. Jamison, and
was bought by his father out of a Rhode
Island slaver, some time before the Revolu-
tion. He is now, as you may suppose,
rather an old man ; and, to all appearances,
would seem a simple and silly one enough ;
but the negroes all around regard him to be
a great conjuror, and look upon his powers
as a wizard, with a degree of dread, only to
be accounted for by the notorious supersti-
tion of ignorance. The little conversation
which we have had with Scipio, in his
partial delirium, has revealed to me what
a sense of shame has kept him from de-
claring before. He believes himself to be
bewitched by Gullah Sam."

" And what do you propose to do ? " was
my inquiry.

" Nay, that question I cannot answer you.
It is a work of philosophy, rather than of
physic, and we must become the masters of
the case, before we can prescribe for it. We
must note the fancies of the patient himself,
and make these subservient to the case. I
know of no other remedy."

That evening, we all returned to the cabin
of Scipio. We found him more composed,

sane, perhaps, would be the proper word, than in the morning, and accordingly, perfectly silent on the subject of Gullah Sam. His master took the opportunity of speaking to him in plain language.

"Scipio, why do you try to keep the truth from me? Have you ever found me a bad master, that you should fear to tell me the truth?"

"Nebber say sich ting! Who tell you, massa I say you bad?" replied the negro with a lofty air of indignation, rising on his arm in the bed.

"Why should you keep the truth from me?" was the reply.

"Wha' trute I keep from you, massa?"

"The cause of your sickness, Scipio. Why did you not tell me that Gullah Sam had bewitched you?"

The negro was confounded.

"How you know, massa?" was his demand.

"It matters not," replied the master, "but how came Gullah Sam to bewitch you?"

"He kin 'witch, den, massa?" was the rather triumphant demand of the negro, who saw in his master's remark, a concession to his faith, which had always been withheld before. Mr. Carrington extricated himself from the dilemma with sufficient promptness and ingenuity.

"The devil has power, Scipio, over all

that believe in him. If you believe that
Gullah Sam can do with you what he
pleases, in spite of God and the Saviour,
there is no doubt that he can ; and God and
the Saviour will alike give you up to his
power, since when you believe in the devil,
you refuse to believe in them. They have
told you, and the preacher has told you,
and I have told you, that Gullah Sam can
do you no sort of harm, if you will refuse
to believe in what he tells you. Why then
do you believe in that miserable and ignorant old African, sooner than in God, and
the preacher, and myself?''

''I can't help it, massa—de ting's de ting,
and you can't change um. Dis Gullah Sam
—he wuss more nor ten debble—I jis' laugh
at um t'other day—tree week 'go when he
tumble in the hoss pond, and he shake he
finger at me, and ebber since, he put he bad
mout' 'pon me. Ebber sence dat time, dat
ugly crow bin stand in my eyes, whichebber
way I tu'n. He hab gray dirt on he wing,
and enty dere's a gray patch on Gullah Sam
jacket? Gullah Sam hab close quaintan'
wid dat same lazy crow da's walk roun' me
in de cornfield, massa. I bin tink so from
de fuss ; and when he 'tan and le' me shoot
at um, and no 'fraid, den I sartain.''

''Well, Scipio,'' said the master, ''I will
soon put an end to Sam's power. I will see
Mr. Jamison, and will have Sam well
flogged for his witchcraft. I think you

ought to be convinced that a wizard who
suffers himself to be flogged, is but a poor
devil after all.''

The answer of the negro was full of consternation.

''Massa, I beg you do no sich ting. Yo
lick Gullah Sam, den you loss Scipio for
eber and eber, amen. Gullah Sam nebber
guine take off de bad mout' he put on Scip,
once you lick em.''

A long conversation ensued among us,
Scipio taking occasional part in it ; for, now
that his secret was known, he seemed somewhat relieved, and gave utterance freely to
his fears and superstitions ; and determined
for and against the remedies which we
severally proposed, with the authority of
one, not only more deeply interested in the
case than any one beside, but who also knew
more about it. Having unscrupulously opposed nearly every plan, even in its incep-
tion, which was suggested, his master, out
of patience, at last exclaimed,

''Well, Scipio, it seems nothing will
please you. What would you have ? What
course shall I take to dispossess the devil,
and send Gullah Sam about his business?''

After a brief pause, in which the negro
twisted from side to side of his bed, he
answered as follows :

''Ef you kin trow away money on Scip,
massa, dere's a way I tink 'pon, dat'll do
um help, if dere's any ting kin help um

now, widout go to Gullah Sam. But it's a
berry 'spensive way, massa."

" How much will it cost?" demanded the
master. " I am not unwilling to pay money
for you, either to cure you when you are
sick, as you ought to know, by my sending
for the doctor, or by putting more sense into
your head than you seem to have at present.
How much money do you think it will take
to send the devil out of you?"

"Ha! massa, you no speak 'spectful
'nough. Dis Gullah Sam hard to move;
more dan de lazy crow dat walk in de cornfield. He will take money 'nough; mos' a
bag ob cotton in dese hard times."

" Pshaw—speak out, and tell me what
you mean!" said the now thoroughly impatient master.

" Dere's an old nigger, massa, dat's an
Ebo—he lib ober on St. Matthew's, by de
bluff, place of Major Thompson. He's
mighty great hand for cure bad mout'. He's
named 'Tuselah, and Gullah Sam fear'd um
—berry fear'd um. You send for 'Tuselah,
massa, he cos' you more nor twenty dollars.
Scipio git well for sartin."

" If I thought so," replied Mr. Carrington, looking round upon us, as if himself
half-ashamed to give in to the suggestions
of the negro. " But, you shall have your
wish, Scipio. I will send a man to-morrow
by daylight to St. Matthew's for Methuselah, and if he can overcome Gullah Sam

at his own weapons, I shall not begrudge
him the twenty dollars."

"Tanks, massa, tousand tanks!" was
the reply of the invalid; his countenance
suddenly brightening for the first time for a
week, as if already assured of the happy
termination of his affliction.   Meanwhile,
we left him to his cogitations.

The indulgent master that night addressed
a letter to the owner of Methuselah, stating
all the circumstances of the case, and solic-
iting permission for the wizard, of whom
such high expectations were formed, or
fancied, to return with the messenger, who
took with him an extra horse, that the journey might be made with sufficient dispatch.
To this application a ready assent was given,
and the messenger returned on the day after
his departure, attended by the sage African
in question.   Methuselah was an African,
about sixty-five years of age, with a head
round as an owl's, and a countenance quite
as grave and contemplative.   His features
indicated all the marked characteristics of
his race, low forehead, high cheek bone,
small eyes, flat.nose, thick lips, and a chin
sharp and retreating. He was not more than
five feet high, and with legs so bowed that
—to use Scipio's expression, when he was
so far recovered as to be able again to laugh
at his neighbor—a yearling calf might
easily run between them without grazing
the *calf*. There was nothing promising in

such a person but his sententiousness and gravity, and Methuselah possessed these characteristics in a remarkable degree. When asked—

"Can you cure this fellow?" his answer, almost insolently expressed, was,—

"I come for dat."

"You can cure people who are bewitched?"

"He no dead?"

"No."

"Bally well—can't cure dead nigger."

There was but little to be got out of such a character by examination, direct or cross ; and attending him to Scipio's wigwam, we tacitly resolved to look as closely into his proceedings as we could, assured, that in no other way could we possibly hope to arrive at any knowledge of his *modus operandi* in so curious a case.

Scipio was very glad to see the wizard of St. Matthew's, and pointing to a chair, the only one in his chamber, he left us to the rude stools, of which there happened to be a sufficient supply.

"Well, brudder," said the African abruptly, "wha's matter?"

"Ha, Mr. 'Tuselah, I bin hab berry bad mout' put 'pon me."

"I know dat—you eyes run water—you ears hot—you hab knee shake—you trimble in de joint."

"You hit um ; 'tis jis' dem same ting. I hab ears bu'n berry much," and thus encouraged to detail his symptoms, the garrulous Scipio would have prolonged his chronicle to the crack of doom, but that the wizard valued his time too much, to suffer any unnecessary eloquence on the part of his patient.

"You see two tings at a time?" asked the African.

"How! I no see," replied Scipio, not comprehending the question, which simply meant, do you ever see double? To this, when explained, he answered in a decided negative.

"'Tis a man den, put he bad mout' 'pon you," said the African.

"How you know dat?" exclaimed Scipio.

"Hush, my brudder—wha' beas' he look like?"

"He's a black nigger of a crow—a dirty crow, da's lazy for true."

"Ha! he lazy—you sure he ain't lame?"

"He no lame."

Scipio then gave a close description of the crow which had pestered him, precisely as he had given it to his master, as recorded in our previous pages. The African heard him with patience, then proceeded with oracular gravity.

"'Tis old man wha's troubles you!" ·

"Da's a trute!"

"Hush, my brudder. Wha's you see dis crow?"

"Crow in de cornfiel', Mr. 'Tuselah; he can't come in de house."

"Who bin wid you all de time?"

"Jenny—de gal—he 'tan up in de corner now."

The magician turned and looked upon the person indicated by Scipio's finger—a little negro girl, probably ten years old. Then turning again to Scipio, he asked,

"You bin sick two, tree, seben day, brudder—how long you been on you bed?"

"Since Saturday night—da's six day to-day."

"And you hab nobody come for look 'pon you, since you have been on de bed, but dis gal, and de buckrah?"

Scipio confessed to several of the field negroes, servants of his own master, all of whom he proceeded to describe in compliance with the requisitions of the wizard, who, as if still unsatisfied, bade him, in stern accents, remember if nobody else had been in the cabin, or, in his own language, had "set he eye 'pon you."

The patient hesitated for awhile, but the question being repeated, he confessed that in a half-sleep or stupor, he had fancied seeing Gullah Sam looking in upon him through the half-opened door; and at another time had caught glimpses, in his sleep, of the same features, through a chink between the logs, where the clay had fallen.

"Ha! ha!" said the wizard, with a half-savage grin of mingled delight and sagacity —"I hab nose—I smell. Well, brudder, I

mus' gib you physic—you mus' hab good
sweat to-night, and smood skin to-morrow."

Thus ended the conference with Scipio.
The man of mystery arose and left the hovel,
bidding us follow, and carefully fastening
the door after him.

This done, he anointed some clay which
he gathered in the neighborhood, with his
spittle, and plastered it over the lintel. He
retired with us a little distance, and when
we were about to separate, he for the woods,
and we for the dwelling-house, he said in
tones more respectful than those which he
employed to Mr. Carrington on his first
coming.

"You hab niggers, massa—women in de
bes'—dat lub for talk too much ?"

"Yes, a dozen of them."

"You sen' one to de plantation where dis
Gullah Sam lib, but don't sen' um to Gullah
Sam ; sen' um to he massa or he misses ;
and borrow something—any ting—old pot
or kettle—no matter if you don't want 'em,
you beg um for lend you. Da's 'nough."

Mr. Carrington would have had the
wizard's reasons for the wish, but finding
him reluctant to declare them, he promised
his consent, concluding, as was perhaps the
case, that the only object was to let Gullah
Sam know that a formidable enemy had
taken the field against him, and in defence
of his victim. This would seem to account
for his desire that the messenger should be

a woman, and one "wha' lub for talk too much." He then obtained directions for the nearest path to the swamp, and when we looked, that night, into the wigwam of Scipio, we found him returned with a peck of roots of sundry sorts, none of which we knew, prepared to make a decoction, in which his patient was to be immersed from head to heels. Leaving Scipio with the contemplation of this steaming prospect before him, we retired for the night, not a little anxious for those coming events which cast no shadow before us, or one so impenetrably thick, that we failed utterly to see through it.

In the morning, strange to say, we found Scipio considerably better, and in singularly good spirits. The medicaments of the African, or more likely the pliant imagination of the patient himself, had wrought a charm in his behalf; and instead of groaning at every syllable, as he had done for several days before, he now scarcely uttered a word that was not accompanied by a grin. The magician seemed scarcely less pleased than his patient, particularly when he informed us that he had not only obtained the article the woman was sent to borrow, but that Gullah Sam had been seen prowling, late at night, about the negro houses, without daring, however, to venture nigh that of the invalid—a forbearance which the necromancer gave us to understand, was

entirely involuntary, and in spite of the
enemy's desire, who was baffled and kept
away by the spell contained in the ointment
which he had placed on the lintel, in our
presence the evening before.   Still, half-
ashamed of being even quiescent parties
merely to this solemn mummery, we were
anxious to see the end of it, and our African
promised that he would do much toward
relieving Scipio from his enchantment by
night of the same day.   His spells and
fomentations had worked equally well, and
Scipio was not only more confident in mind,
but more sleek and strong in body.   With
his own hands, it appears, that the wizard
had rubbed down the back and shoulders of
his patient with corn-shucks steeped in the
decoction he had made, and, what was a
more strange specific still, he had actually
subjected Scipio to a smarter punishment,
with a stout hickory, than his master had
given him for many a year ; and which the
poor fellow not only bore with Christian
fortitude, but actually rejoiced in, imploring
additional strokes when the other ceased.
We could very well understand that Scipio
deserved a whipping for laughing at an aged
man, because he fell into the water, but we
failed to ascertain from the taciturn wizard,
that this was the rationale of an application
which a negro ordinarily is never found to
approve.   This over, Scipio was again put
to bed, a green twig hung over the door

of his cabin within, while the unctuous plaster was renewed freshly on the outside. The African then repeated certain uncouth sounds over the patient, bade him shut his eyes and go to sleep, in order to be in readiness, and go into the fields by the time the sun was turning for the west.

"What," exclaimed Mr. Carrington, "do you think him able to go into the field to-day? He is very weak; he has taken little nourishment for several days."

"He mus' able," returned the imperative African; "he 'trong 'nough. He mus' able—he hab for carry gun."

With these words, the wizard left us, without deigning any explanation of his future purposes, and taking his way toward the swamp, he was soon lost to our eyes in the mighty depth of its shrouding recesses.

When he returned, which was not till noon, he came at once to the mansion-house, without seeking his patient, and entering the hall where the family was assembled, he challenged our attention, as well by his appearance, as by his words. He had, it would seem, employed himself in arranging his own appearance while in the swamp; perhaps, taking one of its thousand lakes or ponds for his mirror. His woolly hair, which was very long, was plaited carefully up, so that the ends stuck out from his brow, as prompt and pointedly as the tails of pigs, suddenly aroused to a show of delightful consciousness on discovering a forgotten corn-heap. Perhaps that sort of tobacco, known by the attractive and characteristic title of "pigtail," would be the most fitting to convey to the mind of the reader the peculiar form of plait which the wizard had adopted for his hair. This mode of disposing of his matted mop, served to display the tattooed and strange figures upon his temples—the certain signs, as he assured us, of princely rank in his native country. He carried a long wand in his hand, freshly cut and peeled, at one end of which he had tied a small hempen cord. The skin of the wand was plaited round his own neck. In a large leaf he brought with him a small portion of something which he seemed to preserve very carefully, but which appeared to us to be nothing more than coarse sand or gravel. To this, he added a small portion of salt, which he obtained from the mistress of the house, and which he stirred together in our presence, until the salt had been lost to the eye in the sand or gravel, or whatever might have been the article which he had brought with him. This done, he drew the shot from both barrels of the gun, and in its place, deposited the mixture which he had thus prepared.

"Buckrah will come 'long now. Scipio gwine look for de crow."

Such were his words, which he did not wait to hear answered or disputed, but taking the gun and leading the way off toward the wigwam of Scipio, while our anxiety to see the conclusion of the adventure did not suffer us to lose any time in following him. To our surprise, we found Scipio dressed and up ; ready, and it would seem perfectly able, to undertake what the African assigned him. The gun was placed in his hands, and he was told to take his way to the cornfield as usual, and proceed to work. He was also informed by the wizard, with a confidence that surprised us, that the lazy crow would be sure to be there as usual ; and he was desired to get as close as he could, and take good aim at his head in shooting him.

" You sure for hit um, brudder," said the African ; "so don't 'tan' too long for look. Jis' you git close, take you sight, and gib um bot' barrel. But fuss, 'fore you go, I mus' do someting wid you eye."

The plaster was taken from the door, as Scipio passed through it, re-softened with the saliva of the wizard, who, with his finger, described an arched line over each of the patient's eyes.

" You go 'long by you'sef now, brudder, and shoot de crow when you see um. He's a waiting for you now, I 'spec'."

We were about to follow Scipio to the field, but our African kept us back ; and leading the way to a little copse that divided it from the swamp, he took us to its shelter, and required us to remain with him out of sight of the field, until some report from Scipio or his gun, should justify us in going forth.

Here we remained, in no little anxiety, for the space of two hours, in which time, however, the African showed no sort of impatience, and none of that feverish anxiety which made us restless in body, and, eager to the last degree, in mind. We tried to fathom his mysteries, but in vain. We heard the sound of Scipio's gun—and set off with full speed toward the quarter whence it came. The wizard followed us slowly, waving his wand in circles all the way, and pulling the withes from his neck, and casting them around him as he came. During this time, his mouth was in constant motion, and I could hear at moments, strange, uncouth sounds breaking from his lips. When he reached Scipio, the fellow was in a state little short of delirium. He had fired both barrels, and had cast the gun down upon the ground after the discharge. He was wringing his hands above his head in a sort of frenzy of joy, and at our approach he threw himself down upon the earth, laughing with the delight of one who had lost his wits in a dream of pleasure.

"Where's the crow?" demanded his master.

"I shoot um—I shoot um in he head—enty I tell you, massa, I will hit um in he

head ? Soon he poke he nose ober de ground,
I gib it to um. Hope he bin large shot. He
gone t'rough he head—t'rough and t'rough.
Ha ! ha ! ha ! If dat crow be Gullah
Sam ! if Gullah Sam be git in crow jacket,
ho, massa ! he nebber git out crow jacket
'til somebody skin um. Ha ! ha ! ho ! ho !
ho ! ki ! ki ! ki ! ki ! la ! ki ! Oh, massa,
wonder how Gullah Sam feel in crow
jacket ? ''

It was in this strain of incoherent exclamation, that the invalid gave vent to his
joyful paroxysm, at the thought of having
put a handful of duck shot in the hide of
his mortal enemy. The unchristian character of his exultation received a severe reproof
from his master, which sobered the fellow
sufficiently to enable us to get from him a
more sane description of his doings. He told
us that the crow had come to bedevil him as
usual, only—and the fact became subse-
quently of considerable importance—that he
had now lost the gray dirt from his wing,
which had so peculiarly distinguished it
before, and was now as black as the most
legitimate suit ever worn by crow, priest,
lawyer, or physician. This change in the
outer aspect of the bird had somewhat confounded the negro, and made him loth to
expend his shot, for fear of wasting the
charmed charge upon other than the genuine Simon Pure. But the deportment of the
other—lazy, lounging, swaggering, as usual,

convinced Scipio, in spite of his eyes, that his old enemy stood in fact before him ; and without wasting time, he gave him both barrels at the same moment.

'' But where's the crow ? '' demanded the master.

'' I knock um ober, massa, I see um tumble ; 'speck you find um t'oder side de cornhill.''

Nothing could exceed the consternation of Scipio, when, on reaching the designated spot, we found no sign of the supposed victim. The poor fellow rubbed his eyes, in doubt of their visual capacities, and looked round aghast for an explanation to the wizard who was now approaching, waving his wand in long sweeping circles as he came, and muttering, as before, those strange uncouth sounds, which we relished as little as we understood. He did not seem at all astonished at the result of Scipio's shot, but abruptly asked of him—'' Wa's de fus' water, brudder Scip ? ''

'' De water in de bay, Master 'Tuselah,'' was the reply ; the speaker pointing as he spoke to the little spot of drowned land on the very corner of the field, which, covered with thick shoots of the small sweet bay tree—the magnolia flacca—receives its common name among the people from its almost peculiar growth.

'' Push for de bay ! push for de bay ! '' exclaimed the African, '' and see wha' you

By American Authors. 341

in de bay ! "

These words, scarcely understood by us,
set Scipio in motion. At full speed he set
out, and conjecturing from his movement,
rather than from the words of the African,
his expectations, off we set also at full speed
after him. Before we reached the spot, to
our great surprise, Scipio emerged from the
bay, dragging after him the reluctant and
trembling form of the aged negro, Gullah
Sam. He had found him washing his face,
which was covered with little pimples and
scratches, as if he had suddenly fallen into
a nest of briars. It was with the utmost
difficulty we could prevent Scipio from
pummeling the dreaded wizard to death.

" What's the matter with your face,
Sam ? " demanded Mr. Carrington.

" Hab humor, Massa Carrington ; bin
trouble berry much wid break out in de
skin."

" Da shot, massa—da shot. I hit um in
crow jacket ; but wha's de gray di't ? Ha !
massa, look yer ; dis da black suit of Misser
Jam'son Gullah Sam hab on. He no wear
he jacket wid gray patch. Da's make de
diff 'rence."

The magician from St. Matthew's now
came up, and our surprise was increased
when we saw him extend his hand, with an
appearance of the utmost good feeling and
amity, to the rival he had just overcome.

"Well, brudder Sam, how you come on?"

The other looked at him doubtfully, and with a countenance in which we saw, or fancied, a mingling expression of fear and hostility; the latter being evidently restrained by the other. He gave his hand, however, to the grasp of Methuselah, but said nothing.

"I will come take supper wid you tonight, brudder Sam," continued the wizard of St. Matthew's, with as much civility as if he spoke to the most esteemed friend under the sun. "Scip, boy, you kin go to you massa work—you quite well ob dis business."

Scipio seemed loth to leave the company while there seemed something yet to be done, and muttered half aloud :

"You no ax Gullah Sam wha' da he bin do in de bay."

"Psha, boy, go 'long to you cornfiel'— enty I know," replied Methuselah. "Gullah Sam bin 'bout he own business, I s'pose. Brudder, you kin go home now, and get you tings ready for supper. I will come see you to-night."

It was in this manner that the wizard of St. Matthew's was disposed to dismiss both the patient and his persecutor, but here the master of Scipio interposed.

"Not so fast, Methuselah. If this fellow, Sam, has been playing any of his tricks

upon my people, as you seem to have taken
for granted, and as, indeed, very clearly appears, he must not be let off so easily. I
must punish him before he goes."

"You kin punish um more dan me?"
was the abrupt, almost stern inquiry of the
wizard.

There was something so amusing, as well
as strange, in the whole business, something
so ludicrous in the woe-begone visage of Sam,
that we pleaded with Mr. Carrington that
the whole case should be left to Methuselah ;
satisfied that as he had done so well hith-
erto, there was no good reason, nor was it
right, that he should be interfered with.
We saw the two shake hands and part, and
ascertained from Scipio that he himself was
the guest of Gullah Sam, at the invitation
of Methuselah, to a very good supper that
night of pig and 'possum. Scipio described
the affair as having gone off very well, but
he chuckled mightily as he dwelt upon the
face of Sam, which, as he said, by night
was completely raw from the inveterate
scratching to which he had been compelled
to subject it during the whole day. Methuselah, the next morning, departed, having
received as his reward twenty dollars from
the master, and a small pocket Bible from
the young mistress of the negro ; and to
this day there is not a negro in the surrounding country—and many of the whites
are of the same way of thinking—who does

not believe that Scipio was bewitched by
Gullah Sam, and the latter was shot in the
face, while in the shape of a common crow
in the cornfield, by the enchanted shot provided by the wizard of St. Matthew's for
the hands of the other.